BLOOD TETHERED

I. S. BELLE

Kindle eBook ASIN: B0DJHHFJ1D

KDP Paperback ISBN: 979-8-304539-59-3

IngramSpark Paperback ISBN: 978-1-067014-19-3

IngramSpark Hardcover ISBN: 978-1-067014-11-7

CONTENT WARNINGS

Underage drinking, consensual blood drinking, *non*consensual blood drinking, mentions of homophobia, burns, murder, gore, suicidal ideation, dismemberment, emotional abuse, bullying, eye trauma, addiction, smoking, child abuse, discussions of self-harm, vomiting.

"It is our duty to be hard. When they bite us, let them chip their damned teeth."

— Guide To Hunting The Accursed Vampyre, volume XXI

———

U STAY SOFT
U GET EATEN

— Kade Renfield's t-shirt

CHAPTER
ONE

THIRTEEN HOURS before Theo Fairgood died, he woke up early to hang party decorations.

This wasn't just any party. This was the Founder's Day party, the wildest night of the year. He was the first sophomore to be granted the honor of hosting, and he wasn't about to waste it.

"Careful," Theo's mom warned him as he teetered on the edge of a chair, stretching to the next hook with a line of wildflowers. "Any further and you'll fall and crack your head and die."

"He's fine, Carol." Theo's dad, Victor, looked up from where he was holding the chair steady. "Dead yet, son?"

"Not yet." Theo concentrated, straining further.

Victor sniffed a flower knotted into the decoration and grimaced. "These are strong. Where did you buy them from?"

"Just the garden place in town," Theo said quickly. Like he didn't know the store—*Rose's Goods*—and each employee by name.

Carol laughed, dropping another sweetener into her coffee. "He grew them himself, Victor. Got the seeds months ago."

Victor looked up at Theo disapprovingly. "Theo. You *didn't*."

"Busy, Dad!"

"You know what we've told you about your little gardening habit," Victor continued in a warning voice that made Theo fight a shiver.

"It's not a habit, Dad," Theo assured him, making sure to keep his voice even and respectful. "This was a special case, I'm the first sophomore to host this party. *Ever*, Dad. The whole school will be here. Don't you want things to look perfect?"

Theo didn't dare look down, but he heard Victor sigh in resignation.

Carol made a noise into her coffee mug. "Honey, we need to remember to drop by the Yancy house for a friendly chat."

"Got it," Victor said.

Theo kept his gaze on the hook he was stretching toward. *Friendly chat* meant they were intimidating someone to win their case. Crack legal team Fairgood & Fairgood were on a twenty-year winning streak, marred only by a few unlucky cases where they couldn't talk, bribe or steal their way out of it. One day, Theo would join his parents' ranks.

Theo stretched even further, wincing as a joint popped. The banner eased reluctantly onto the hook.

Carol sighed in relief and went back to her morning coffee, stirring it with the end of her Fairgood & Fairgood pen.

Victor slapped the chair. "*There* we go. Now hurry up, I didn't give you the Lexus so you could be late for school."

Theo jumped down, a stray petal brushing his ear. "Got it, Dad. I said I won't—*oof.*"

His arms came up automatically, surprised and a little wary as Victor hugged him. Victor had a reason for everything, and hugs were usually to cushion the blow of something hard coming at him.

"You're representing this family," Victor said in his ear. "And Fairgoods are—"

"Vicious," Theo replied. "I know, Dad."

"We don't waste time on *wildflowers.*"

"I know, Dad."

"Good." Victor leaned back, ruffling a hand through his hair.

Theo tensed, waiting for the hand to clench—but it never came. Sometimes a hair ruffle was just a hair ruffle, Victor fluffing up the blond curls they proudly shared.

Then Victor's hand drew back. A petal sat between his fingers, so white it almost glowed.

Theo held his breath, waiting.

"You can tell people we ordered it in," Victor told him. He crushed the petal between his fingers and strode off. "Go knock 'em dead!"

"Always do," Theo replied, relieved.

He scooped up his backpack and ran out the door.

It was, Theo considered as he ran down the garden path towards his car, the perfect house for a party.

Beautiful colonial-style architecture, originally built when the first settlers rolled into town. Pristine garden gardened all-year around. Not to mention the cliffside view.

Theo looked over at the lake. It was a soft, calm blue in the morning light, and it would have been peaceful if not for the sheer drop between him and the water. Theo used to pretend to fall off the cliff when he was a kid. He cut that out when he almost slipped and tumbled to a watery grave, saved only because his dad was around to grab him.

Theo spared the steep drop another wary glance. He would have to give a speech at the party tonight. The last thing they needed was some idiot classmate getting drunk and falling off the cliff into the lake. His parents would kill him.

A friendly voice cut through his worrying. "Theo!"

Theo looked over to see the gardener straightening up in the flowerbed.

He raised a hand. "Hi, Russel!"

Russel waved back with a trowel. He was a decade older than Theo's dad, skin burnished with tiny scars from a lifetime of odd jobs involving sharp implements. Theo had never seen him wear anything but jeans and rubber boots.

"Hey kid," Russel replied, going back to digging through the flowerbed. "How'd the wildflowers go?"

Russel had been taking care of the gardens since Theo was a baby, and he never told Theo's parents about his ongoing gardening habit. Even when he was eleven and messed up the azaleas enough for his mom to complain to Russel about the sudden drop in service quality.

I don't get why they're hard on you about it, Russel had told him once. *It's sweet that you like plants so much.*

"They went great," Theo replied. "Thanks, Russ."

Russel shot him a distracted thumbs-up. "Everyone's gonna love it. Don't worry."

"Uh-huh," Theo replied, glancing pointedly back at the house. He didn't *think* his parents could hear, but he could never be sure.

"Right." Russel raised a dirt-streaked finger to his lips. "Never mind. Hope the party's good, kid."

"It will be," Theo told him, full of bone-deep confidence he wouldn't feel for a long time after today. "It's mine."

· · ·

Ten hours before Theo died, he tripped another sophomore in the halls.

The boy sprawled to the ground with a grunt. Theo swallowed down his first instinct to apologize. It was an accidental collision as he turned the corner toward History—but that didn't matter. People were watching, and there were *rules*.

So Theo laughed. He even meant it, once he saw who it was. Kade Renfield could always be taken down a peg or two.

"Oh no," Theo said mockingly. "Did you chip a claw?"

His friends sniggered behind him. Felicity leaned into Aaron, giggling, mouth forming into that perfect half-crinkle they taught her at the modeling agency. Next to her, Aaron smiled. He even showed teeth.

Kade lifted his shaved head from the linoleum with a glare. He raised his hands, hooking his nails toward Theo like they really were claws.

"I don't know," he said in that lazy British accent that had faded with his years in the states. "What do you think? Still think I can rip some fair maiden's throat out or are my rampaging days over?"

Felicity giggled even louder. She liked it when they fought back. If they did a good enough job she could even be convinced to change sides, jeering at her friends and talking up someone she'd been laughing at thirty seconds previously.

Theo made sure his smile stayed in place. Talking to

Kade always made him feel like he was walking a tightrope, and any moment Kade could shake it and send him plummeting down.

"Your guess is as good as mine, Monster." He scraped a sneaker against Kade's shoulder. "Gonna get up or are you gonna take a nap?"

Kade hissed and wiped his denim-clad shoulder, like Theo had contaminated it with his spotless sneakers. He'd dyed the denim black, just like everything else he was wearing: black jeans, black Doc Martens, black choker around his neck. The only spot of color was on his shirt in small, white letters: *U STAY SOFT, U GET EATEN.*

One thing we can agree on, Theo thought, and nudged Kade again. "Nap, then. Have fun, Monster."

"Sure to, golden boy," Kade hissed.

Felicity stepped around him to follow Theo, turning to talk to him in a determinedly awful British accent. "Pip-pip and cheerio, old mate."

"Never said any of those words in my life, Sloan," Kade called as she stepped around him. "Go back to making fun of British dentistry or something."

Aaron took the easier, crueler path and stepped on his stomach. Kade doubled over, wheezing. He was one of those pale, scrawny kids who always had an excuse to get out of PE class. Theo used to think one good punch would probably take him out. Then Kade started getting into fights. Theo had seen the aftermath often enough, heard the stories, but he'd had only seen it once in person: Kade's eyes ringed with purple in the movie theater parking lot, blood in his grin as Aaron held him against the hood of his car.

He started it, Aaron told him as Theo iced his nose later. *I just punched back.*

After that, everybody started calling him Monster. Kade leaned into it—hissing, snarling, even barking.

Everybody paused as Aaron stepped off him, waiting to see if Kade would take the bait. Sometimes he did. Other times he just made a joke and limped off. You could never tell which way he'd lean until it was happening.

Kade uncurled, resting his shaved head against the linoleum. He looked over at Aaron and bared his teeth, snarling like a dog.

Felicity barked back. A few passersby followed suit, everybody eager to join in. Lock was a town of many traditions, and one of them was taunting Kade "Monster" Renfield.

Aaron laughed, low and dangerous. "You don't wanna do that, queer."

"Ooh," Kade hissed. "Disappointing. Girlfriend's gonna yell at you again."

"I just want him to be more creative," Felicity said waspishly. "Homophobic slurs are *so* 2010s."

Another round of sniggers went up from passersby. Everybody remembered Felicity going off on her boyfriend in freshman year, telling him to quit being homophobic or lose a girlfriend. What they *didn't* know was it was prompted by a three-way confession where Felicity drunkenly confessed her bisexuality and Theo awkwardly followed, and Aaron acted really weird about it for weeks before mumbling something that sounded like yet another bisexuality confession, but he quickly took it back and refused to talk about it since.

Aaron ignored them and bent down, looming over Kade. "Remember what I told you would happen if you talked to me again, Monster?"

Kade growled.

The bell rang. Theo grabbed Aaron and slung him forward, toward History. "Do *you* remember promising you'd come around and help me clean the kitchen?"

They turned the corner, Felicity on their heels.

Kade vanished from view. He still hadn't moved from the floor.

Aaron fixed Theo with a fond, if irritated, look. "I don't, actually."

"No? Guys?" Theo looked around at Felicity. "You remember promising me, your *best friend* since *childhood*—"

Felicity batted him with the hand that wasn't stuck in Aaron's pocket. "I remember you whining about how much work it was going be."

"We're still burned out from spring break," Aaron pointed out.

"That's the *point*," Theo insisted as they streamed into History. "We *rally*. Founder's Day is our biggest town tradition, we *have* to come together and get shitfaced!"

A cheer went up from the rest of the class. Theo turned to them, fist raised, white teeth flashing in a grin.

A throat cleared behind him.

Theo turned, smile already apologetic. "Sorry, Mr. Hawthorn."

"Apology accepted, Theo. Go sit down." Mr. Hawthorn adjusted his glasses, trying to look stern. It didn't last. By the time he made it to his desk, his amused smile was shining through.

"Alright. As our favorite rising basketball star was saying, it's Founder's Day today. Can anybody tell me the year our town was founded?"

He shot the class hopeful finger guns. They got less and less hopeful the longer the silence stretched. He sighed. "Come on, gang. 1832! See, this is why they should've made a song. Everything rhymes with two. Who wants to make up a song that the future generations of Lockians can sing?"

Theo stifled a laugh as Mr. Hawthorn hummed a few bars. He wasn't the only one. Mr. Hawthorn was in his late thirties, the youngest and most beloved teacher at Lock High. Everything about him stunk of genuine care and heart in a way that Theo was obligated to make fun of, but deep down he wished all teachers were like Mr. Hawthorn. It would be nice if more teachers actually gave a shit.

Mr. Hawthorn stopped humming. "No? Alright. Easier question: who knows our town's spooky origins? Theo! You were so excited earlier, you *must* know."

Theo groaned. Aaron leaned over to kick him, and Theo kicked back until Mr. Hawthorn gave them a good-natured warning look.

Theo leaned back in his chair. "Okay, uhhh. These vampires set up shop in the woods. They terrorized the surrounding towns until a gang of heroic vampire hunters rode in and saved the day. They killed most of the vampires, but not the leader. They cursed her to burn for eternity, locked her in a coffin and buried her deep under the earth, because they were a bunch of sick freaks! Anyway they made a town on top of her and that's why we call it Lock."

He stood up and bowed. Another cheer went up, a few classmates even clapping. Felicity raised her hands over her head and whooped. Theo glanced up at Aaron, who rolled his eyes but joined in.

Mr. Hawthorn waved them down. "That was great, Theo. You should look into joining the drama club. Now: how do we think this story originated?"

Theo eased back into his seat. "I don't know, some old-timey cops tracked down some weirdo and buried her alive for some reason. Or burned her."

At the back of the room, Felicity shuddered. "Ugh, I hope that's just the story. I think I'd rather burn. When I was a kid I watched this Ryan Reynolds movie about being buried alive—"

Mr. Hawthorn clapped again. "Great, thank you Felicity! Before we get into the actual class, let me do the ol' count…"

Theo admired the black tattoos peeking out of his rolled-up sleeves as Mr. Hawthorn counted heads. Mr. Hawthorn had worn a turtleneck every day since he moved here, even in the hot months.

He stopped at the only empty desk in class, frowning. "Has anybody seen Kade?"'

Aaron sniggered. He didn't even hide it. Theo stared down at his desk, trying not to picture Mr. Hawthorn's sad look if he found out. *I'm not mad, I'm just disappointed. You have the potential to be such a sweet kid, Theo.*

"He'll turn up," Felicity said. Her pink lips twisted in a smirk, tossing her pale hair over her shoulder. "Unless he's finally gotten a clue and dropped out."

"Hey." Mr. Hawthorn gave her the look Theo was dreading. "We don't talk like that about our classmates."

"Right. Sorry, sir." Felicity waited until he'd turned around, then shot her friends a sardonic look. Theo returned it, trying not to picture Kade still there in the hallway, gray eyes closed.

FIVE HOURS before Theo Fairgood died, Kade was getting out of detention.

Trying to, anyway. If Coach Cheech had his way, Kade would be stuck here until graduation.

Kade slouched against the desk as he waited for Coach Cheech, asshole supreme, to deem his detention essay good enough to let him escape.

"Off," Coach Cheech said, not looking up.

Kade straightened resentfully. He drummed a beat into his T-shirt, smack-dab in the *O* of *SOFT*. The stitching was coming apart. Soon it would say *STAY SUFT.* He'd have to fix that tonight. *Then* he'd get to the new patches he'd been planning on sewing into his favorite leather jacket. Or the circle scarf he'd promised his aunt as a late birthday present. Or the blanket he was crocheting, festooned with tiny skulls. Kade's projects were vast and never-ending, most of them done in the dead of night when he couldn't sleep. Luckily, Kade had a *lot* of trouble sleeping.

Coach Cheech sighed, scratching at one scraggly sideburn. He let Kade's paper drop to the ground like it had personally offended him.

Kade grinned. "So? Do you set me free? Are my shackles falling from my slender wrists? Is the cage cracking open?

"This is the worst piece of shit I've ever read," Coach Cheech said. "And I taught kindergarten."

"I bet they loved you," Kade whispered.

Coach Cheech picked up his terrible paper and threw it at him.

Kade leaned out of the way, giggling. "You gave me an hour, mate! How am I supposed to summarize all my complicated, tender feelings about the utter uselessness of friars in Shakespeare in an *hour*? Come on, just let me go."

"I hoped if he gave you a topic you could complain about, you'd actually *try*." Coach Cheech groaned, rubbing again at his sideburns. Kade wondered if anyone had told him about worry beads. If anyone needed them, it was Coach Cheech. He was forty but looked older, on the constant verge of a heart attack. If you annoyed him enough his bald head would pop with a vein. Kade had seen that vein a *lot* in his two years at Lock High.

"Never mind." Coach Cheech picked up the paper

and threw it in the trash. To Kade's surprise, it landed, circling the rim once before toppling in.

"Whoa," Kade said. "Nice shot."

"You continue to disappoint me," Coach Cheech said. "And yourself, and your family, and this school, and the taxpayers that paid for this school to stay afloat."

Kade tossed him a peace sign and skipped out. *Properly* skipped, just to hear Coach Cheech groan in annoyance after him. He was born and bred in Lock, but he reminded Kade of every teacher he'd had in the UK: rude, tired, and more suited to a job where you sat out the back and didn't talk to anyone. But he apologized the one time he made Kade cry, which meant he wasn't a total pile of shit. Just...mostly.

Kade was used to finding piles of shit in this town. He'd lived here for six years now, and it seemed like Lock was full of nothing but steaming piles of shit.

He turned into the hallway, reaching into his pocket for his cigarettes when he slammed into someone.

Kade hit the ground ass-first, cigarette pack bouncing over the linoleum. He sat up snarling, shoulders hunched protectively. "Watch it, asshole!"

He stopped as soon as he saw who it was.

"Oof," said Mr. Hawthorn, adjusting his glasses and politely pretending not to notice Kade swearing directly in his face. "That looked like a rough fall. Sorry about that, Kade! Let me help you up."

He held out a hand. Kade had to stop himself from flinching. *It's Hawthorn*, he reminded himself. *Chill the hell out. He's about the only person at school who wouldn't laugh about knocking you over.*

"Thanks," Kade said as Mr. Hawthorn hauled him up.

"No problem. Are you alright?"

Kade made a show of brushing himself off. "No damage that wasn't already there."

"Ha, ha." Mr. Hawthorn looked past him into the detention room. "Did they make you write an essay this time?"

"Yup."

"Fun." Mr. Hawthorn waved into the detention room. "Hi, Coach!"

Coach Cheech grunted. He didn't like Mr. Hawthorn, which just went to show how much of a dick he was. *Everybody* liked Mr. Hawthorn.

Mr. Hawthorn bent down again, picking up Kade's cigarette carton.

"These things will kill you," he said with a wince.

"Fingers crossed, sir." Kade stuffed the carton into his jacket and hooked a thumb down the hallway. "Well, gotta get back to the salt mines."

He turned. Mr. Hawthorn stepped in front of him, and Kade had to stop himself from flinching yet again.

"Look," Mr. Hawthorn said, so kind and understanding Kade's stomach squirmed. "I know high school can be rough. But it's such a small part of your life. Alright? You're destined for great things, Kade. I know it."

Kade stared down at his shoes, feeling his cheeks heat. Mr. Hawthorn did this sometimes—gave him little pep talks when he sensed Kade was going through a particularly tough time. And he never made jabs at Kade's accent, which was a rarity with people in this town.

Kade hated the pep talks. Kade also wished he did them every day.

He thumbed at the hallway again. "I still...I gotta..."

"Right." Mr. Hawthorn raised a hand like he was going to give Kade a friendly tap on the shoulder. Then he dropped it. "Have a great night, champ."

"Always do," Kade mumbled. He strode off, chin still tucked into his chest to hide his red cheeks. Mr. Hawthorn was the only person in Lock, barring his aunt, who could get away with calling Kade champ without getting his head bitten off. Because Hawthorn wasn't condescending, he wasn't making fun of Kade. He was just that genuine and dorky. Like he watched *Dead Poets Society* too many times when he was getting his teaching qualifications.

A correction: Lock was full of steaming piles of shit, barring one history teacher.

Four hours and forty-five minutes before Theo Fairgood died, Kade met Felicity behind the science building and gave her a twenty-dollar bill.

"Ah-ah," she warned when he reached for the paper bag in her hands. "Price is up. Fifty bucks."

Kade laughed through a cloud of smoke. "*Fifty?* You're joking."

Felicity shrugged her slim shoulders and cocked her hip, all nothing-curves that once made her the best gymnast in town. Once she ran circles around everyone in track and did somersaults in the playground and placed silver in statewide gymnast competitions. Then she threw it all away to start modeling, a move that apparently made her mother foam at the mouth. Kade was half convinced Felicity spent so much time chasing her modeling career just to piss her off.

"Deal's a deal," Felicity chirped. "Take it or go shoplift from the liquor store. Ooh, actually you *should*. You know he keeps a gun under the counter, right? He could do us all a favor and take you out."

Kade clutched his chest. "Is Felicity Sloan...making *fun* of me? Woe! Pain! How will I go *on*?"

Felicity cackled. Over the years Kade had realized she enjoyed their interactions the way one enjoyed watching a suffering lion perform in a circus. She wanted to watch him bare his teeth and jump through hoops. Sometimes their interactions even bordered on friendly. Then she'd grin while he was getting whaled on, or hike up the price of her stolen booze, and Kade would remind himself that she still sucked.

She dangled the bag out of reach. "Fifty or eat buckshot, Monster."

For a second Kade considered shoplifting. But he'd promised his aunt he wouldn't get arrested again, and the liquor store owner *did* shoot the last person who tried to rob him.

He sighed, shelling out another thirty bucks.

Felicity snatched it, showing off all her shiny teeth, whitened after she signed with the modeling agency. "Pleasure. I'll let you know next time my mom stocks up. Thank youuuu."

She flounced off, pale ponytail bouncing.

Kade flipped her off and unpeeled the brown bag. It was whiskey. Not his favorite, but it was better than the miniature schnapps she'd given him a few months ago. He'd drunk that whole tiny bottle and barely got a buzz. For *thirty dollars*. In comparison, a liter of whiskey was a steal.

He walked off with a skip in his step, a cigarette pinched between his teeth, whiskey clinking in his backpack, and a stubborn reminder in his head: all of this was backstory to his great adventure. No matter how bad the bullying got, how many people barked at him in the street or tripped him in the halls or told him to crawl into a dark hole and die—he just had to get through two more shitty years, and then he was out of here. Off to live his story, his *real* story, wonderful and strange and far away from Lock.

. . .

Three hours before Theo Fairgood died, Kade was drunk.

Not tipsy—drunk. *Good* drunk. Only a few shots from absolutely shitfaced.

He was blaring music in his room, jumping around and enjoying how his head spun, when a knock on the door broke his carefree haze.

"Shit," he hissed. He raced to screw the cap back on the whiskey and tossed it under his pillow. Then he swished a mouthful of mouthwash he kept next to his bed for this very reason, running over to the window to spit it out.

He opened the door with a sunny smile and a casual lean, spinning a knitting needle. "Howdy, miss," he said in a terrible cowboy accent. "You're looking mighty fine tonight."

His aunt, Sundance, snorted. She reached up as if she was going to tweak his hair, like she used to do when she was a kid. Then her stout hand faltered. Muscle memory didn't catch up in time for her to remember he hadn't had that big bush of black hair for a while now.

She rubbed her knuckles against his scalp instead. "So rough. Like a cat's tongue."

He bent down, butting his head into her cheek until she squawked and pulled back.

"You're home early," he said, throwing the knitting needle back onto this bed.

"Everyone got sent home. Sally burned her hand. It

was pretty damn bad." The tired look came back, the one she pretended didn't exist and he pretended not to notice. "I'm gonna have to pull some extra shifts."

"That's fine. It's *fine*," he repeated when that tired look only got worse. "I'm a big boy. Sixteen whole years old. I can reach the taps and everything. If I strain, I think I can even use the microwave."

"Yeah. Well, not tonight." She headed down the narrow hall toward the kitchen. "I'll get the potatoes ready. You do the meat. I'll even make us some fancy gravy, no packet needed. Sound good?"

Kade chewed his cheek. He had his heart set on a night of solitude, whiskey and Netflix. Then possibly some drunken sewing, which never turned out great. He wasn't the best at changing tracks unexpectedly. But if he stayed home, she'd want to watch something, or talk, and he'd have to fake being sober. Another thing he wasn't good at.

"Actually..." He bit his lip. "I'm going out."

Sundance turned around, shock written in every wrinkle and gray hair he'd given her. "Oh? Does my nephew have a social life?"

"Ha, ha. I was surprised too." He scratched at the badly painted doorway. His pinkie nail dented. A memory floated back: *oh, no. Did you chip a claw?*

"I'm going to the Founder's Day party," he said.

She blinked.

I'm as surprised as you are, Kade thought.

Sundance put a stern hand on her hip. "Don't get

into any trouble. No fights, no crazy drinking, and I do *not* want to get a call from the cops."

"Got it."

"Good." She looked him up and down, giving him a sniff. Kade was glad he'd bothered with the mouthwash.

She leaned back, apparently satisfied. "Are you going to wear a nice outfit?"

Kade scoffed, motioning at himself. "Don't I always?"

She smiled and ducked into the kitchen. He watched her go, his stomach twisting in a way that had nothing to do with whiskey. *It might be nice*, he thought. *Staying home, eating dinner with her for once. I could even fix that shirt.*

Then he closed the door and went to pick out an outfit.

CHAPTER
THREE

TEN MINUTES BEFORE THEO DIED, he was drunk.

He would be hungover tomorrow, he reasoned, because he mixed beer and liquor (never sicker). But for now, he was warm and happy and his basketball teammates kept pulling him into hugs or cheering or telling him what a great party it was.

Life was good.

Then Skeeter Bass ran into him and spilled beer all over his good sneakers.

"Watch it," Theo snapped, recoiling. He shook his feet, disgusted. "God, it's in my *socks*."

Skeeter cowered. She was a straightlaced sophomore with braces on her teeth and a cross around her neck. The braces were necessary, the cross was to make her parents happy.

"Um," she said. *Um* was one of the cornerstones of her vocabulary. "I'm so sorry. I'll clean it up."

She bent down like she was going to wipe his shoes with her bare hands. Theo stepped back, almost banging into the wall.

"Just forget it," he said. Then, when she wiped uselessly at his sneakers: "Hey, no, forget it. Get out of here."

Skeeter stood cautiously, still cowering. Her braces glinted in the dim light.

"Like, leave?"

"No! Just go...away from me."

"Oh. Um, okay." Skeeter fiddled with the cross around her neck. "Um, I'm sorry. I hope you guys win the game next week. Go Nightfowls."

"Go Nightfowls," Theo echoed automatically. He shook his wet shoes, not bothering to watch Skeeter vanish into the crowd. He felt a little bad for snapping at her. He also felt bad for not going harder—if his parents had seen that, they'd want Theo to demand payment for his ruined shoes. Which Theo thought was a little unnecessary. They could buy new shoes; the Bass family were on food stamps.

He was so busy shaking his wet shoes he didn't notice Felicity creeping up behind him until she slung a slim arm around his shoulders, teeth closing around his ear.

Theo yelped, shoving at her. "Liss! What the hell?"

She grinned. "Couldn't find Aaron. Got bored. What was *that* about?"

"Nothing. Gotta do some laundry later." Theo wiped spit off his ear, unable to keep the fond smile off his face. Aaron was his best friend, but Felicity had been his first. He didn't even remember life without her. Even though he had a burning crush on her during middle school, he was almost glad Aaron dated her instead—high school dating inevitably meant a breakup. Theo much preferred getting over his crush and keeping her as a friend. Even if she'd been pulling away from him since she started dating Aaron, preferring to spend time out of town with her new modeling friends or hanging one-on-one with her boyfriend. No time for her childhood best friend unless they were at school or at a party.

Felicity flicked him in the face with her ponytail. "You didn't even need us to help clean, you dick. I could've spent *way* longer on my makeup."

"It wouldn't have helped." Theo dodged the elbow she threw at him and laughed.

Felicity's eyes caught on something over her shoulder and widened. "Those flowers over the door are *so* pretty. Where did you get that from?"

Theo paused, trying to remember his lie. It was harder after this many beers.

Felicity gasped, a wicked grin curling her lips. "*No.* Did you *grow* them?"

"No," Theo said, but it was too late. Felicity grabbed him again, squealing.

"Our favorite little gardener," she cooed, squeezing his cheeks. "Golden boy, *gardener* boy—"

Theo pushed her off, glancing around to check if anyone had heard. The chatter was too loud, the music too thick. He breathed a sigh of relief.

"I got it from the garden store," he insisted. "So shut up, alright?"

She rolled her eyes. Her floral perfume tickled his nose.

"Boooring," she singsonged. She pressed a wet kiss to his face and bit him in the chin. "I'm going to go find someone *interesting*," she growled, and flounced off.

Theo snorted, rubbing the fading bite mark on his chin. As soon as her pale hair vanished into the crowd, a thick, familiar hand landed on Theo's shoulder.

"Aaron," Theo said, not needing to turn. "Dance with me."

"What? No." Aaron stepped into view, distracted. "Have you seen Liss around?"

Theo pointed into the crowd. "Just missed her."

"Shit." Aaron scratched his mouth, which was slick with beer. "Has she broken anything yet?"

Theo slung an arm around his shoulder. "She's *fine*, man. You worry too much."

Aaron muttered something, too low to catch. His steely gaze roved the crowd, looking for a flash of Felicity's blond head.

Theo's smile faded. Aaron got *weird* about Felicity sometimes, especially at parties. Granted, Felicity had become a bit of a wild card in the past few years. But it didn't warrant Aaron getting all annoyed and worried, monitoring how many drinks she was having and telling her to stop dancing on tables.

"I worry enough," Aaron barked, still scanning. "*You* didn't see her start a knife-throwing contest at Kenny H's house last month."

Theo blinked. "I thought you guys were having a double date."

"We were," Aaron said dryly. "It got intense. Hope Kenny enjoyed digging his steak knives out of his living room wall."

Theo didn't ask why they hadn't told him earlier. There was a lot going on between Aaron and Felicity that they didn't tell him about.

"I just...if she hurts herself doing something stupid, *again*..." Aaron's face clouded. He shook his head, twisting out from under Theo's arm. "Anyway. Came over here to tell you Monster's skulking around the cliffs next to the house."

It took a moment to click. "Kade Renfield? He's here?"

"Yeah, little gate-crashing shit." Aaron scowled at the window, where the cliffs and the forest waited. "Let's go show him what happens when he crashes a *Fairgood* party."

Visions of broken noses and police sirens danced in Theo's head.

He caught Aaron's elbow before he could storm off. "Whoa, hey. I'm the host. Let me do it."

Aaron frowned. Or, an Aaron version of a frown, mouth turning almost imperceptibly down at the corners. "You don't want backup?"

Theo didn't want a repeat of last year. Aaron's parents had been so pissed at him for getting into a fight, especially with a lowlife like Kade "Monster" Renfield, no matter how many times Aaron insisted Kade started it.

"I want you to take a load off. Enjoy yourself, bud." Theo pulled him in, knocking their foreheads together.

Aaron laughed. His teeth showed, just a glimpse beyond his slim mouth.

"Text me if you need backup. And if it's Monster, you *will* need backup. I was always the better fighter."

"You wish," Theo replied. "Go make sure Felicity isn't throwing my parents' good knives, please."

He slapped Aaron's back and headed for the front door. The crowd parted easily around him, people reaching out to clap his arm or offer him a drink. The town's golden boy, bright and gleaming, everybody wanting a glimpse.

One minute before Theo died, he walked toward the cliff that plunged into a steep drop next to the house.

A figure stood at the edge. Not at the bushes, which were a sensible distance away. But the *edge* edge, right on the precipice, the one-more-step-and-you're-dead edge. If Kade moved a little further he'd be falling into the lake.

"Hey," Theo yelled. "Get back here, dumbass. I did a whole speech, didn't you hear it? You know how many people have died in that lake? A *lot*, and not because of the fall. Those rocks will mess you *up*."

The figure turned, stumbling. Theo couldn't see his face. The light from the house spilled out onto the cliff, but not far enough to reach them. All they had was the moon, half-full and obscured by mist.

Theo squinted. That was definitely Kade—same skinny frame and dark clothes. He had lacy fingerless gloves and black shorts and dark tights with holes ripped up the front. He even had eyeliner, in black streaks down his cheeks.

"Hey, dipshit..." Theo's yell trailed off as he got closer. The black streaks weren't a fashion statement. Kade was crying, his gray eyes wet in the moonlight.

Theo jerked to a stop. "Oh. Uh. I'll—"

Leave you alone never made it out of his mouth. One, he realized it probably wasn't a good idea to leave a crying crazy guy on a cliff edge. And two, Kade's face shifted from embarrassment to fearful shock. But not at him: Kade's wet, horrified eyes were aimed over Theo's shoulder.

Theo turned. A burst of black rushed at him. Hands closed around his torso and he was lifted into the air.

The world blurred. Someone shrieked. It sounded like Kade.

Up and up and *up*. Theo tried to turn, tried to see who—*what*—was holding him, but it was dark and they were moving so fast. The ground was far away now, the cliff a pinprick, the forest faraway specks. Even the lake was small.

Am I on drugs? Theo thought deliriously. *Is this what tripping is like? I don't think I like drugs if this is what drugs are like.*

White hot pain flared in his neck. Theo screamed. The pain moved, spreading through his veins. It was the worst thing he'd ever felt. Then the figure pulled back, pushing a cut wrist against Theo's mouth. Something terrible trickled from the wound, black and viscous. It flowed and flowed, filling Theo's mouth until he had no choice but to swallow.

The figure whispered in his ear. Its voice was distorted, inhuman, like it was talking past a thicket of thorns. "I'll see you soon, Cyth."

Then Theo was falling.

He screamed again, the noise filling with tears. *Please be a drug trip,* he begged silently as the lake water rushed toward him, rocks looming. *Please be a dream, I know it hurts but sometimes dreams hurt, right, please—*

He hit the water with a loud crack. More pain, incredible and strange.

He passed out. When he opened his eyes he was groggy and deep underwater and he couldn't tell which way was up. Everything hurt but nothing felt broken—he'd missed the rocks.

There, in the distance: light. The moon, half-full and misty. He swam toward it, but his lungs ached and every inch of his skin burned, every muscle, every shred of sinew and the back of his throat and his heart pounded slower.

He opened his mouth, sucking in water.

It didn't take long after that.

FORTY MINUTES before Theo Fairgood died, Kade was shitfaced.

Properly. *Beautifully*. Blurry vision, slow reflexes, calm-before-the-massive-fall shitfaced. He was going to be devastatingly hungover tomorrow, even if he hadn't chugged two cups of that cheap beer from the drinks table.

"Beer before liquor," he sung under his breath as he found an empty room to sit in, turning on the light to find a freakishly clean laundry room. "Never sicker. Liquor before beer—oh shit, maybe I'm fine."

He stood still, considering. The freakishly clean laundry room spiraled around him.

"Not fine," he muttered, sagging against the washing machine and setting his cup down behind him. He dug his knuckles into his eyes. He was going to have to do some serious puking before he walked home. Maybe he'd be spiteful and do it on somebody's bed.

He fumbled in his pocket for his cigarettes and came up empty. Right. He'd smoked them all on the way here.

The door opened. Kade looked up to meet the startled green eyes of Aaron Fletcher. As startled as Aaron got, anyway: dark eyebrows raising slightly, slim lips parting. Practically a gasp from Aaron. Felicity hung off his arm, mouth stuck in a surprised grin that definitely meant trouble.

Kade sprawled back against the washing machine. "Excuse *you*. This room is occupied. Go do jock things with your jock buddies."

Felicity snorted, propping her chin on Aaron's shoulder. "Since when do you crash Fairgood parties?"

"I'm a party person," Kade growled.

"You're a freak," Aaron said quietly.

The door creaked closed behind them. Kade eyed it warily, adrenaline creeping in through the drunken haze.

"You know," Aaron said. "I never did get you back for what you did to me in the movie theater parking lot."

Kade bit his tongue so hard he tasted blood. "What *I* did to *you*?"

"You gave me this scar." Aaron tilted his head back. A thin white line stood out under his jaw, barely visible in the dim laundry room light.

"Great," Kade said. "Wish I made it bigger."

Felicity nodded at the crinkled red cup behind him. "Thought you had your own liquor. Still crashing parties for more?"

"You know me." Kade flashed his teeth. "Can't get enough."

Aaron detached Felicity from his arm and stepped closer. He was unfortunately handsome, if you liked expressionless assholes: steely green eyes. Gelled hair. Assured swagger, like everything was going his way forever and he knew it.

The distance got less and less. Kade backed up against the washing machine, Aaron's strong thighs brushing his.

Kade swallowed, making sure his voice wasn't as high pitched as it wanted to go. "Are we going to fight or kiss? 'Cause I'll be honest with you, Aaron. I'm not sober enough for either."

Felicity laughed. "Oooh. I'd actually like to see that."

"*Liss*," Aaron hissed. "Jesus."

Felicity shrugged, twirling a strand of blond hair around her finger. She always struck him as someone he could like if they met each other ten years down the line. She was smart, vicious, and annoyingly funny. If you got to any house party after eleven, she was guaranteed to be doing something dangerous and interesting. Plus if the rumors were true, she was a fellow bisexual. If she stopped being such a colossal bitch, Kade would actually admire her.

Aaron turned back to Kade, sending shivers of

anxiety through Kade's whiskey-sodden body. Having the full brunt of Aaron's attention was always bad.

Kade tried to square his shoulders. It didn't go well. One of the reasons he snarled at people: he couldn't exactly intimidate them with his skinny stature.

Aaron leaned in until their noses almost brushed. "I can't believe you thought you could get away with coming here."

"Free country," Kade mumbled. "Right? That's what you Yanks are always going on about."

"I can't believe you'd think, for a second, that you're welcome," Aaron continued, still with that low, infuriating voice. "That we'd let you anywhere near us. Why did you even come? You knew what we'd do to you."

Kade twisted to hide the heat burning behind his eyes. He always cried easily, and he always hated it. There was nothing easier to tease than a boy who cried. Somebody like Theo Fairgood, who was all performance and annoyance, Kade could almost ignore. But Aaron... Aaron was quiet. Serious. No lofty performance, just malice. If they were alone, he could reduce Kade to tears in seconds.

Kade tried, "Aaron, piss off or I'm going to hit you."

Aaron shook his head. His thighs pressed hard into Kade's, his solid chest pressing into Kade's skinny one.

Kade looked behind him. Felicity stood at his shoulder, toying slowly a clumsy braid she had twisted into her hair. She tugged at it, gaze wary as she watched the exchange. She'd step in if it got too bad, Kade was pretty sure. She didn't like watching her guy get banged up.

She caught him looking and winked. Kade couldn't tell if that was good or bad.

"I still think you should kiss," she said.

"*Liss,*" Aaron said, shifting uncomfortably. "Come *on*."

"Aaron," Kade tried. "Do you really think this is smart? You know what I did to you last time."

The fighting was new. Just in the last few years. He got tired of waiting for that first punch. That, and he'd discovered that even if he was awful at everything else, there was one thing he was very, very good at: destroying things.

Aaron's breath stunk of cheap beer, warm and gross on Kade's cheek. "You know what I think, Monster?"

"What?" Kade snapped.

Aaron leaned in, beery breath washing over Kade's ear. "I think somebody's gonna die tonight."

Kade punched him in the stomach.

Aaron doubled over. Kade gut-punched him again, then once in the back for good measure. Aaron crumpled to the ground, groaning.

Felicity let out a strange shriek-laugh, her kitten heel stuttering out like she couldn't decide if she wanted to trip him or not. Kade leapt over it, almost slamming against the door as it spun around him. He fell into the hallway.

Aaron glared at him, pulling himself up to his knees. "I'm gonna get you for that, Monster."

Kade snarled. "Goddamn try it. I'll bite your nose off."

Felicity giggled and did the *Forrest Gump* voice. *"Run, Monster, ruuuun!"*

Kade ran.

Monster. He didn't pick it, and he didn't particularly like it. But *god* if he didn't play the part well, growling and snarling and launching himself into fights. His ripped black clothes and cheap cigarettes; his strange jewelry and his head shaved down to the prickly scalp. There were so many rumors, and Kade rolled with every one.

He slammed the door, ignoring Aaron's muffled threats as he wobbled down the hall, which was alight with noise and people. It was longer than he remembered it being, and wetter. He raised a hand to his cheek. That wasn't the hallway, he was just crying. Great.

Classmates danced and chatted and laughed as he squeezed through them, pausing to shoot Kade disgusted or curious looks. Kade hated all of them. He reached the bottom of the stairs that led up to the second floor. There was a rope barrier and a sign that read DO NOT ENTER.

Kade ducked under. The noise was dulled on the second floor. Muffled music and the occasional *whoo!* from whatever idiot was having fun tonight.

Kade stood against a window and seethed. Assholes, all of them. Pieces of shit. He couldn't take another two years in this place. He'd rather eat his sewing machine. He'd rather—

He blinked. The window was cool against his forehead. Beyond it sat the forest, the cliffs, and Fairgood Lake. Not its official name, but the name everybody knew it by. You couldn't get to it from up here, you had to walk down the cliffs. If you jumped from the cliffs next to the house...

"Huh," Kade said, and stumbled back toward the stairs.

Three minutes before Theo Fairgood died, Kade was staggering toward the cliff edge.

This will show them, he thought. *Those shitheads. Those asshole jackasses. Those pricks, this'll show them.*

He didn't think about his aunt. He didn't think about the drop. He didn't think about much at all except the seething anger in his gut.

He got to the edge and peered out.

"Bloody hell that's a long way down," he blurted. He wavered at the edge, testing his courage.

This suddenly seemed like a bad idea. Surely throwing himself off the Fairgood roof would work better? The fall would be shorter, and he wouldn't have to drown.

"Hey," a voice barked behind him. "Get back here,

dumbass. I did a whole speech, didn't you hear it? You know how many people have died in that lake? A *lot*, and not because of the fall. Those rocks will mess you *up*—"

Kade turned. It took some effort to stop turning, and he stumbled.

"Hey, dipshit..." the voice trailed off. It was Theo, Kade realized. Theo flushed and startled, his fluffy blond hair white with moonlight.

"Oh," Theo said. He stopped walking. Had he been coming to pull Kade back?

Theo said more, but Kade wasn't listening. There was a shadow in the tree line. Way back behind Theo, near the house. Then, all at once, it moved out of the trees. Too fast. *Inhumanly* fast, limbs blurring like something out of a horror movie.

Kade opened his mouth, but it was too late. The shadow grabbed Theo and dragged him into the air, up over the lake. It had *wings,* white and broad and terrible.

"*Ohshit*," Kade heard himself say, twisting to watch Theo climb higher and higher. Was this a prank? This seemed like a really elaborate prank. How were they even up there, a crane?

A distant scream. The small shape of Theo writhed in the sky, held by a figure that Kade couldn't see even if he wasn't far away and wasted.

"*Ohshit*," Kade said again. He bent over and vomited. It dripped over the cliff face, down toward the lake.

When Kade straightened up again, Theo was plummeting. He hit the water with a pitiful splash.

"SHIT!" Kade screamed.

Then, for reasons he wouldn't be able to explain for months, he fumbled his dress jacket off and jumped.

The next few minutes were a blur. Screaming the whole way down. Miraculously missing the rocks. Swimming. Finding Theo's hand just before it sank under. He gulped lake water as much as air, cursing himself and Theo and whiskey and water as he finally dragged Theo onto the grass.

He leaned over Theo and checked his pulse. His wrist, then his neck. Pressing harder and harder, trying to find a thump. Finally he held his hand in front of Theo's still mouth, his heart sinking as it confirmed what he already knew.

Theo Fairgood was dead.

THE MORNING AFTER THEO DIED, he awoke in the woods.

He sat up. A deer carcass lay next to him, its head pillowed neatly on his legs. Its throat had been ripped out.

Theo screamed. He shoved the deer head off him and stumbled up. He was alone. His clothes were sodden with water and blood. The last thing he remembered...

Kade's startled face, drained of color. Being dragged up into the air. A searing pain in his neck, fire in his veins. Then the plunge.

Theo felt his neck. The skin was smooth.

"Okay," he croaked. "So I got drugged. I saw stuff. This is fine."

This was when he realized he wasn't breathing. He sucked in a breath. Blew it out. The more he did it, the less natural it felt. Like flexing a muscle you didn't normally use.

He wiped the worst of the viscera off his shirt and started walking. He could hear cars in the distance, rumbling toward town. Far-off animals snuffling at bushes. Birds in distant trees. Breathing got more annoying, but he made himself keep doing it.

He emerged through the tree line. The cliff lay to one side, the lake looming underneath. Next to it sat the house, just as Theo remembered it. He could actually hear his mom inside, making coffee. She said something to his dad about depositions.

Theo blinked. It was impossible. This whole *morning* was impossible.

He sucked in a breath and realized he'd forgotten to inhale for the last minute and a half.

"I am having a bad trip," he told himself. "I need to sleep it off, and I'll be fine."

He headed toward the front door. Then he paused, looked down at the blood staining his clothes, and headed to a tree around back so he could climb in his bedroom window.

The shower was weird. Theo turned the heat up as high as it would go, but even with steam leaking under the shower door, he was still cold.

Also, he had no pulse. He only realized it after getting dressed and googling NOT BREATHING

WHAT DO I DO?? No matter where he pressed—throat, wrist, ankle, the back of his knee—no pulse thudded back at him. He held his breath for as long as he could and found himself getting bored around three minutes. Exhaling was not a relief. He should be sweating in panic, but the only dampness on his skin was from the shower.

He lay in bed for twenty minutes, trying to sleep. None came. He was in the middle of texting Felicity *hey what's a drug trip like* when his parents' murmurs drifted up from the kitchen.

"So strange," Carol said. "Why kill him? Jeremiah was a strange one, but he never did anything to anybody."

Theo froze. There was only one Jeremiah in Lock—Jeremiah Lemmings, a sixty-something man who lived at the edge of town and never left his house.

Victor sighed. "Wrong place, wrong time, I guess. More stevia?"

"Thanks." Clinking noises. "And they didn't even get a description?"

"No. Whoever did it was *fast*. Messy, too. They said there was blood everywhere."

Theo's unbeating heart sunk into his stomach. Someone had been killed last night. Murdered by someone fast. Blood everywhere.

I didn't, Theo thought. *I couldn't. Right?*

But the bite. His still heartbeat. The *deer*, its throat ripped to ribbons.

"Okay," he told himself when yet another Google search—*vampires real or bullshit??*—turned up useless. "Kade was *there*. Obviously he had something to do with this. He's a monster, right? Maybe he's...an *actual* monster. And he did something to me."

It wasn't the best theory he'd ever had. But it was the only one he had.

He thought about climbing back out through the window. Then he remembered he sort of died last night, and his parents were probably worried. Not to mention royally pissed off about the mess.

He steeled himself in the hallway, glad he couldn't sweat. Then he poked his head into the kitchen. "Morning, I'm going out, I'll clean when I get back."

"Hold it," Victor said.

Theo winced. He tugged his hoodie up over his head and turned back to the kitchen, ready to accept his fate. Cold fear gripped his stomach. They seemed like they were in a good mood, but that never stopped them from coming up with punishments.

Victor leaned back against the kitchen island, tapping a newspaper against his hip. He never had breakfast—it made him queasy—but he liked to sit in the kitchen with them and do his crossword. It looked less fun now the kitchen was trashed, plastic cups piled on the floor and in the sink, various liquids staining the countertops. Carol sat across from him, a stranger's bra perched next to her morning coffee as she read a stack of papers.

Victor cleared his throat. "What's a four-letter word for *shirking his responsibilities?*"

Theo tensed. "Theo. I *really* have to go, I swear I'll clean when I get back, I know this is *totally* unacceptable—"

"Someone puked in my favorite vase," Carol told him. "You said you'd make sure people knew this was a *calm* party."

"I tried, mom! There's only so much you can control teenagers!"

"At least *you* didn't drink," Carol said, narrowing her eyes at him.

"I would never," Theo assured her nervously as he headed into the front hall. "I'll clean that up later, love you, bye!"

"Wait," Victor called, jogging after him.

Theo groaned. He'd just seen the main door. Half of the flower decoration he'd spent so long putting up had been torn down. Battered wildflowers dripped petals into the front hall.

Victor sighed. "*Don't* tell me you're upset."

"Of course not," Theo replied, and turned.

Victor was looking at him strangely.

Theo pulled his hoodie up, defensive. "I'm *not* upset. I just—I put a lot of time into it. To make the house nice. It was an important party."

"What?" Victor blinked. "Right."

He fiddled with the top button of his dress shirt. Theo had never seen him in a T-shirt, and he rarely saw him without a tie. *Appearances above all else*: another Fair-good family motto. He always gave Theo's hoodie and sweatpants judging looks. This wasn't judging. This was...confused.

Victor came closer. "You look different."

"What? No I don't."

Victor stared at Theo a second longer. Theo tensed as Victor tugged the hoodie down, ruffling a hand through his blond curls.

"Guess you're just getting older." Victor didn't sound convinced, but he dropped his hand.

"Guess so," Theo said. His throat clicked. "I really gotta go."

"Sure," Victor said.

Theo's shoulders sagged in relief. He didn't know why Victor was being so lenient—he was surprised Victor had even let him get out of that kitchen without cleaning up—but he wasn't about to complain. Whatever punishment was waiting for him, he could deal with that later. As long as they let him leave now.

"Bye," he said, and rushed out. He heard his dad snicker in the front hall as he jammed the keys into his car, heard him mutter *crazy kid*.

"You don't know the half of it, Dad," Theo said to the windshield.

Kade's house was on the other side of town. *The poor*

side, his mom would say after a few drinks, and Victor would hide a smirk and tell her not to be so crude.

Theo only knew it because Aaron followed Kade home last year, after Kade threw a dodgeball in Aaron's face during one of the only gym classes they'd seen him attend.

We're just gonna scare him, Aaron had said.

They'd left a burning bag of crap on the porch. Theo didn't know that happened outside of movies, but they did it. They knocked on the door and sped off in Theo's car. But not fast enough to miss the door opening, Kade's pointy, guarded face collapsing in shock as he realized what was happening.

Theo didn't go to the front door this time. He didn't even take a second to admire the wisteria twisting around the porch, vivid and gorgeous. He crept around the back, following Kade's scent: smoke and sweat and metal blending to mask something that he knew instinctively was Kade, despite not even being in the room with him. It smelled...soft.

Kade's room was a mess: laundry scattered every-where, mugs and shoes piled in strange corners, posters of abstract symbols and models in strange clothes. Kade lay on his bed, an arm draped over his eyes. As Theo watched, Kade rolled over, uncapped a bottle of Gatorade sitting on the nightstand, and took a swig.

He slid the window open and eased in. It was surpris-ingly easy to creep silently to Kade's bed and loom. As he stood, something strange itched in his stomach. It bled out into his veins, like the fire from last night's bite. His hands twitched at his sides. Kade was so *pale*, the veins blue and prominent on his translucent skin.

Kade opened his eyes and screamed.

"Shut *up*," Theo hissed. He tensed, waiting for a parent to come running. Nothing came. Did Kade even *have* parents? He had an aunt, right?

Kade struggled up, pressing a hand to his chest.

"You scared the shit out of me," he croaked. "Holy shit, mate, I thought—"

Theo grabbed him by his shirt. It was another stupid one, black with pink stitches spelling out *WAIT I HAVE ANOTHER BAD IDEA*, and Theo almost ripped it as he hauled Kade up and slammed him into the wall.

"I know what you did," he growled.

"What?"

Theo shook him. "Do you know what happened to Jeremiah Lemmings?"

"The old guy who watches his yard from a peephole in his living room wall and screams if you get too close? What happened?"

"He's dead!"

"He's OLD," Kade yelled. "Did you go to the hospital?"

Theo blinked. His grip loosened. "What?"

Kade strained away from him. "You woke up and you just—walked off! I thought you were *dead*, man.

You—you had no *pulse*. You were underwater for a while. Your *eyes*...what does Jeremiah Lemmings have to do with any of this?"

You were underwater for a while. Theo remembered the burn in his lungs, almost imperceptible in the burning everywhere else in his body. Did he...drown?

"Wait," he said. "I woke up? Where was this? How'd I get to the forest?"

"I just...I..." Kade ducked his head. His shoulders were stiff. He had a mole at the base of his neck Theo had never noticed before, a small dark smudge against all that white. A vein beat next to it, thin and blue.

"I dragged you out," Kade said. His face twisted. "Ugh, that sounds so stupid. I was really drunk, you know. *Apocalyptically* wasted. Jumping in after you seemed like a good idea at the time."

"You jumped in after me," Theo repeated. "*You* jumped in. From the *cliff*. To save *me*."

Kade grinned anxiously. "Did I mention I was wasted?"

Anger flared in Theo's gut, almost as hard as the hunger. He lifted Kade up higher and higher and *higher*, and suddenly Kade was pressed against the ceiling. He screamed. Theo screamed with him.

"What is HAPPENING?" Theo yelled.

"I don't KNOW!" Kade slapped him on the shoulder of his hoodie, hard. "Put me DOWN!"

Theo let go. Kade fell on the bed and rolled onto the worn carpet with a yelp.

Theo landed next to him. "So you're not...you didn't do this to me?"

Kade shook his head. Theo remembered when Kade had long hair, an untidy puff of black curls haloing his head. He never took care of it. Theo used to stare at it in class, annoyed, thinking of putting hair care pamphlets in his bag just so he didn't have to look at all those split ends. He'd been relieved when Kade showed up to school with a buzzcut six months ago.

"Is this real?" Kade croaked as he got up. "Is this some really screwed up prank?"

Theo sighed. "What were you doing on the cliff?"

Kade's wiry shoulders came up again. "Having a bad trip."

Theo had to force himself back on track. The vein in Kade's neck was thumping even louder now. His skin was so thin. So breakable.

"Um," Kade rasped. He backed up against the wall. "Theo? What's going on here, mate, you look weird."

Theo grabbed Kade's jaw. He heard another yell as he twisted Kade's head to the side, the sizzle of burned flesh—but he didn't pay attention.

He sank his teeth into Kade's neck. He hadn't even noticed his teeth sharpening until now, but they pierced Kade's skin effortlessly. Blood surged into his mouth, hot and welcoming. A soft buzz worked up his cheeks, flowing into his teeth like electricity through telephone wires.

He let go of Kade's face, fisting his shirt to pull him closer.

The yell faded. A soft moan replaced it, Kade's trembling hands coming up to grip Theo's sleeves.

Theo hummed happily. There was a bitter taste that was a little like whiskey, but it was a whisper in the cacophony of blood. It pulsed into his mouth, swallow after swallow. He'd thought Kade would be cool to the touch. He was wrong. Kade was all heat, Kade was a volcano, Kade was a forest fire, Kade was party drugs lighting him up from the inside, Kade's hands were slipping from Theo's sleeves, head flopping back drunkenly—

Theo lurched back. Kade made an unhappy noise, leaning into him. Blood leaked from his neck. His eyelids fluttered. There was a lumpy circle burned into his neck where Theo's mouth had touched him, another puffy mark on his cheek where Theo had held him still.

"Crap," Theo said. "Oh, shit. Shit!"

He let go. Kade crumpled to the ground with another upset noise, trying and failing to get his arms under him.

"'M good," he mumbled, his British accent even more obvious when he was out of it. "'M good, gimme another one."

A drop of blood rolled into his shirt, staining the *W* of *WAIT*. Theo stepped forward, everything in him screaming to lean down and drink. Then Kade reached up, hand flopping like that drunk girl who had propositioned Theo last year at his birthday party. Theo hadn't gone through with it, too uncomfortable with how out of it she was.

Also, said the last sensible shred of Theo's brain, *blood loss usually leads to death*.

"Crap," Theo repeated. "One second!"

He ran out to the kitchen, grabbed a cup from the drying rack, and filled it with water. He opened the cupboard and took the first sugary thing he saw—a jar of loose M&Ms—and carted them back to Kade. Water and sugar was their go-to when his mom passed out from *her* blood thing.

"Here," Theo said. He tipped the glass against Kade's lips, careful not to touch his skin.

Kade mumbled something against the glass.

Theo pulled it back. "What?"

A grin spread over Kade's face, loose and blazing. "That was one *hell* of a high, Fairgood."

The burn marks stood stark on his skin, bright red and puffy. The ones on his neck, he could hide. The ones on his *face*...

"I'm so sorry," Theo blurted, and he fled.

CHAPTER
SIX

KADE SPENT the rest of the weekend nursing bottles of Gatorade and googling vampires and burn scars. He borrowed one of Sundance's scarves, weaving it around his head and lower face and calling it a fashion statement when she caught him in the kitchen.

"Whatever you say," she told him. "But I want it back."

He agreed. Then he went to wash out the blood spots that had transferred from his bite wound. He spent a long time with the scarf off, staring into his bedroom mirror with the door locked.

The bruising was *bad*. The world's worst hickey with puncture wounds in the middle. Not just two neat holes, either—Theo had bitten with *all* his teeth, leaving a rosy ring of red. And outside it, a puffy circle where his lips had been. Then on the other side of his face were five neat finger marks, spanning from the underside of his jaw to the bottom of his ear. The ones on his jaw weren't *that* deep—they would blister and then heal. But the one on his neck was so dark it was almost black, and after a few hours it hurt so much Kade considered drinking to make it go away, even though he'd just throw it all up. Stupid blood loss.

It didn't stop him from daydreaming of Theo's mouth on his neck. It was the venom, he decided. It had to be. Once the pain went away, the venom made it the best high he'd ever had. Like what he imagined heroin was like. He'd always promised his aunt he'd never try it, but she never said anything about vampire bites.

Where to buy vampire venom had twenty million hits on Google. Kade gave up after the fifth page.

He kept his scarf tight around his neck and jaw all through homeroom on Monday. He wasn't an idiot—a guy wearing a green summer scarf in high school wasn't going to have it on him long, especially one as low on the totem pole as Kade "Monster" Renfield.

He kept his head down. When he saw Aaron Fletcher and Felicity Sloan come his way in the hallway, he walked on the other side.

They followed. Kade's prey instinct lit up. He walked faster, ducking around a corner. But at the end of the day, he was a lanky kid who couldn't run a mile no matter how much time you gave him, and Aaron was on the basketball team.

Aaron grunted as he heaved Kade up against a locker. Felicity stood at his side, looking uncharacteristically exhausted. Her eyebags showed even through her makeup, her smile razor-sharp to distract from it.

"So?" Aaron asked. "Did you do it?"

"Do what?" Kade snarled. A crowd was forming. Never a good sign. Adrenaline flowed through Kade's veins, readying him for a fight.

Aaron smirked. "Kill old man Lemmings."

Kade froze, the fight draining out of him. In all his panic he'd forgotten to look up the guy Theo had been yelling about.

"*That* didn't look promising," Felicity said, not as excited as he expected. She was only half watching him, her gaze darting over to her boyfriend with an expression Kade couldn't decipher.

She nodded at Kade and said in a terrible British accent: "Hey, guv'nor."

"Guv'nor," he replied, wishing for the thousandth time that she wasn't so awful so he could actually like her as a person.

Aaron gave Kade a shake, dragging his attention back to the angry guy in his face. "Didn't expect you to fold so easily, Monster. Should we call somebody?"

"Nope," Kade snapped, straining against his hold. No use. He'd have to start kicking or go limp. "Come on, I'm not in the mood. Everybody go home, folks! Monster show's over!"

"I don't think so." Aaron's green eyes glinted. "Everybody says the wound is...weird. Not very knifey. You left the party right before he died. What'd you do?"

"Weird," Kade repeated, an icy chill coming over him. *Oh shit, did Theo* kill *a guy after he ran off into the woods?*

"Look," he tried, glancing around at the crowd that was forming. He stared at Felicity pleadingly. "Usually I'd play along but this is serious shit, mate. And I'm not really in the mood."

Aaron dug his finger into the bandage on Kade's jaw. The scarf had slipped down when Aaron shoved him into the locker.

Kade cried out as the burn marks flared with agony.

Felicity startled, stepping back.

"Whoa," Aaron said. He looked surprised, like he hadn't expected it to hurt so much. For a moment he almost looked guilty. Then his grin came back, not as big as before.

"Did the old man fight back?" Aaron whispered. "Didn't expect that, but I also didn't expect him to come out of his house. They said they went all the way outside his gate before he got shanked. How'd you talk him into it?"

"Didn't do anything," Kade gritted. His eyes watered. He blinked hard.

Felicity peered at the bandages peeking out from Kade's scarf. Her snub nose wrinkled.

"Um," she said. "Aaron?"

But Aaron was already talking over her, grip tight on Kade's jacket. "Aw, you feeling guilty?"

He wasn't going to let up, Kade realized. He'd have to go all in.

He grabbed Aaron's cheeks and bared his teeth. "If you really think I killed a guy over the weekend, do you really want to be doing this? Who knows what I could do, Fletcher? Could coax you out your back door next."

A gasp went up in the gathering crowd. Nervous laughter.

Felicity let out a shocked huff and nothing else. Disappointing. Kade had hoped it would be a good enough dig that she changed sides for a few seconds, like she had been known to do if the diss was good enough. Loyalty was nothing to Felicity in the face of a good joke.

Aaron's eyes widened. For a second it was just shock. Then something appeared behind it, dark and dangerous. A memory flashed back: Aaron's face at his ear, beery breath against his cheek. *I think somebody's gonna die tonight.*

"I don't think you realize—" Aaron stopped as a big hand landed on his shoulder.

"We need to get to class," said Theo Fairgood. "Save it for lunch."

Theo looked...normal. A little pale, like he hadn't

gotten enough sun. But his curls were intact, his eyes clear. No blackness bleeding into them like when he'd woken up after the lake, or when he bit Kade in his room.

Kade let go of Aaron's face and kicked him lightly in the knee. "Yeah, go on, Aaron. Be a good lackey and follow your golden boy."

"I can't be late again," Theo said as Aaron whipped back to glare at Kade. "Come on, man."

Felicity nudged Aaron with her forehead. "Babe. Your parents will be pissed."

Aaron stood perfectly still. Then, all at once, he dropped Kade's jacket and walked off, slinging his arm over Felicity's slim shoulders. Theo followed them. Kade almost expected a glance, for that guilty look from the weekend to return, or for Theo to toss him some kind of thinly veiled threat.

But Theo just kept walking. Kade watched that bright, fluffy hair turn the corner and thought, *maybe that's it. The whole craziness was just one weekend. I never have to talk to Theo Fairgood unless he's tripping me in the hallway.*

An hour later, Theo dragged him into a closet.

"Oh god don't kill me," Kade babbled, all instinct and primal fear. "Don't get me wrong, mate, that was the best high ever, but if you killed Lemmings that's *not* a great hit on your track record."

"I didn't kill Jeremiah Lemmings," Theo hissed. He looked confused, like he'd expected Kade to growl at him. He moved back, but there wasn't much room to move around in a broom cupboard. His sneaker immediately clanged into a mop bucket.

Theo swore. "Look, I don't remember what happened after I hit the water. I woke up with a dead deer on me."

"A *deer?*"

Theo shushed him.

Kade slapped the wall of the broom closet. "Who's gonna hear us in here?"

"There's a teacher down the hall." Theo tilted his head, listening. Kade watched him, caught between incredulity, fear, and deep excitement. His neck throbbed.

Theo's gaze returned to him. "I thought you might have done something to me. Or that you'd know what happened. So I came over, and...look, I'm sorry for biting you."

Do it again, Kade thought.

"And...burning you." Theo winced at the bandages peeking through the wilting scarf. "I don't know what that was. I didn't burn my parents when I touched them. Or Felicity, or Aaron. Or the other deer I ate."

"Do you...feel better? After the deers?"

"Kinda." Theo made a face, tongue moving in his mouth. "They taste gross, and it doesn't fill me up properly. Like eating brussels sprouts when you want a steak."

I'm the steak, Kade thought giddily. "Did *I* taste nice?"

Theo's jaw worked. When he spoke, his voice was as flat as Aaron's. "It was fine."

It brought Kade crashing back to reality: he was stuck in a closet with a jock who wouldn't piss on him if he was on fire. Sure, he'd brought Kade snacks and water after he mauled him. And Kade wanted to get mauled again. But this wasn't...safe. *He* wasn't safe. Theo had *killed* someone this weekend. For all Kade's reckless behavior, he *did* have a sense of self-preservation. It sounded a lot like his aunt sighing in the back of his head when he drank too much or flung himself at a bully when he could've just run. *You're not really going to do this, are you?*

Kade pulled back as far as he could. "Did Lemmings actually die from a bite? Or was it, like...a weird stab wound?"

"The official story is that he got knifed," Theo said, strained. "But...I don't know. The timing is...and nobody gets killed in *Lock*. He got attacked around two a.m. I don't remember what I was doing then."

"Chasing deer, hopefully. Did you see who, uh, *turned* you?"

Theo shook his head. "It was a guy. I didn't recognize him, he was all...growly. He called me...sith?"

"Maybe he's a Star Wars fan."

"What? No. It sounded familiar, though." Theo paused. He scratched his head, thick fingers raking through those fluffy blond curls that made Kade think of boy bands. "Do you want to look into it? With me? Lemmings's murder, and all the...vampire stuff?"

This is it, Kade thought deliriously. *It's happening. My backstory is over, the story is finally starting. It's starting in a broom closet and everything stinks like cleaning fluid and floor polish, but it's HAPPENING. Why couldn't it have happened with a guy who was less of an asshole?*

It didn't stop the thread of excitement from leaking into his voice. "You're bringing me along on your little vampire adventure of discovery?"

"What? No, come on." Theo ran another hand through his hair, hissing when he almost knocked over a spray bottle. "I can't ask anyone *else*. Nobody knows."

"And nobody will know." Kade gave him a two-fingered lesbian salute. "I'll take your secret to the grave. Which will be very far away."

"Sure," Theo said distractedly.

Kade watched him tug on his lustrous fringe and wondered if anyone had told Theo about worry beads.

"Well," Kade said. "I should..." He was reaching for the doorknob when Theo spoke up.

"You really dragged me out of the lake?"

Kade glanced up. Or, he glanced *over*. They were actually the same height, though it was easy to forget with all the tripping in halls and being shoved into walls and pulled into closets.

Theo still looked tense. Like he was waiting for Kade to snarl or laugh in his face. Kade thought about it. Then he remembered gagging next to Theo's cold, drenched body, sobbing and wondering how he was going to explain any of this to the cops. Suddenly Theo had sat up, and Kade had screamed. Babbled something about an ambulance, about waterlogged lungs, about how he should've tried CPR. And Theo had just...stared at him, his brown eyes all pupil. He'd shuddered, leaned in, and for a second the fear had come back, Kade's entire body screaming at him to run.

But he hadn't. And Theo had shuddered again, head whipping around toward a rustle in the bushes. He'd stumbled toward it. He was sprinting by the time he vanished into the trees, ignoring Kade calling after him, asking what the hell was going on.

It would've been terrifying, waking up after that. It would've been terrifying being dragged up in the air, being gnawed on and dropped a hundred feet into a lake.

Kade's weekend had been scary. But Theo's must've been worse.

"Yeah," Kade admitted. "I...yeah."

Theo was silent. Then he said, "Surprised you could do it. You look like a toothpick."

"Hey, under this skinny form lies a musclebound *beast*." Kade thought about flexing, but he was tired and Theo was a dick and it was too small in this closet anyway. "I had an adrenaline rush, Fairgood. Google it."

If Theo understood the reference, he didn't show it. He just nodded, like he would actually look into adrenaline rushes, and stared down at his sneakers.

"Thank you," he mumbled. "You didn't have to."

Kade had to take a second. Apparently big and bashful did it for him. Even when it was attached to a jock.

"Return the favor sometime," he told him, and reached again for the door. "Uh. Is the coast clear?"

Theo nodded.

"Good. Meet me behind the science building after school." Kade flicked him another salute and strode out, hands in his jeans pockets, whistling, craving a cigarette so badly his teeth itched. It didn't matter how hard he was playing cool, he realized as he strolled toward class. Theo and his new vampire ears had to hear his heart thundering in his chest.

CHAPTER
SEVEN

THEO EXPECTED Kade to make a bigger deal out of walking on the opposite side of the road as him. And he did, at first. Laughed in Theo's face, asked if Theo wanted him to wear a fake mustache and talk in another accent. Then he spoke in an awful Russian accent until Theo crossed the road and started toward Lockhart Books.

He checked behind him on the way, expecting Kade to be ducking behind lampposts just to annoy him. But Kade was walking normally. Thin shoulders slumped, one hand in his pocket, the other cradling a cigarette. Eyes scanning in case he had to duck out of the way of—or into, depending on Kade's mood—someone's fist.

Must be tiring, Theo thought. *Always having to look out for someone who wants to give you trouble.*

It made his stomach twist. He didn't look at Kade

again until he was inside Lockhart Books, pretending to browse the poetry collection.

The bell over the door jingled. Theo looked up from the poetry book he wasn't reading and watched Kade stroll the aisles. He reached Theo's aisle and gasped, hand flying to his chest. Today's shirt was another winner: black lace with red letters spelling out *SMALL-TOWN BOY,* with a little heart instead of an *O.*

Theo rolled his eyes. *Here we go.*

"By my stars and garters," Kade said, which didn't make any sense to Theo, but so did most of what Kade came up with. "Doth my eyes deceive me? Fellow class-mate, Theo Fairgood—"

"Okay."

"Trawling the aisles of ye olde local bookshop, home of all things weird and strange? Reading a secondhand copy of"—His arched brows rose even higher—"Richard Siken's *Crush?* Bit, uh, *abstract* for you, but alright."

It *was* a bit abstract for Theo. He had skimmed two sentences about melons and dreams before he started feeling like he was sitting an exam he hadn't studied for and let his gaze go fuzzy. That didn't mean he appreci-ated Kade's mocking tone. He wasn't *stupid.* He studied too hard for that.

"Of course you know *poetry,*" he sneered.

"Food of the soul." Kade grinned that sharp smile Theo was used to, adjusting the scarf so it covered his bandages better. "Okay, where's the vampire section?"

Theo shushed him.

"It's an empty *shop*, Fairgood." Kade spun in a circle, narrowly avoiding knocking over a display of first-edition books about witch hunting.

"There's someone out back," Theo hissed. She smelled like dust and ozone and something else Theo couldn't identify, old and dark and dripping.

"Shit. She's coming—" Theo clicked his mouth shut as a woman pushed through the beads that separated the counter from the back room.

Kade gaped. Theo couldn't blame him. One of Milly Hart's eyes was white, the other so pale gray it might as well have been white. She had long, flat brown hair with a streak of grey and a deep scar bisecting her cheek and brow. There was a tattoo on her wrist, a spiky green fruit that Theo didn't recognize. A worn friendship bracelet sat over the tattoo, a tiny skull knotted into it.

Theo's sole memory of the Lockhart bookshop owner was being five years old and getting spooked by her in a supermarket. He'd tugged on his dad's hand. *Dad, what's wrong with that lady's face?*

Don't stare, his dad replied. *It's rude.*

But he'd been staring too. Theo still remembered the look in his dad's eyes, curiosity tinged with disgust, before he dragged Theo into the next aisle.

Kade's smile came back, less sharp and more excited. "Oh my god, *hi*. We're doing a school project about the town founders. Do you have any books about that?"

Milly didn't look at him. She was too busy staring at Theo, unblinking, her white eye somehow wider than the other.

Theo shivered. Maybe he really *did* look different. He'd noticed it a few times when he looked in the mirror over the weekend, but only when he was in the middle of looking away: a flash of something off, something *wrong*, pale and rotting and dead. Then he'd look back and find his face staring back at him the same as ever.

"Um," Kade said. "Hello?"

Milly blinked, jerking back from wherever she'd been. "Hi. Hello. Sorry, you reminded me of something I have to do later. I can absolutely get you books on town lore, we've had a few local historians collect records. But if you'd like an overview, I can tell you whatever you'd like."

Her speech was stiff and timid, like she'd taken a seminar on how to do customer service and was still getting the hang of it. But her face was warm. Friendly. Not quite open, but it hinted that it would *like* to be open, one day.

Kade strode up and leaned on the counter in barely restrained glee. "We would love that. Regale us, oh lady fair."

She blinked again. Her mouth twisted, like she didn't know if this strange goth boy was making fun of her or not.

"I mean ma'am," Kade amended. "Regale us, *ma'am*. Sorry, we get so *pumped* about history. Right, partner?"

He turned to look at Theo, who ripped his gaze away from Milly's scar and nodded.

"Can't get enough."

Milly brushed her hair back behind her ears. It showed off even more of the deep scar, which wrapped down around her jaw. If Theo had a scar like that, he would never push his hair behind his ears again. Like Felicity and the scar she got when she broke her arm during gymnastics practice in fifth grade, the bone shooting straight through the skin. She wore long sleeve shirts whenever she could get away with it. They had to photoshop it out of her model photos.

Theo shot a guilty look over at Kade, that stupid scarf tight around his head. Kade pulled him out of a lake and what did Theo do in return? Disfigured him for life. Probably. Theo didn't know how burn scars worked.

"One second." Milly ducked back behind the beads. Theo listened as she shifted books around. Above him, a fly buzzed in the rafters. If Theo closed his eyes and concentrated, he could hear it rubbing its legs together.

A loud snap made his eyes fly open. Kade stood in front of him, face bright like it had been for a few seconds in the closet. *You're dragging me along on your little vampire adventure?*

"This is insane," Kade whispered, bouncing on the spot. "She's *perfect*. She's right out of a Stephen King novel. Is she going to be our sage guide or is she secretly in charge of the vampire cult that will kill us all?"

"What are you talking about? She's just a lady who owns a bookshop. Stop *jumping*."

Kade stopped. His goofy grin didn't go away as Milly emerged and threw a book down on the counter. It was thick and black, the pages yellow with age. It had no title, just a chipped gold flame embossed into the black cover.

"Cool!" Kade squeaked.

Theo nudged him.

Kade cleared his throat, tone turning flat and unaffected. "Cool. So, you're gonna give us the Cliff notes?"

"I'm going to do my best." Milly tipped the book open, revealing spidery text crammed from margin to margin. Half of the book was burned, more of it was stained. Not much was legible, and only if you could read cursive that curly, which Theo couldn't.

"So, you know the basics—vampires moved into the land, terrorized surrounding villagers. Hunters tracked them down, killed them, trapped the leader in a coffin, lit her on fire and buried her deep underground. They built a town on top and called it Lock."

Kade whistled, rocking on his heels. "I gotta say, for a town with a history so metal I expected Lock to be less boring."

"It's small-town America," Theo said. "What did you expect?"

Milly kept flipping until she hit loose paper: ledgers and dates and what looked like an old diary entry.

"The stories get filed down over the years," she continued. "Simplified. No thorny complications."

Kade and Theo spoke in one. "Complications?"

The book fell open to a drawing: men with spiked mouths, snarling from the dark. On the other side, lit by the sun, stood a group of men with torches and axes. The stains and burns blurred half of each group into a cracked mess.

"The hunters never left," Milly said. "They stuck around, passing the mantle down to the next generation. Vampires are still drawn to this place and their old leader, still burning under the earth. The fight has been going on for centuries, right under our noses."

Kade let out a delighted snort.

Theo dug an elbow into his side.

"I'm cool," Kade hissed. Then, to Milly: "So the hunters would have to be a family who have been here since it was founded, right? Like the Fairgoods?"

Theo nudged him again, harder. "The hell, man!"

Kade rubbed his side. "What? I'm just throwing out options!"

"Half the *town* has been here since it was founded," Theo argued. "And my parents didn't even grow up here! They only moved back once I was born!"

"Convenient."

"Shut up!"

Milly cleared her throat. "The Fairgoods don't get

mentioned. Actually, all the names are in code. One group goes by the title *Warrens*. Something about rabbits."

Kade cocked his head. "Theo. Doesn't your best pal, Aaron Fletcher, go out to shoot rabbits with his family every year? A tradition spanning countless generations?"

Theo glared at him. Kade's shit-eating grin grew even bigger.

"But this book doesn't make it clear if the Warrens are the hunters or the hunted," Milly continued. "It's... difficult to put together."

She lifted another page. The corner flecked off, too charred to hold. She closed the book carefully, resting her scarred hand over the cover. For a moment her face emptied, eyes going half-lidded. Then she looked up and the stiffness was back.

"Whoever wrote this was *very* dedicated to keep up the fiction. I wish they got to write our other history books. Centuries of vampires and hunters chasing each other would make Gerabaldi's *History Of Lock, 1800s To Now*, much more interesting."

Kade laughed. Theo joined in, but it was dry, scraping up his throat. The golden flame gleamed under Milly's fingers. If vampires were real, then the founders story could be too. Hunters could still be among them, wanting to...what? Kill him? Shove him down there to join the vampire leader? A shudder worked up his spine as he imagined the tight space of a coffin, flames licking his skin for eternity. If the story was true, then she'd been down there all this time. She was burning right now.

"Theo?"

Theo looked over. Kade and Milly were watching him, waiting.

Theo shook his head. "Sorry, what?"

"I said it makes for a good story," Kade told him. "Doesn't it? Centuries of hiding and fighting. Generations rising and falling. It's like an epic poem."

Dust drifted between Milly's fingers, onto the golden flame. Theo could see dust motes. He could see each pore in their faces. If he focused, he could hear termites in the wall of the next store, he could hear the blood rushing in Kade's veins, tantalizing, *waiting* for him...

"I've never been much of a poetry guy," Theo mumbled. He kept his lips over his teeth, just in case.

Kade ghosted his hand over the golden flame embedded in the black book. "Shame about old man Lemmings, huh?"

Theo shot him a look. Kade shot one back, defensive. *We're investigating,* he mouthed as Milly busied herself behind the counter, refilling the receipt machine.

"Jeremiah? Yes, it's terrible. He ordered from here sometimes."

"Oh?" Kade gave Theo another look, far too smug. "What did he read?"

"Elizabethan history, mostly." Milly clicked the

receipt machine closed and looked up at them again, white eye gleaming in the dim store. "Are you going to his funeral?"

"Maybe," said Theo, who knew his parents would rather listen to Theo talk about wildflowers for an hour than attend an old hermit's funeral.

Kade hummed. "Theo, isn't there just one funeral home in Lock right now? The other one folded after everyone in the family business—"

He mimed a gun under his chin.

"I guess," Theo said through gritted teeth.

"So I guess all dead roads in Lock lead to that funeral home."

"What's your point?"

"No point," Kade said, staring at Theo like he could scream directly into his soul with nothing but eye contact. "Hey, do you want to head out? I think we have enough for today. Thanks a bunch, Milly."

CHAPTER
EIGHT

"WELCOME to Hersay's funeral home, how can we..."

The receptionist's smile melted right off her face once she saw who it was. Her name tag said CLARA, with a flower sticker after the *A*. She was in her late thirties with a bad dye, boob, and nose job, and Kade had no idea why she already hated him. Most of the hatred came from his classmates, and some of their parents. Maybe she'd seen him hissing at them around town. Or she took offense with his shaved head and painted nails, or she didn't like that he had the demeanor of a feral cat. Maybe she overheard someone call him Monster, took one look at him and thought *yeah, makes sense.*

Kade beamed at her. "Hi! I was wondering if you guys are hiring? I'm passionate about the death business."

Clara's expression soured even more, snub nose twisting in displeasure.

"Hiring," she repeated. She gave him another once-over: crooked teeth, chain on his wallet, miniature swords dangling from his ears. "We don't really..."

"Come on," he wheedled. "There's gotta be somewhere I can drop in my CV. Sorry, *resume*. You don't have a job application box back there? Something to let the manager know I'm interested...wait, do you guys have managers?"

"We have a director." Her lips pulled up, strained with Botox and how much she wanted to tell him to get out. "We don't have an applications box. It's a small job pool."

Kade nodded and pointed. "What's that?"

"What?" She turned to follow Kade's pointing finger.

Kade glanced over his shoulder in time to see a blur flash past the counter and into the back rooms, the door opening and closing with barely a whisper. If they were going off door noise, Theo would ace Sneaking with flying colors.

His inhuman sprint was another matter. Passing the desk at supersonic speeds had caused loose papers to fly everywhere.

"Hey!" Clara frowned, looking around in confusion as papers scattered around the counter.

"Whoa," Kade said, bending to scoop them up from the floor. "Windy today! Hate it when that happens. So can I email somebody my resume, or...wait, you guys do part-time, right? Because I can only do weekends."

Clara straightened, papers clutched to her staff uniform. "Do you have any qualifications?"

"I'm a sophomore."

Clara stared at him. She sucked her lipsticky lips against her teeth, pressing hard enough to leave teeth marks. "Maybe come back after you graduate."

"I look forward to it," he said sagely, and left.

The back door cracked open as Kade hurried gleefully up the ramp. *The ramp they used to wheel bodies up.*

"Get in," Theo hissed.

Kade ducked inside.

Theo pulled the door shut behind him. "Okay. The body drawers are over—why are you *smiling*? We're in a funeral home!"

"We're *breaking into* a funeral home," Kade corrected in a whisper. "For our strange adventures! Who knows what we'll uncover? What dark secrets await?"

Theo stared at him. Kade regretted not wearing his platform boots. It would be funnier if that incredulous stare was directed upward.

"I think I like you better when you're barking at people," Theo said.

Kade woofed quietly. Theo shushed him.

The funeral home was less impressive than the ones on TV. It was smaller, for one, and less...bare. There was a vase of plastic flowers on a desk near the doors, and a painting on the wall of skeleton dogs playing poker. Someone had stuck a magnet on one of the storage drawer doors that said CRACK OPEN A COLD ONE.

Kade sniggered. "I should get that on a T-shirt."

Theo made a face. "Is it a necrophilia joke?"

"What? No, it's about opening...the body fridges..." Kade trailed off uncomfortably, scuffing a boot against the peeling floor. "Huh. I should still get it on a T-shirt."

Theo led him over to a storage drawer in the corner. "I think he's in here."

"Can you smell him?"

Theo hesitated. "Sort of. I smell *something*. Like...old meat. Not-yet-decay."

"*Awesome*," Kade said. He reached for the handle and paused. "Wait. I thought funeral homes had a freezer for bodies, not these tray things. Trays are *morgues*. Who designed this place?"

Theo stared at him. "*Why* is that something you know?"

Kade shrugged and yanked the handle. He slid the tray out, stopping as soon as they saw the man's head. His eyes were gouged out, the lids removed except for a stray shred of eyelid at the corner of his eye. Somebody had done a bad job cleaning up.

Kade gagged.

"Don't," Theo warned, but his voice was tight. He

turned around, hands on his hips, then on his face, then his hips again. "Oh my god."

"Oh shit," Kade agreed. "I wasn't—I wasn't expecting that."

"No?" Theo cleared his throat. "Mr. Death Guy doesn't get a kick out of no-eyes old dude on a slab?"

Kade shot him a look. Theo was busy pinching his nose, glancing at Jeremiah and then away with a wince. It didn't feel like a jab. It felt like...desperately trying to say something normal.

"I'm not a big eye trauma guy," Kade said. "Now, the *stab* wound. Let's see that puppy."

Theo made a noise in the back of his throat. Not quite a laugh, not quite vomit.

Kade snorted. "*Can* you even puke? Wait, can you eat human food?"

"Let's not find out," Theo said, and pulled the tray further until they could see the man's ribs.

There was a deep gash over his heart. The meat inside was strangely black.

"Not-yet-decay," Kade repeated uncertainly.

Theo shook his head, leaning over the wound. "It's not rot. Not...properly."

"Sure. But humans don't have black blood, right?"

"No," Theo said. He leaned back, a faraway look on his face. "How old would you say he is?"

Kade considered. "Forties? Which is weird, I always heard he was *old*."

"Me too," Theo said. "I thought he was in his eighties. He's lived in town since before my parents moved back. *Way* before."

They traded a look. Kade felt the excitement creep back despite the faint but persistent urge to puke.

"He's a *vampire*," Kade said. "He—oh."

His excitement dimmed at the tight panic in Theo's face.

"I'm sure *you'll* be fine," he tried. "Like...if you just keep a low profile. Nobody's gonna stake you. Or... gouge your eyes out."

He shuddered at the man's empty sockets. That little shred of eyelid was killing him. It was like when he had half a cuticle come off, he couldn't rest until he bit the rest of it off. Even if it made him bleed. *Especially* if it made him bleed. There was something satisfying about hurting after a job well done. It made it feel more real.

Theo bent down, peering further into the container.

"Uhhh," Kade said. "Are you...trying to look at his junk?"

"No, jackass, there's something else in there." Theo dragged the shelf out some more, revealing the man's stomach.

It was slashed. Not deep, like the hole in his chest. These were shallow cuts, black meat showing past the skin. Each cut formed a wonky letter:

WATCH OUT

BLOODSUCKERS

The last *S* hooked deeper, showing a flash of white hipbone. Kade looked at that bleached white and thought, *that is the gnarliest thing I've ever seen.* Then he gagged again.

"Kade."

"I got it," Kade croaked, shielding his mouth, just in case.

"No, someone's coming." Theo shoved the tray closed. Jeremiah Lemmings vanished back into the cold dark.

Kade straightened. "What? Shit, let's—"

Theo said something. It sounded like *hold on,* but it was too fast for Kade to make out. Then his legs were being swept out from under him, Theo's arms under his knees and his back as he streaked out of there.

Kade didn't see shit. Vague color, wind on his scalp, and suddenly they were standing half a block away in an alley and Theo was tipping Kade out of his arms.

Kade stumbled to his feet. The trip hadn't helped his nausea, and he blinked until black spots faded from his eyes.

"Screw *golden boy*," he managed. "They should call you *vamp taxi*. Hoo, that was a rush! Can we do that again?"

"Did I burn you?"

Kade paused. He'd been riding the adrenaline rush since he crept up the ramp into the funeral home. Now that he focused, his arm hurt. A small sting on the white of his elbow. He held it out and saw a shiny burn just starting to show.

"Huh," he said.

Theo nodded. He was still staring at Kade's arm.

"What?"

Theo shook his head. "Why you?"

Kade turned his arm, watching the evening light bounce off the burn. "Maybe I'm special."

Theo snorted. "Sure. Monster's *special*. That'll be the day."

Kade smiled at him, razor-sharp. "Well, I'm *something*," he snapped. "Or you wouldn't burn me every time you come close."

Theo stared at him. For a second, something impossible happened: golden boy looked *sorry*. Like he wished he could take the words back. Like he gave a single iota of shit about Kade "Monster" Renfield's feelings.

"Fine," Theo said quietly. "Maybe you *are* something. *Maybe*. Now can we get out of this alleyway? Everything smells so much worse this week."

"AT LEAST WE know *you* didn't kill him."

"Yay," Theo said dryly. "Great."

He slumped down against a rock, staring at his hands. If he cut his palm open right now, what would ooze out? Black blood, like the vampire who had turned him? If he slashed his stomach open would his organs be dark, like the old man cut open in the funeral home? What *was* he?

"Soooo," Kade said. He toed at a patch of moss near Theo's foot. "Are we going to talk about the whole Fletcher thing?"

"There's no Fletcher thing," Theo told him. "You're reaching."

Kade spun a lit cigarette in his fingers like a small, dangerous drumstick. "I'm not reaching, I'm suggesting. You got any other ideas about possible hunter families who suit the title *Warren*? Because I sure don't!"

"But—"

"I'm not saying walk into school and sink your teeth into your childhood bestie. I'm saying let's look into it! Let's unravel this dark little mystery and see where it leads!" Kade sucked on his cigarette and whirled, tipping his stubbled head back to whoop at the trees. It went long and loud, birds startling and taking off en masse. Kade cheered louder, cupping his hands around his mouth so his yell followed the birds as they vanished into the sky.

"THIS IS THE COOLEST THING TO EVER HAPPEN IN THIS STUPID, SHITTY LITTLE TOWN!"

Theo shot to his feet. "This is *not* cool. Somebody wants to *kill* me. Someone killed Jeremiah Lemmings! They basically carved YOU'RE NEXT, THEO, into his chest! How are you excited about this? I'm doomed!"

"You're not *doomed*," Kade told him. His mouth curled like he wanted to sneer, but the grin got in the way. "You just need to keep it quiet. Lemmings was a vampire for who knows how long, and we had no murders, so obviously you can keep eating deer! And while you munch on bambis, we can dive deeper down this rabbit hole and find out what's going on. Who killed the old man? Why the warning? Who the hell turned you? God, I can't wait. It's so cool. I wish it had happened with someone who wasn't an *asshole*."

"Back at you," Theo snapped. "You know I could die, right? I *did* die! You're acting like this is a movie!

This is my LIFE! No wonder you don't have any friends."

Kade's teeth clamped around his cigarette. His grin sharpened into the thing Theo was used to seeing in school: the smile that appeared before he threw himself at someone with his fists up, ready to lose.

"At least I don't spend my whole day worried about what people think of me," Kade said, voice thin and dangerous. "You pretend you don't care what everybody thinks but it's so obvious you do, *all* of you jocks do, that's why you're bullies. Guess what? People who are secure in themselves don't bully people, they just get on with their lives and let other people BE!"

Theo's chest heaved. "At least I don't antagonize people every second of every day just to feel something."

"Antagonize," Kade repeated. He ripped the almost-finished cigarette out of his mouth and stamped it into the dirt. "How the hell do I *antagonize* people?"

"You do it every day! You open your mouth and it's some stupid quip, or a reference nobody understands, and—" Theo gestured down at his clothing. "What is this? Just dress like a normal person! *Let people be.* If everybody *let you be* you'd start screaming for attention by the end of day one."

Kade's eyes shone. His cheek dented inwards, and Theo smelled blood.

"Right," Kade spat, stalking forward. Theo jerked back, but Kade kept going until they were nose to nose.

His breath was hot and smoky on Theo's cheek. "So it's good that people trip me in the halls? Steal my textbooks? Leave burning *shit* on my front door? Make fun of me every day, say I should *drop dead*, call me a creep, a freakshow, a *monster*—"

"If you hate me this much, why are you still here?"

Kade stuttered to a stop. He lifted a hand to his scarf, touching the bandage through the fabric.

Theo winced. He forced it out of his expression before Kade could look at him again, his father's voice clear in his head: *never let them see you flinch.*

Kade lifted his head, defiant. As if there was any other way for Kade Renfield to be.

"You know what," he snarled. "You're *right*. It's time I got out of your swoopy boyband hair. But! I want one thing before I go."

Theo opened his mouth to tell him good luck getting anything from him, but Kade was too fast.

"I want another bite," Kade said.

Theo stopped, watching for any sign of his usual sarcasm. There was none. Kade was serious.

"*Why?*" Theo asked. Then a memory came back— Kade in the closet, babbling. *Best high I ever had,* he'd said. Kade on his bedroom floor, slurring for more.

Kade unwound the scarf from his head. He pried the cheek bandage off first, and Theo held back another wince as the finger-shaped burns were revealed. Then the bandage in the dip of his neck. The bruising was terrible, the bite was worse. Theo marveled at the angry shades of red and purple.

Theo started, "But—"

Kade let out an ugly laugh. "What, you're worried about hurting me *now*?"

"It's *bad*," Theo tried. "Like, it's—dude, it's *so* bad. People will see."

"Oh, if people will *see*," Kade muttered. He twisted his head, baring his burned throat. "Come on. You look tired. This is *way* better than deer."

"This is why you agreed to come with me to the funeral home," Theo said, his cold heart sinking. "It wasn't about helping me, or turning your life into some stupid mystery story. You wanted me to bite you again."

Kade shrugged. "Now use 'em or lose 'em, vamp boy."

The blood was so close underneath his battered skin. That was all bruises were: blood, pooling. A dozen different shades collecting on Kade's long neck. There was that mole he'd spotted in Kade's bedroom, hidden under stark purple.

Theo swayed in and hesitated. "You're sure?"

"What am I, your prom date? *Yes*, I'm sure. Now shut up and—"

Theo lurched forward and bit him in the neck, right over the worst and most delicious of the bruising. Kade cried out at the sharp pain, fighting instinctively as Theo pressed his hands against Kade's shoulder blades.

Theo sucked, his jaw humming with vibrations.

Kade's cry melted into a groan. Theo clutched him, sucking harder. *This* was what he was missing when he ate those deer—animal blood tasted stale, almost sickly. Kade tasted like fine wine. Liquid gold. Warmth in a blizzard.

Kade sagged against his shoulder.

Now, Theo told himself. *Stop.*

He allowed himself one more drag, blood flowing thick into his mouth. Then he pulled back, and the tingling in his jaw died down. He held Kade steady as he tried to lean back in, a whine spilling from his pale lips.

Kade's eyes cracked open, gray barely visible around his full pupil. For a moment he just looked at Theo, dazed.

As if in a dream, Theo reached up and touched the bite wound on Kade's neck. His fingers buzzed, but he barely noticed. This strange new version of Kade made Theo feel protective. Kade was an asshole, sure. But he was so vulnerable like this, and Theo wanted...

He blinked. The skin under his fingers wasn't torn. The jagged bite wound on Kade's neck was gone, the burned skin healed except for the places Theo's fingers were touching. As Theo dropped his hand, the burn marks vanished from his touch vanished.

He was healed.

Kade turned. "Whazzat?"

Something stung Theo's cheek, hot and sharp. He leapt back with a hiss. "What was *that*?"

Kade swayed on the spot. "What? Give a guy a

second to—" He stopped, eyes going huge as he saw Theo's face. "The hell?"

Theo rubbed his stinging cheek. It felt like a burn. Thin and shallow, right next to his nose.

"What even..." Kade trailed off. He reached up to touch his earrings—twin silver swords with vines twisting around the hilt. Long and thin, just like the burn.

"No," Theo said. "Come *on*. Silver, really?"

Kade took an earring out and stared at it, considering. Then he lashed out, still clumsy with blood loss, zapping Theo in the forehead with the tip of the earring sword.

Theo reared back with another hiss as pain bloomed under his hairline. "Quit it!"

Kade snickered, going to flick him again.

Theo caught his arm. "I said cut it *out*. You got what you wanted, now leave me alone."

Kade's smile faded. He jerked his arm out of Theo's grip. "Right. Well, see ya, blood boy. Wouldn't wanna be ya. Eat shit, etcetera. *Can* you even eat anymore? Questions I'll never know, because digging into this shitty little mystery is *not* worth hanging out with you."

He fumbled at his scarf, fingers stubborn and clumsy as he tried to wrap it back around his head. He didn't realize he'd been healed.

"Wait," Theo called as Kade turned away.

Kade paused, wobbling on his lanky legs.

"Your burns," Theo said. "They're gone."

"They're what?" Kade felt his face, gingerly at first, then shoving at his unblemished skin. "Bloody hell. When did that happen?"

"Before *you* burned *me*," Theo said. "I didn't—I touched the wound. And it…"

He shrugged. He didn't know how to explain the buzzing in his hand—so much like the vibration in his jaw when he pushed venom into Kade's bloodstream—and more importantly, he didn't want to. If Kade wanted out of this nightmare, good riddance.

Kade wavered. His gray eyes gleamed, unreadable. For a second Theo thought he'd ask, and Theo prepared to shoot him down.

"Great," Kade said flatly. He threw his scarf around his neck, fast and careless, like he did everything else. "Well, see ya, blood boy. Wouldn't wanna be ya."

He walked off, flicking Theo a middle-finger salute.

Theo watched him vanish into the trees and reached up to touch the burn on his forehead. Super speed, super strength, flight—he had to have super healing, right? Any moment now, these burns would fade into smooth skin.

He pressed harder. They kept stinging.

He dropped his hand with a sigh, thinking about one of the last things Kade had said: *could* he even eat anymore? He always liked eating. The idea of never getting to do it again depressed him.

He'd go out and buy something, he decided. Then he'd figure out what he was doing next.

He had barely made it out of the woods when he spotted Felicity heading down the long path that led to his house.

He jogged to catch up with her. "Liss!"

She startled, whirling around. Her long blond ponytail almost snapped him in the face. She was wearing sweatpants and no makeup, two things she hadn't done in public for years. She stunk like deodorant and sweat and something else he couldn't identify.

"Oh my god," she said, her grin strained. "Make some noise when you walk!"

She shoved him. It was about as effective as a canary shoving an elephant. Theo moved with it anyway, glad she wasn't actually annoyed. Felicity walked on the knife edge of playfully irritated, but when she got genuinely pissed off, her wrath was deadly.

"What's up?" he asked, glad for the distraction. "Where's Aaron?"

She struck an unsteady model pose, eyelashes fluttering. "What, am I not enough?"

"You're great," he assured her. "I was just—we haven't hung out for ages. Just you and me."

Felicity toyed with her ponytail. "And whose fault is that?"

Yours, Theo didn't say. He'd tried to initiate all their usual hangs after she started seeing Aaron. She was the one who made excuses, pulled away, brought Aaron along to all their hangouts. After a while he just assumed that if he saw Felicity, Aaron would come along too. Which was fine. Aaron was their best friend, too. Had been for years. But he still hung out one-on-one with Aaron. He missed his Felicity time. Now she had a boyfriend and a career and out-of-town model friends she saw on weekends.

Felicity frowned, pointing at his face. "What are *those*?"

"What are what? Liss, are you...okay? Is your mom hassling you again?"

Or are you partying too much, he thought. He'd thought Aaron was being overprotective, but maybe Theo needed to take Aaron seriously and add it to her list of issues.

Felicity peered at him, her blue eyes striking in the afternoon light. Her hand flashed out.

Theo caught it automatically.

Felicity stared at it, then at his face. "Wow. Now with super kung-fu grip. You been watching karate tutorials along with that mushroom foraging ASMR?"

"It's not ASMR," Theo argued, dropping her hand.

"Uh-huh. And those aren't burns." Felicity pointed to his face. The small burns from Kade's earrings stung. "What did you do, make out with some nettle?"

"Allergies," Theo lied.

"Since when do you have allergies?"

"People can get them later in life," Theo insisted. When she tried to argue, he continued: "I was going to get McDonald's. Want to come?"

She blinked. He waited for her to ask if he was having a cheat day, to teasingly threaten him about telling his parents.

"Okay," she said instead.

Theo drove them to McDonalds in his Lexus. They ate in the parking lot, Felicity propping her feet up on the dashboard while Theo made a mental note to clean it later. His dad got him this car, after all. He had to take care of it.

Felicity stabbed a fry into his hand. "You aren't eating."

"I'm getting to it." Theo dug a fry out of the carton resting in his lap. He held it up, considering. Hot. Salty. Crunchy. He and Felicity used to sit in the parking lot—no car, this was before either of them could drive—and eat one small fries each after school. The only junk food they had all week. They used to hold it over each other when they fought—*I'll tell your family about our McDonald's trysts!* They never meant it. There were some secrets they'd take to the grave.

Kade's voice rang through his head. *Can you even eat human food?*

One way to find out, Theo thought.

He slid the fry into his mouth. It tasted like cardboard.

Felicity adjusted her shoes on the dashboard. Her sweatpants fell down her calves, and Theo spotted an impact bruise he hadn't seen for a long time.

"Whoa," he said. "Where did *that* come from? Did you pick up gymnastics again?"

Felicity twisted her leg, following his gaze. He expected a snort, some fun-slash-worrying story that Aaron was going to stress over. But Felicity just held her leg up, examining the bruise with a bitter look in her eyes.

"Actually, yes," she said. She gave him a wry grin. "Mom wanted me to keep working on my falls tonight. Decided to sneak out here instead. I'm going to a party later, want to come?"

He frowned. "But...you told your mom you'd never do it again. She *begged*."

"A girl can't change her mind?" Felicity stretched and winced. "God. I forgot how much it messes with your muscles. So, you coming?"

The idea of being in the midst of so many people made Theo want to crawl into a hole.

"Next time," he said. He looked her up and down, all that gymnast muscle replaced by a model's willowy thinness. "Will they even let you into competitions after you've been gone this long?"

"Not doing it for the competitions," she said dully. "It's about the *discipline*."

She made a face, like she was quoting something she didn't fully understand.

Theo started, "But—"

She cut him off. "How was the rest of the party last weekend? Totally lost you after, like, ten."

He eyed her warily. She picked at her fries, jaw tense. She wanted him to let it go.

"Wasn't feeling it," Theo replied finally. "Went for a walk."

"Ooookay," Felicity said, in a tone that meant *tell me more, dipshit*. Which was rich, considering the weird news she'd just dropped on him without elaborating.

Theo ate another fry. It was awful. A wave of sadness overtook him at the knowledge that he could never enjoy McDonald's again. He didn't want fries anymore. He wanted Kade Renfield's neck, warm and tantalizing, his blood better than any animal, his scent more powerful than anyone else's in town.

Felicity stabbed him with another fry. He'd zoned out again.

"You know you can tell me anything," she said, sounding so sincere it worried him. "I know we haven't...like. Yeah. But you can tell me anything."

"I know," Theo lied. He ate another fry, wishing he could open his blunt teeth and let all the vampire crap spill out. Once, they had no secrets from each other.

"You can tell me anything too," he said. "Seriously."

"I know," Felicity said, too fast. She popped another fry into her mouth and rearranged her feet on the dashboard. Theo watched her wide, easy sprawl and thought about Kade curled up tight and cramped in the backseat so no one would see him.

Guilt churned in his stomach. Kade was an asshole, but he didn't deserve Theo snapping at him. *No wonder you have no friends.* He wasn't *that* bad. He'd dragged Theo out of that lake. And his over-the-top jumpy enthusiasm in Milly's bookshop was...weirdly endearing, if Theo was being honest with himself. Annoying, but endearing. He hadn't seen it before this week. Usually Kade was all snarls and jeers, flipping teachers off or careening around a party yelling along to the music.

Watching Kade jump up and down waiting for Milly to tell them the great big secret about Lock had been... cute. It made Theo want to scratch at that thorny surface and see what else was hidden underneath. And seeing Kade all floppy and vulnerable after biting him made Theo want to...*protect* him. Curl around him and growl at anyone who dared to come close. As if Kade needed protection. As if he was Theo's to protect.

Theo sighed. "Do you ever get the feeling you're not what your parents want? Like, deep down."

"You *are* what your parents want," Felicity replied bitterly. "You're hot, you're smart and—how do your parents put it? *Vicious.* You're the whooole package."

Theo shifted uncomfortably. "I really thought your

mom was getting over it. The gymnastics thing. You *said* you'd never go back to it."

"We're not talking about me," Felicity snapped. She rubbed her thigh, and Theo remembered the callouses she would get from the bars, the bruises on her sides and knees and legs and elbows from hitting the mat.

She turned to him, smiling thinly. "You're exactly what your parents want, Theo. Don't worry your pretty little head about it."

Theo thought back to Kade sagging against him. Of holding him up, easy as anything, his hands embarrassingly gentle.

"But what if I'm not?"

Felicity stared at him. She didn't look surprised. Theo had a sudden fuzzy memory of having this same conversation with Felicity in middle school. There was an uncanny sense of déjà vu when she replied: "Then get good at pretending."

She smiled at him again. Theo smiled back, wishing with everything in his dead body that one of them could say something, *anything* true. What her mom had said to convince her back into gymnastics after all these years. Why she was partying so much lately. Even something as small as why she was stressed enough to wear sweatpants and no makeup in public.

She reached over and touched his face. "Your allergies cleared up fast."

Theo rubbed his cheek and forehead. They were smooth again, no trace of Kade's earrings left.

"Just in time," Felicity said, leaning back into her seat and flashing him that smile that got her recruited to her modeling agency. "Wouldn't want your parents asking questions."

"Got that right," Theo said.

His stomach churned.

He ate another fry.

CHAPTER
TEN

THEO RETCHED. Another thread of black bile landed in the toilet. He imagined Kade standing next to him in the school bathroom stall with a notepad. A novelty one with a black unicorn on it, or something equally stupid.

Ten hours, imaginary Kade said. *Interesting. Eat this watermelon next. No, whole. You can't unhinge your jaw? Boring.*

"Screw you, Renfield," Theo gurgled. His stomach cramped. Another string of black bile dripped into the toilet bowl. He hadn't even gotten the opportunity to puke it out overnight. He'd spent last night watching cooking shows—he *had* to find better things to do now that he couldn't sleep, and working out felt useless now—and got ready for school feeling better than he had in days. It was on the drive to school where everything went wrong. By the time he pulled into the parking lot his stomach was churning. He'd ducked into a bathroom on the way to Homeroom, just in case. The second the door closed behind him his stomach did a barrel roll so intense he fell over onto the tiles.

At least it hit after I got to the bathroom, Theo thought. *Throwing up black bile in the middle of the hall would have sucked.*

He waited for the next spasm. It didn't come.

Someone cleared their throat. Theo startled. He'd been so caught up in puking he hadn't heard anyone come in.

"It's just me," said Mr. Hawthorn. "Are you sick? I can help."

"Not sick," Theo croaked. "It's me. Uh, Theo. Fairgood."

"Theo, hi. You seem like you're having a rough morning."

Theo groaned into the toilet bowl. "You could say that."

"And you're not sick?"

"Nope. No, I'm fine."

"Right." Mr. Hawthorn paused. Theo listened to the soft step of his polished boots, lingering near the sinks. "I read this study recently, about how sports kids are at higher risk of EDs—"

"I don't have an eating disorder, Mr. Hawthorn." Theo unpeeled his forehead from the toilet, expecting sweat. There was none. One bonus of vampirism.

"Oh. Good!" Mr. Hawthorn's boots squeaked against

the tiles. He smelled clean, like pine needles. "How was the Founder's Day party?"

Theo frowned. "What? Fine. I...I kinda wandered off."

"I heard."

Theo sighed. The troubles of living in a small town: everybody knew everybody's business. Especially a teacher who heard his students gossip whether he liked it or not.

"Sounds like you've had a difficult week," Mr. Hawthorn continued. "Do you want to come out of there and talk about it?"

Theo eased to his feet. His stomach settled. He rolled up a wad of toilet paper, wiped his face clean of black goo, then flushed it down the toilet.

When he emerged, Mr. Hawthorn was leaning against the sinks, shirtsleeves pushed up to his elbows, tattoos peeking out like they always did in the summer months. Theo still didn't know what those black tendrils were. An octopus?

"Hi," Mr. Hawthorn said, with that easy, understanding smile. "So, tell me—"

The door swung open. Coach Cheech walked in, tired and sweaty as usual, fiddling with his watch and swearing under his breath. His swears trailed off as he noticed the two of them standing next to the sinks.

He raised his bushy brows. "Did I interrupt an important bathroom talk?"

"Of course not," Mr. Hawthorn said smoothly. "We were just—"

Coach Cheech cut him off. "Great, then get out. I want blissful silence during my piss, it's the only quiet time I get all day."

He strode toward the urinals. Mr. Hawthorn gave Theo an apologetic smile and led him outside. If he disliked Coach Cheech—an opinion shared by most staff and students—he didn't show it. Then again, Theo had never seen Mr. Hawthorn treat anybody with anything but patient respect.

"So," he started once they were in the halls. "Want to tell me what's on your mind?"

Before Theo could figure out what he could say, the bell rang. Theo winced at its shrillness.

Mr. Hawthorn frowned. "Are you sure you're okay? I can call your parents."

"No! Seriously, I'm fine." Theo smiled as convincingly as he could. The last time his parents had to pick him up from school, he got the silent treatment and left alone for three days to fight a fever. Well, not *alone*—his mom brought him soup and water, and she even stroked his forehead a few times. But his dad would just come and stand in the doorway, check he was alive, and look disappointed.

I really expected you to be over this by now, he'd said.

I know, Theo had replied miserably, wheeling in and out of consciousness. *I'm sorry.*

"I should get to Homeroom," he said as Mr. Hawthorn opened his mouth. "See you in class, sir."

Mr. Hawthorn nodded. "Anytime you need to talk…"

"I know. Thanks." Theo waved as he left, pushing into the wave of students trying to get to class.

It should've been a relief, playing basketball out the back of Aaron's house several days later. They'd done it a million times before. But there was none of the adrenaline Theo was used to, no endorphins, no blood pumping.

Basketball was easy now. Too easy. Theo made basket after basket without getting winded. Aaron tried to laugh it off, but Theo could see him getting frustrated.

"What, you taking steroids now?"

Theo laughed. "Sure, man. All day, every day."

Aaron pulled his shirt up, wiping his face. His chest was flushed. Theo watched the blood rise under his tan skin. *He's not a good guy,* Kade had said. But of course he'd say that. It'd be hard to think of anyone as a good guy if your only interaction with them was them slinging insults at you.

Kade hadn't been at school in the days since the bite. Theo was trying not to think about it.

"Hey," he said, batting the ball against the concrete. "Is Liss, like…okay? I thought she'd never get back into gymnastics. Her mom brought up the whole 'it's what your dad would've wanted' and she *still* didn't give in. What happened?"

Aaron's face flattened out. He dropped his shirt back down. "I don't know. She won't talk to me. Just showed up exhausted with blisters on her hands."

"Weird," Theo said. He'd keep a closer eye on her in the next few weeks. If he was too busy with vampire shit and something slipped through the cracks, then Aaron would pick up his slack.

He asked, "You got any guys named Warren in your family tree?"

Aaron gave him an odd look. Probably expecting more Felicity questions. "I don't think so."

"Cool. Your family loves rabbits, right? Or, like... you've killed a lot of them."

"You gunning to get invited hunting, Fairgood?" Aaron flashed his teeth. "It's pretty exclusive. Even our girlfriends don't get to come. Just wives."

He feigned right. Theo followed him easily, stealing the ball and throwing it toward the net. It sailed through effortlessly.

Theo whooped. "There it is! How does it feel?"

"Lucky shot," Aaron said waspishly, the smallest frown twisting his thin lips.

"Or maybe I'm just that good," Theo taunted.

He turned to run after the ball. It had rolled off the court and toward the forest, where the Fletchers' one and only greenhouse was hidden behind the house.

Theo gave it an interested once-over, as always. The

point of a greenhouse was to let the sun in, but the material around this greenhouse was so opaque Theo couldn't even see what was growing in it.

"I don't care how much my parents like you," Aaron called from the court. "They're not letting you see the ghost."

"Or the drugs," Theo called back.

"Or the bodies," Aaron replied, grinning.

They had come up with many reasons for the mysterious locked greenhouse hidden on the back of the property none of them were allowed to enter. Even the gardener was barred from entry. Aaron had only seen his father go in once, and he'd snapped at Aaron when he'd asked about it.

The ball rolled dangerously close to the door.

Theo gave the locked greenhouse one last longing look and then snatched the ball before it could touch the milky white door. Then he jogged back to Aaron, throwing him the ball.

"Let's go," he said.

Aaron paused. His eyes flickered down Theo's body, taking in his absolute dryness where Aaron's skin was dewy with sweat.

Crap, Theo thought. He'd have to be more careful.

He flexed his leg. "Hey, actually I'm, uh, getting a cramp. Raincheck?"

He hooked a thumb back at the house. It was only a few long, winding roads over from Theo's, the lake in the distance, the greenhouse tucked in at the mouth of the forest. Like Theo's, it was the only house in a quarter mile.

Our own little wilderness, Mrs. Fletcher liked to say.

No one can hear you scream, Mr. Fletcher would continue, shooting their guest a wink.

Mr. Fletcher was sitting at the kitchen island when they walked in, humming and soothing a hunting knife down a whetstone. His grip was confident and quick, knife flashing easily against the shiny stone.

"Hello," he said distractedly, tossing them a smile as Aaron headed toward the fridge. He caught sight of Theo and his smile grew. He was always smiling and chuckling, laugh lines carved deep in his face. It was a stark contrast to his only son—Aaron moved his face so little he'd probably make it to fifty without a single laugh line.

"He*llo*! Theo, I thought you'd gone home. I saw you out there on the court, you were incredible."

"Ah, you know me," said Theo, more pleased than he should be. His new skills weren't earned from hard work, after all.

"Gonna kill those Wayside Hawks on Friday," Mr. Fletcher continued. He nodded over at Aaron, focus already drifting back to his whetstone. "You need to work on your blocking. And you jumped like a pansy."

Theo averted his eyes. It wasn't the most homophobic thing Mr. Fletcher had ever said, but it never failed to make him uncomfortable. He looked over at Aaron hidden behind the fridge door.

He wished Aaron would actually talk about this stuff. The closest they came to it after Aaron's not-quite bisexuality confession was that one time he asked Aaron if he thought an actor was hot, and Aaron had given him a look like Theo had betrayed him.

It's fine for you and Liss, he'd said later, so rushed Theo almost missed it. *Like, your parents might be disappointed but they'll deal. My parents will kill me, man.*

Aaron leaned around the fridge door, a carton of orange juice in hand. "Dad, Theo wants to get an invite to the next hunting trip."

Mr. Fletcher chuckled. "Like hell, kid. Why the sudden interest? I thought your family didn't hunt."

"We hunt," Theo said hastily. Neither of his parents were ardent hunters like the Fletchers, but Theo's dad had taken him to hunt deer during middle school. They'd shot exactly one deer—his dad's kill, after Theo's shaking hands and shitty aim lost them a buck—and Theo had to hide his rising nausea as his dad showed him how to skin it. He hadn't hidden it well enough, apparently. Whenever his dad brought it up, he looked at Theo like he'd failed a test.

I worry sometimes, he'd told Theo as he washed the blood off his hands with the garden hose, *that you don't have the killer instinct to make it in this world. You do know that's what it takes, right? Kill or be killed. Be the prey or the knife.*

I know, Theo had replied, watching all that red trickle into the dirt. *I have what it takes, Dad. I promise.*

But they'd never gone out for a hunt again. Theo's dad didn't bring it up, and Theo tried not to show his relief.

Aaron resurfaced from his orange juice carton. A drop of sweat rolled down his neck. Theo could smell the salt.

"Also wanted to know if we have any Warrens in the family tree," Aaron said. "Don't bore him too much, old man."

Mr. Fletcher blinked rapidly. Then he grinned. "*Ohhh*, you'll regret asking me about the family tree, boy. You know I love my family history. Let's see... Warren...I don't think we have any. Why?"

Theo mumbled something incoherent. What was he doing, questioning these people he'd known his whole life? Kade was reaching for something that wasn't there. And Theo didn't have to report back to him anyway— he'd taken himself out of their shitty little mystery. Theo was on his own now, free to make his own conclusions. So what if he didn't have any other leads? He'd come up with some.

Aaron hummed into the orange juice container. "Why'd you pull me away from Monster the other day? Thought you'd like to see him shaken around a little."

Theo froze, darting a look over at Mr. Fletcher. He was a cheerful guy, but he could turn on a dime sometimes, and Theo wasn't the best at figuring out when that was.

Aaron's parents were mysterious when it came to their son pushing people around—the general rule was *as long as you don't get caught, anything goes.* But there were no hard rules.

"I just don't want you to get in trouble," Theo said slowly.

"Glass," Mr. Fletcher said, eyes on his strop as he pressed the knife against the leather.

Aaron groaned, slumping toward the kitchen cabinet for a glass.

"Knocking some people down a peg is worth a little trouble," Mr. Fletcher continued, frowning down at his blade. He ran a thumb over the sharp edge, then returned it to the leather. "God knows that queer needs a little shaking up. Needs a lot more than that, after what happened to that old man."

Aaron snorted.

Theo frowned. "You don't think he actually did it, right? Killed Lemmings?"

"Why not?" Mr. Fletcher shrugged.

"Kade doesn't have the guts," Aaron protested as he poured his juice. He wiped at his sweaty neck, and Theo's empty stomach clenched. "He's a coward, deep down. That's why he throws himself into all those stupid fights. Funny if he did do it, though. Then he'd go to jail. Two losers taken down in one week."

He shared a conspiratorial look with his dad, who looked back at him like he'd said something he shouldn't, but not something he disagreed with.

Theo laughed nervously. "Since when do we not like old man Lemmings? He's weird, sure. *Was* weird. But he didn't deserve to die."

Aaron snorted again.

Mr. Fletcher held his hunting knife up to the light, examining the shine. "Some people deserve to die," he murmured, distracted.

Before Theo could ask him what the hell that meant, Aaron had downed the last of the juice and was running at him, slapping Theo in his chest.

"Rematch," he called, running out the door. "Catch up, steroid boy."

Mr. Fletcher watched, amused, as his son pelted out of the room. "Kick his ass, kid."

"Always do," Theo said. He pinned a smile up, like his stomach wasn't churning with wariness and hunger. He was playing basketball at Aaron's house, a house he knew almost as much as his own. *Everything is fine,* he told himself as he slowed his steps and let Aaron sink basket after basket. He repeated it to himself every time his gaze fell to the vein beating hard in Aaron's neck, hot and appetizing as a steak.

The empty feeling in his stomach only intensified on the walk home. It was growing claws, scraping his veins. Hunger in his fingertips, his skin, his tingling scalp. He felt weak but somehow still restless with energy—

basketball had done nothing to fix that. He wanted to lie down on the backroads and rest.

He stepped off the road and walked toward the forest, hands shaking. He wanted to run as fast as he possibly could. He wanted the trees to streak past, he wanted to run until his mind was quiet, he wanted to *chase*. He wanted—

His nostrils flared. There was a scent drifting out of the forest, soft and liquor-sour and strangely metallic. Not like a hunting knife. Cheap metal, crappy jewelry painted silver.

Kade Renfield emerged from the trees, pale and slumped. His skinny knees showed through his torn jeans, the laces of his combat boots undone. He looked just as exhausted as Theo felt, with none of the jumpy adrenaline. He startled when he saw Theo, jerking like he was about to turn around and head back into the woods. Then his gait smoothed out as he headed toward Theo with tight shoulders. An animal with its haunches up.

"You haven't been at school," Theo called as Kade came closer.

That dangerous smile gleamed across Kade's face, less sharp than usual. "Aw, you worried about me, Fairgood?"

"No. Just wanted to check you weren't..." Theo tried to find something that didn't sound ridiculous. "I don't know. Infected, or something."

"Nope! Been great since you bit me." Kade smiled

harder, like that would distract Theo from his trembling hands and the bags under his eyes. He gestured at his face, long fingers tapping his own cheek. "My earrings didn't permanently scar you, huh? Tragic. They'd really fix that boy band look."

Theo sighed. "What are you doing here?"

Kade laughed bitterly. "What, am I not allowed in the rich kid neighborhood? Afraid I'll get my *poor* stink on you?"

Theo gritted his teeth against the onslaught of *salt-liquor-metal-soft* that assaulted his nose. "It's just not your regular haunt."

"You can say *that* again." Kade shoved his hands in his thin pockets. "Didn't mean to end up here. Just started walking. I...needed a distraction. What about you, hanging at Fletcher's place?"

"Basketball practice," Theo said.

"Yeah?" Kade's flinty gaze flickered over him. "Bet everyone is impressed by your sudden and unexplainable rise in talent."

"Shut up."

"No, I bet you're loving it. The star goes *supernova*."

"I'm the best," Theo tried. "People know that."

Kade snorted. "Yeah, but go jumping higher than humans can physically jump and the hunters who killed Lemmings will put two and two together."

He cocked his head. His pulse beat in his neck. Theo could see it flutter under his pale skin.

"You good, mate?" Kade asked, the mockery audible underneath the fake concern. "You look hungry."

"I'm fine," Theo snapped.

You look sick, he didn't say. He didn't want to drag this out. If Kade kept arguing with him, Theo didn't want to know what would happen. Not now, with this hunger sizzling under his skin. It had been days since he fed on Kade, but it had only been one day since his last deer. Surely he didn't need to feed every *day*. He'd run out of deer.

"I have somewhere to be," he said. "Try not to get your stink on any of our houses."

Kade sneered. Then he twisted to look at the woods he'd just walked out of.

"*I have somewhere to be,*" he mimicked. "The deer of Lock better watch out."

Theo thought back to being twelve years old, hands trembling around a gun. *Move*, he'd mouthed at the deer as he held the gun up. *Run.*

And it had. After Theo fired a round into a tree right next to it. He told himself he'd meant to hit it, but he still wasn't sure.

"I have to go," Theo said stubbornly, and stalked past him.

Kade called, "Happy hunting, blood boy!"

Theo ignored him. Everything in him wanted to turn around, rush back, sink his teeth into Kade's neck. He breathed deep, inhaling the scent of dirt and bark and bugs, the trees waiting up ahead. Anything was better than Kade's scent, strange and heady and overwhelming, beckoning him back.

KADE FELT LIKE HAMMERED SHIT.

It had been four days since Theo sunk his fangs into his neck. Three days since the tremors set in. Then sweating. *Then* nausea.

He was out of sick days. And he'd gone to school hungover before. This was basically a terrible hangover, he told himself as he shivered on his walk to school. A hangover that felt suspiciously like withdrawal symptoms, even though he'd never drunk enough to have withdrawals, and drinking didn't do *shit* to fix it.

"This has nothing to do with Theo Fairgood," he told himself in the bathroom mirror before the bell rang for second period. "Even if it does, screw him. He can suck shit. Let him figure out this shitty town's weird-ass mystery by himself."

A shudder wracked his lanky frame. He gripped the bathroom sink and fought down a wave of nausea.

"This is just a fever," he blurted. "Totally normal fever. Just need to sweat it out."

He grabbed a paper towel from the dispenser and wiped his forehead. He missed his hair, black and frizzy. It was annoying, but it was great to hide behind. He couldn't hide anything with his buzzcut.

The bell rang.

"Be cool," he hissed at the mirror.

His reflection stared back, pale and sweaty, hands shaking at his sides.

"Great," Kade muttered, and stumbled to the bathroom door.

Kade had ditched class for less. Who cared that he had no more sick days? Or that he'd promised his aunt he wouldn't ditch so much this year after they threatened to suspend him?

He ditched because he was bored. Or he had a craft project he wanted to finish. Or the idea of sitting in a room with people who hated him made him want to claw his skin off.

And here he was: sitting in Biology, sweat dripping down his back. Trying desperately not to gag at the dead frog in front of him, its belly cut open but not yet pulled apart. He should've bolted the second he saw those poor dead things get wheeled into class.

"Everybody calm down," called Mrs. Twigg dryly, adjusting her milk-bottle glasses. "We'll get through this together. Now, if you look at the board, you'll see how to properly pin..."

She trailed off as Theo stalked into class looking like someone pissed in his designer sneakers. His enraged stride only faltered as he took in the trays of frogs on the desks, everyone crowding around them in pairs.

"Fairgood," said Mrs. Twigg, scanning the classroom. "You're with...hmm. Who doesn't already have a partner?"

Oh no, Kade thought, churning stomach sinking to his shoes. He shrunk down in his seat, but it was too late.

"Renfield," she said, his name souring like it did every time she had it in her mouth. "Good luck," she added. It was unclear who she was saying it to.

For a moment Theo just stood there, white-knuckling his backpack. His jaw twitched. Kade hoped against hope he'd turn on his heel and storm out, save them both the strife. Instead he walked—all six feet of rigid, seething jock—down the rows until he reached Kade's lab table.

Kade averted his eyes as Theo sat down, hoping it came across as 'cool and unaffected' instead of 'nervous prey in the presence of a lion.' But not before he noticed Theo's chalky skin, his limp hair, the tightness around his eyes. He looked almost as bad as Kade, minus the sweat.

He glanced at Felicity, who was at the table next to them and should have been smirking at her friend's misfortune. But she wasn't even looking over them, bent over her own frog with weary determination and shockingly oily hair. Aaron sat next to her, watching her pin the frog with a concern that almost made Kade think that Aaron had a heart underneath all that jock bully bullshit. Felicity had looked *rough* for the past week. There were rumors she'd started gymnastics again, but that didn't explain her exhaustion unless she was really, *really* overdoing it.

Kade turned back to his own table, twisting one of the pins between his fingers. "You look like crap," he told Theo.

"Shut up and pin the goddamn frog," Theo snapped.

Kade huffed, trying not to gag as he pinned the frog's front legs down. "Thought you ate yesterday," he said, voice tight as his throat flexed against bile. "You look like you want to suck this frog."

"It's..." Theo lowered his voice. "It's *cold*."

"Right, I forgot. *That's* gross." Kade bent over the frog, wishing for a full head of hair more than ever as he felt Theo's piercing gaze on the side of his face. There was only so much he could hunch into his jacket, the leather squeaking against his sweaty skin.

"You look like shit, too," Theo said.

Kade thought fast. He tossed Theo a twisted grin. "I think you gave me a vampy STD."

"What?" Theo's annoyance gave way to uncertainty. "That's not a thing. Right?"

Kade couldn't help himself. He snickered.

"Should've worn protection," he whispered, noise lost under the flurry of grossed-out teenagers cutting a dead animal open. "Dental dam. Or those plastic fangs kids wear on Halloween."

"Stop talking." Theo grabbed the pins from the tiny tray of tools and pinned the rest of the frog's limbs into place. He grabbed the tiny pair of forceps and paused. "It's not *actually*—"

"No, dipshit, it's a regular-ass fever. I just need to sweat it out." Kade tried to look stoic and badass. His sickly shudder ruined it.

"Looks like you're on top of that," Theo said slowly. "You're dripping on the frog."

Kade lurched back, but not in time to stop a line of sweat from dripping off his chin and into the frog's open stomach. He winced. "Oh shit, poor Victor."

"You named it Victor?"

"What, you don't think he looks like a Victor?"

Theo gave him an incredulous look, eyes narrowing like he wasn't sure if Kade was joking. "That's my dad's name."

Kade barked a laugh. "Really? That's awful. Does he wear a sweater vest?"

"He's a very important lawyer," Theo snapped.

"So that's...a yes?" Kade aimed another grin at him. "I don't know the lawyer to sweater vest ratio."

Theo sucked in a breath through clenched teeth. Kade could pinpoint the exact moment when he realized a hungry vampire breathing in a room full of people was a bad idea—metal cracked in Theo's hand, the forceps splitting in Theo's iron grip.

"Shit," Kade said, watching Theo's hand shake in pure rage around the ruined instrument. "I'll, uh...Mrs. Twigg, we need another pair of forceps."

He raised his hand. A combination of panic and weak, shaky limbs made his elbow sweep out, too wide. It caught on the frog and tool tray, and Kade watched helplessly as Frog Victor careened down to the linoleum, tools following him down. The tools hit the ground with a clatter, Frog Victor splatting to a wet stop.

The classroom chatter died. Mrs. Twigg pursed her lips, not a hint of surprise on her face. Kade Renfield, screwing up class again.

Kade knew his lines. This was the part where he flipped everyone off or picked Frog Victor up and made him dance while everyone cringed and threw things at him. But he was so *tired*. Also, he was pretty sure if he made Frog Victor dance, Theo would rip out his throat right there. He looked about five seconds from doing it anyway, screw all the witnesses.

"What... you..." Theo bared his teeth, thankfully still blunt. "What the HELL is wrong with you, Renfield? Can you not get through one class without fucking it up for the rest of us?"

Shocked gasps went up around the classroom. A moment too late, Felicity let out a tired giggle, twisting her pale hair around her manicured fingers.

An ugly feeling bloomed in Kade's churning gut as Kade sat there, trying not to sway in his lab seat. He didn't want to be here, surrounded by people who hated him, his head swimming with fever. A voice not unlike his aunt's told him *stay quiet, don't yell back, stop being a problem.*

That didn't sound like Kade 'Monster' Renfield.

He bared his teeth back. "Aw, didn't you hear? Fucking things up is my specialty."

Felicity's giggle turned into an exhausted laugh. "Preach it, Monster."

Theo jerked around to glare at her. "Shut *up*, Liss."

Felicity's plucked brows shot up her tanned forehead. Beside her, Aaron's face twisted.

"Wow," Felicity said flatly. "Fuck you too."

Mrs. Twigg snapped her fingers, two sharp clicks that dragged everyone's attention back at her. "You know the rules," she said, pointing up to the rule board that had been hanging over the board since the start of time. "No swearing in my class. All three of you—detention."

Felicity let out a disgusted groan, "But I didn't..."

Mrs. Twigg snapped again. "Pick up your frog, boys."

Kade ignored her. He was too busy listening to the exchange behind him, Aaron leaning in to tell Theo, "Bad luck, man. Don't let this make you late for warm-ups."

"I'll be there," Theo muttered. Then, to Kade: "Are you gonna clean up your mess or do I have to do it?"

Kade didn't want to chance bending down right now. He wasn't sure if he'd be able to stand back up. But he couldn't let Theo know that, so he just shrugged and hoped he came across as an asshole rather than someone fighting off the urge to faint.

Theo jerked his chair back, grumbling under his breath as he bent to scrape Frog Victor off the floor. His foot came down hard, clumsy, right on top of Kade's half-open backpack.

A sharp *crack* rang through the classroom. Kade looked down and saw a pair of knitting needles jutting out of the zipper at an awkward angle. They were his good ones. More fool he for bringing them to school, hoping to finish a project while he shut himself up in the bathrooms. For an exhausted second he thought he might burst into tears in front of everyone. Then he looked up and saw Theo's face, eyes wide with shock. He looked like he wanted to be anywhere else, almost as much as Kade.

Tired, Kade realized. *And lacking control.* He looked down at the snapped pair of forceps lying on the desk.

"Great combo," he mumbled.

Theo straightened, dumping the trays back onto the desk. "I...what?"

He stooped like he was going to touch the needles protruding from Kade's backpack. "Are those *knitting needles?*"

"Nope," Kade snapped. He kicked his crumpled backpack under his desk and nodded down at their frog's body on the ground. "Are you going to let him lie there or what? Let's get this over with."

Theo paused. Then he bent down and picked up the frog, fingers spasming around it, like he was having to hold himself back from crushing it entirely.

"Welcome back," Coach Cheech said, not bothering to look up from the board as Kade slouched into detention only a few minutes late. Pretty impressive, considering how much he wanted to curl up in a dark corner and cry himself to sleep. The detention turnout didn't make him want that any less—it was just Felicity and Theo, together at the back of class, Felicity smug and tired and still trying to be as acid-hot as ever, Theo glaring like Kade forced him to swear in front of stuffy Mrs. Twigg.

Coach Cheech stepped back from the board, where he'd written SHUT UP TIME: 45 MINUTES.

"Sit down, jackass. No one's making you write anything today."

Kade slumped gratefully toward the nearest seat. He still felt bad for Frog Victor. Little guy didn't deserve to get his body tossed around like that. And even after they put him through all of that, they'd still dissected him, Theo trying not to snap and bite someone, Kade trying not to sweat or puke. It was the worst class of his high school career, including that gym class where someone pissed all over his gym shorts and Coach Cheech yelled at Kade until he wore them.

Kade's head swam as he walked. He stumbled, arms coming up to catch himself. Unfortunately, the nearest thing to steady himself was Coach Cheech.

"Whoa," Coach Cheech said, grabbing Kade's shoulders. "The hell, Renfield?"

"Sorry," Kade said. It came out slurred. He straightened up, unclenching his hand from Coach Cheech's shirt. He'd accidentally pulled the shirt collar down, exposing chest hair and a necklace Kade had never seen before. He froze as he noticed the shape: it was a golden flame, the same symbol that was on the book Milly Hart had shown them in her bookshop.

Was Coach Cheech involved somehow? He couldn't be a vampire, he was too sweaty. Vampires didn't smell like Cheetos and onions. Was he a hunter?

Kade shrank back as Coach Cheech scrutinized him, muddy brown eyes pinning him like poor dead Victor. It was a strange look for Cheech—Kade was used to him looking at everything through half-lidded eyes, dull and careless.

"Seriously," Coach Cheech said, voice low. "You drunk?"

"Unfortunately not," Kade rasped.

"You sick? I can't have you infecting my players."

"Since when do you give a shit about your players, Coach?"

"Since that team gets the school a third of its funding." Coach Cheech nodded at the front row of seats. "Don't infect my star player, Renfield."

Kade fell into a chair. He waited for Coach Cheech to return to his desk at the front of the class, then turned to glance back at Theo, surprised to find him already looking. His limp blond hair was a mess, like he'd been running his fingers through it. He looked unhappy, and...concerned?

"You look dead, guv'nor," Felicity told him in a terrible British accent. Her voice was oddly soft.

Kade tore his gaze away from the displeased twist of Theo's mouth. Usually he'd sling an equally terrible accent back, but he wasn't feeling it today.

"Not all of us can be models, Sloan," he said flatly.

"Yeah, but you look like you're about to keel over. Better not have infected Theo in class today, the town will riot if the golden boy can't play tonight." Felicity leaned forward, resting her pointy chin on her elegant hands. Her knuckles were bruised, faint purple through the foundation.

She asked, "Going to the game tonight? You could germ-bomb the rest of the school."

Kade snorted, resting his head on his desk. He could already feel the sweat leaving a mark on the wood.

"You know what," he said. "Maybe I will. Might see something stupid. Even stupider than basketball usually gets."

Felicity narrowed her eyes at him, waiting for a joke.

She didn't know what he was getting at. But Theo did. Kade watched his jaw twitch angrily. Theo was the *best*. He'd always been the best, and there was no way he was going to let his new vampire powers stay dormant during the big game. He was going to do something stupid. And people would notice. And when the right people noticed the town's golden boy was a vampire...

"Like," Kade said. "*Lethally* stupid. But hey! Not my problem."

Theo scowled at him. Kade grinned back, mind whirling: with fever and darkness; an impossible fall into a lake; Theo's cold skin; burns blooming on his face; words carved into a dead man's chest; the symbol on Cheech's necklace; a hundred terrifying possibilities dancing just out of reach.

THE GYM CHANGING rooms smelled infinitely worse now that Theo was a vampire. He pinched his nose hard as he waited for Milly to pick up the phone.

"Come on," he growled as it rang yet again. "Come *on!*"

"Hello?"

"Do vampires *need* human blood?" Theo blurted. "Like, is animal blood not enough? Because if that's how it works, that's stupid. Blood is blood!"

There was a long silence. Theo bounced from foot to foot, letting go of his nose. It was useless—he could taste the stale sweat every time he opened his mouth.

"Uh," Milly said. There was the sound of something boiling in the background. Making dinner, Theo supplied. Like everybody in town who wasn't in the gym right now, waiting for the basketball game to start.

"In a lot of lore they can *survive* on animal blood,"

Milly said. "Human blood is just...better. Quenching in ways animal blood isn't. I don't know what our town lore says, that book I showed you is badly damaged, there isn't—"

Theo cut her off. "So you don't have anything new?"

"I'm sorry. I thought you said your project was due in a few weeks?"

Theo tried to remember what Kade had told her while Theo was dragging him out by his shirt. He'd been tuning Kade out by then.

Somebody knocked on the gym bathroom door. Mr. Hawthorn's voice drifted through: "Theo, are you still in there? Coach sent me. The game's about to start."

Theo ground his teeth.

"I have to go," he snapped. "Thanks for your help."

He shoved his phone into his bag, leaving it on the stained wooden bench as he stormed out.

Mr. Hawthorn blinked as the door slammed open. "Wow. The Wayside Hawks really have it coming."

"We'll kill 'em," Theo said, barely keeping the tremble out of his voice. He had *no* leads. No clue where to look next. He still didn't know how this vampire shit worked, or who turned him, or why, or who killed Lemmings, or if they wanted to kill him next. No idea why he burned Kade when he touched him. And his hunger just kept getting worse. He wasn't sure how long he was going to be able to ignore it. It only got quiet in the days after he fed on Kade.

Mr. Hawthorn paused, halfway down the hallway. "You feeling alright?"

Theo ignored him. "You're a history teacher."

"Ye-es?"

"Do you know the stories about the hunters who stayed in Lock?"

"Stayed in Lock? They all cleared out once the vampires were dealt with. No more threat."

"I heard there were other versions of the story. Old ones. Like, eighteen-hundreds."

Mr. Hawthorn's face lit up. "Oh! Sorry, I deal so much with the town-approved stuff I kind of forget about the unofficial versions. They don't pay me to do dramatic retellings of that on Halloween." He glanced behind him, toward the door. The gym would be full now, Theo could hear the chatter. They were facing the Wayside Hawks, Lock's sports nemesis since before Theo was born.

"Can't this wait?" Mr. Hawthorn asked. "Coach Cheech was pretty eager to get you out on the court."

"Just tell me fast."

Mr. Hawthorn chuckled. "Hope this sudden history passion will carry over to your assignments! Let's see, hmmm. My grandparents had this story they heard as kids. Get this: it's a love story."

Theo nodded, digging his nails into his palm. *Talk faster!*

"There was this vampire woman and her lover. I can't remember their names. The man was...god, I really don't remember. And the woman...Cynthia? Cissy?"

"Cyth," Theo offered, too fast.

Mr. Hawthorn gave him a surprised look. "That's it! Anyhoo, she was the leader. Her lover was her second in command. Very loyal, they'd been alive for centuries. Anyway, when the hunters tracked them down, they caught Cyth and stuffed her in that burning coffin, but her lover escaped. He vowed to come back one day and find her. Over the next hundred years he came back to Lock with these outlandish plans, and none of them worked. They chased him off every time. Then around the turn of the century he vanished. Poof! Never seen again."

"That we know of." Theo swallowed, hunger pounding through his gut, up into his still heart. "Thanks, sir. I gotta go."

"Of course." Mr. Hawthorn raised an awkward fist, stepping out of the way for Theo to walk past him. "Go Nightfowls!"

The gym was overwhelming, all lights and noise. Adrenaline and salt hung heavy in the air, a hundred warm bodies in the stands. His parents, Aaron's parents, all of them waiting eagerly. Felicity had gone home after detention, saying she didn't get enough sleep the night before.

There was no Kade. *Might see something lethally stupid,*

he'd sneered. He couldn't even bother showing up? Sure, he looked ready to fall over in a puddle of his own sweat, but *still*—

"Fairgood," Coach Cheech shouted from the sidelines. "What the hell are you doing?"

Theo blinked. The referee stood between him and the head of the opposing team, watching him expectantly.

"What?" Theo barked. "Throw the ball!"

The referee snorted, but threw. Theo bounded up, slapping the ball halfway down the court into Aaron's gut. Aaron doubled over, breath slamming out of him, hands barely coming up in time to grab the ball.

Theo sprinted down the court toward him, weaving around the Wayside Hawks with an ease he'd ever had before. He was good, when he was alive. The *best*. But this was something else. The impressed murmur of the crowd rose to a roar as Theo caught the ball Aaron threw him, then leapt up to the basket.

Too high. Theo sailed up and up and *up*, past the net and then the backboard. Until it was less jump and more *fly*.

He dropped, twisting to throw the ball into the basket as he fell past it. He landed on the polished floorboards lightly, grinning as he turned to look how high up he'd gotten.

Theo whooped. The crowd whooped back, a few confused mumbles lost under the cheers. Theo glanced at his parents and found them clapping hard, no confusion, just pure pride. It made Theo want to jump a thousand feet, *ten* thousand. Enough of his parents' applause and he could fly to the moon and back.

The ball went back to the opposition. Rusty Legard, a freckled senior with a perpetual scowl stood in front of Theo in the center of the court.

"Fancy jumps, rich kid," Rusty jeered. He smelled like hair gel—not overwhelmingly, like Aaron, just a hint of it at the tips of his hair. His heart rate was already up, sweat beading under his armpits, a fine sheen coating his speckled neck. Theo wanted to yank his lightly gelled head to one side and—

The whistle blew. Rusty tossed the ball at a teammate to his side, but Theo was too fast. He snatched it out of the air, speeding down the court. Four members of the Wayside Hawks crowded him, arms up, like that could stop him. Like Theo couldn't plow right through them. Their arms were blood-warm and right there, the vulnerable crooks of their arms gleaming pale and unmarked...

A yell rang around the stands. *Kill 'em!*

I might, Theo realized, and it was like being doused with a bucket of ice water. *Holy shit, I actually might.*

More boys crowded in front of him, blocking, waiting, warmth radiating from their skin. Theo's mouth filled with saliva. The ball creaked in his grip, rubber about to give way. He stood perfectly still, *predator* still, as the crowd screamed and teammates yelled for him to pass or go for the basket.

Theo's head swam. He needed to get out of here. No, he needed to finish the game. He needed—

A familiar scent cut through the crush of sweat and adrenaline. Theo jerked around to see Kade, sallow and lanky, wobbling around the corner of the gym hallway. He looked even worse than he did in detention, like he was seconds away from falling down right there on the floorboards.

"THEO," boomed Coach Cheech from the sidelines. "WHAT ARE YOU WAITING FOR? THROW THE DAMN BALL!"

Kade grinned. His heartbeat thudded hard and loud, drowning everything else out.

"I need to go," Theo said, barely audible over Kade's thundering heartbeat.

Theo didn't look at Coach Cheech, still yelling, as he stumbled off the court. He didn't look at Aaron, who tried to get in the way and got pushed aside for his troubles. He didn't look at his parents in the stands, the Fletchers next to them, their pride turning into something corrosive Theo would have to endure later.

He only looked at Kade. Gray eyes, chapped lips, long fingers shaking at his sides.

Theo barreled into the hallway, past the changing rooms, hauling Kade around the corner by his shirt. Theo expected a quip, some sharp barb, but there was nothing. Just a gasp, lost in the thud of the door to the disabled bathrooms shooting open.

Theo kicked it closed and shoved Kade into the mirror, blurring with speed.

Kade's breath hitched. His pupils were dark pools, his heartbeat singing in Theo's ears. Theo's hunger mirrored in Kade's face.

Kade twisted his head. His neck gleamed with sweat, vein pumping away underneath. That small mole glinted, dark and beautiful.

Theo lunged. Kade choked out a moan, but Theo barely heard it. He was lost in the taste. It was just like the first time, clutching Kade close, digging his fingers hard into his back, hardly noticing the smoke rising from Kade's skin.

Too soon, Theo pulled back. He pressed a fumbling hand to the wound, another small noise slipping out of Kade's slack lips as the sizzling stopped, the burn and tear turning to smooth skin.

Theo looked up.

The unhealthy pale tinge was gone from Kade's skin. Gone, too, were the dull eyes. Kade's gray eyes were bright, his cheeks glowing with a healthy flush. His hands were steady as they twisted in Theo's shirt, his mouth twisting like he was trying to sneer but couldn't get past the grin.

"Hey, blood boy," he rasped. "We gotta talk."

CHAPTER
THIRTEEN

KADE FELT GINGERLY at his neck as Theo drove them down the back roads of Lock. No burns or tears from Theo's mouth. Just smooth skin. Like it never happened.

Theo pulled the car off the road, driving far enough into the grass that no one could see them. Only then did he turn the car off. He'd been strangely quiet as he drove out of the school parking lot. It freaked Kade out. Like he was the victim in a horror movie.

He sat up in the backseat. "Did you bring me here to kill me?"

Theo twisted to stare at him. "*Why* would I do that?"

"I don't know! You bite me, you drag me to the backseat of your car, drive me out to the middle of nowhere..."

Theo made a noise through his teeth. "Are you this annoying on purpose? No, I'm not killing you. I...we..."

He jerked a hand through his hair. It was already glossier than it was at school today, his skin more pink. Kade looked down to see his arms were no longer shiny, all the sweat was old. He could make a fist without his fingers trembling. No more chills.

Theo sighed. "We...*need* each other. Alright? Animal blood isn't enough. I thought I was going full beast mode in that game, I was five seconds from chowing down on Rusty Legard. And if you don't get venom..."

Kade groaned. "What kind of DARE shit is this? Two hits and I'm hooked? Full-on...*venom* withdrawal, complete with shaking and sweating and almost barfing in the cafeteria? That's bull."

"Yup." Theo toyed with the hem of his basketball shirt, that ugly blue and orange mesh that Kade wouldn't be caught dead wearing. Not even Theo Fairgood could make it look like a fashion choice.

"At least you get a nice high. And you're officially dragged into my..." Theo's straight nose twisted. *"Little vampire adventure of discovery."*

Kade cackled. He couldn't help it. Theo was an asshole, but he could be funny sometimes. Also, he was pleasantly surprised Theo listened to him enough to repeat that phrase days later.

"So," Theo continued. "I know you were...*out* of all this. But you were so excited about solving mysteries. Did you dig into anything?"

He was so hopeful. He was trying to hide it, but Kade could see it behind that careful cool.

"You still have no idea what's going on," Kade said flatly.

"I know things," Theo argued. "I...I can't eat human food! The vampire's leader, Cyth, had a lover who vowed to bring her back! He might still be around!"

"Oh. Shit."

"Oh shit," Theo agreed, triumphant. It wasn't his usual smug triumph, either. This was...bigger. More relieved. Like a golden retriever who finally found a stick after hours of searching. He rubbed the steering wheel, which was covered with scratches. Like he'd been pushing his nails in, not noticing his newfound strength until the plastic peeled away.

Kade offered, "Coach Cheech is wearing a necklace that has the creepy book symbol. The one Milly showed us."

"Coach..." Theo squinted at him. "Coach *Cheech*. You're saying Coach Cheech is...what, a hunter? He can't be a vampire, he smells like food all the time. Are you screwing with me?"

"I *said* I saw it."

"When? I've never seen that necklace, and I'm around the guy ten hours a week."

"When I almost passed out against him in detention today!"

"Oh." Theo looked surprised, like he couldn't believe that had happened *today*. "So we...shit, we can't talk to him now, he'll be *so* pissed I walked out on the game. We could go to Milly's? No, she said she doesn't have anything new. Also I don't know where she lives. We could...go to the Lemmings house? Look for clues? He was a vampire, he must've had...I don't know. *Stuff* around the house. Stuff that could tell us what the hell is going on. Maybe a diary?"

Kade rubbed the newly healed skin of his neck. He'd been under the impression Theo would drop him home, save the actual investigation for later. He was tired. Not bone-tired and shaky, like he'd been before getting another sweet, sweet dose of venom—but he'd like a rest before they headed out to the next thing.

But Theo looked so lost, and something in Kade tingled excitedly at the idea. *Look for clues.* Like they were in a mystery story, and anything could be lurking around the corner.

"Hell yeah, Scooby," Kade said. "Let's go."

"I'm not Scooby," Theo told him, relieved. "*You're* Scooby. *I'm* Fred. Wait, no, you're—"

"Shaggy," Kade finished in unison with Theo. He felt a strange urge to grin at him. He bit his cheek instead. He refused to have a moment with Theo Fairgood. Even if he *was* stuck with him now.

"Get down," Theo told him.

Kade rolled his eyes and lay down in the backseat. "Right. Can't let anybody see Monster in golden boy's backseat."

"Got that right." Theo started the car and pulled

back into the road. Then, so fast Kade almost missed it, he said: "So, you knit?"

Kade stared at him, uncomprehending. Then he remembered the broken knitting needles jutting out of his backpack, Theo's shocked face after his foot came down.

"Don't tell anyone," Kade insisted.

He waited for Theo to laugh. Hold it over him as leverage. Make a shitty jock joke, at the very least. It *was* funny—the big bad goth, hiding his knitting needles in his backpack so he could knit in the school bathrooms.

But Theo just watched the road, voice surprisingly quiet as he said, "I won't."

He drove in silence for several seconds. Then, wonder of all wonders, he spoke again.

"Sorry for saying you had no friends."

Kade blinked, lashes brushing the leather seats. "What?"

"In the woods," Theo explained, as if he needed to remind Kade about something that had him sniffing back tears as he walked away from Theo.

"I shouldn't..." Theo hesitated. "I was *really* freaked out. But I shouldn't have yelled. Or said that shit. You're a good guy, when you aren't barking at people. You don't deserve that shit."

Kade's mouth went dry. He bit down on his cheek again, hard and gnawing, only stopping when he remembered Theo would smell blood if he bit through the skin.

"I can take it," Kade said, and pressed his head back hard into the leather seat.

Jeremiah Lemmings' house was on the edge of town.

A blight on the landscape, people called it.

Kade thought it was kind of cool. The windows were painted over black, and water stains turned the rear wall into a bloated white mess. If Kade squinted, the house looked like a mushroom growing on an otherwise impeccable street.

The house had no garden, just an overgrown lawn filled with daisies and stinging nettles. Kade was protected by his long jeans, but the nettles brushed Theo's exposed legs as they crept through the rotting back gate. Kade watched the nettle leaves graze his skin and waited. Theo didn't even twitch.

"I expected yellow tape," Kade whispered as they reached the back door.

"Why? It's not a crime scene. He got stabbed on the sidewalk."

Kade peered in the back window, the only one without black paint blocking the view. "Okay. What are we thinking? Break a window?"

Theo took the door handle and yanked. The door cracked open. He had broken the lock.

"Awesome," Kade whispered. He grinned. "Nice work, muscle man."

"I like that better than *blood boy*."

Kade waved into the dark hall with a flourish. "You first, blood boy."

Theo rolled his eyes, but Kade thought he saw his mouth twitch.

He led Kade into the living room and flicked on a lamp. "For your weak human eyes."

"Ha, ha," Kade said distractedly. He was too busy staring around the room, looking for something that hinted at the man who had lived here.

But there was nothing. Any suggestions of vampires were nonexistent—it was just a room. A room full of dust and darkness, the paint on the windows so thick none of the evening light seeped through. The walls were bare. A pile of magazines was rotting wetly behind the door. A battered armchair sat in the corner, pointing toward an old TV. The biggest thing in the room was the bookshelf. Kade touched a small succulent resting on top of a stack of mystery novels. It couldn't survive here—the old man must've moved it recently. The dust around it was disturbed, like it had been placed down in the last week.

"This is *depressing*," Kade said.

Theo nodded, staring at the doomed succulent under Kade's hand. "No family photos, no hobby stuff except books. Might as well have boarded up the windows. How long did he live like this? How could *anybody* live like this? He locked himself in here for decades."

"I don't know." Kade wiped a finger along an ornate mirror on the mantelpiece. It had been painted over, white instead of black. He picked flecks of paint and dust out from under his nails and continued, "I kinda get it. World obviously got too much for him."

Theo snorted. "You could never do that."

"I do it all the time." Kade scratched a line into the mirror, exposing a gleam of streaked glass. "I was out of school for a month last year."

"I remember. It was quieter."

Kade snorted and kept scratching, white flecks falling to the moth-eaten carpet.

"What happened?" Theo asked. "Were you sick?"

"Kind of," Kade said, squirming. He could change the subject, make some stupid joke. Find a fake clue and make Theo hide a smile again.

"Your aunt let you skip that long?"

"She didn't LET me, I just...refused to leave. Couldn't face it."

"School?"

"The world. Life. I don't know." Kade stood back. He'd cleared a patch of mirror, enough to show glimpses of his face. He smiled, pale skin and patches of his teeth back at him. He shouldn't have said it. He could see Theo's reflection in the dull glass, eyes big and pitying.

"Are you okay now?" Theo said.

Kade forced an eyeroll. First Theo was apologizing

for saying he had no friends, and now he was asking if Kade was okay after his depression spiral. Maybe the vampirism really had changed him.

"Can't you tell? I'm *great*," he said, dripping with fake levity. "Are you hungry *again*?"

Theo blinked. "Huh?"

"You're staring." Kade cocked his hip, his wallet chain jingling. He hoped he looked aloof and cool, like he was aiming for, and not like he was misdirecting the conversation to escape the vulnerability he'd just injected into it. "Am I just that delectable?"

"Shut up," Theo said reflexively. "Let's...let's go check his bedroom, maybe there will be a diary like you said. Or he's got a giant, mysterious crate in the attic."

There was no diary in the bedroom. No *anything* in the bedroom. The attic was full of moths and tools and not much else. The bathroom was a lost cause, and the kitchen looked like it hadn't been used in decades.

"Except by rats," Kade said, closing the closet in disgust.

"I thought you'd be happy to see them," Theo said mildly. "Don't goths like rats?"

Kade scowled. "Hey, I like rats. *Tame* rats. Those guys would give you the plague just by looking at you."

Theo started, "Maybe you should pet one and—"

He stopped.

Kade turned, scowl falling off his face once he saw Theo's startled expression. "What? What is it?"

Theo shushed him. He cocked his head, and Kade thought of golden retrievers again.

"Something's here. In the house."

"Some*thing*," Kade repeated, voice cracking embarrassingly.

"It…" Theo swallowed. "It doesn't have a heartbeat?"

Kade stared at him. "Do we check it out?"

"I mean…" Theo shrugged. "We did come here to find stuff? This is…stuff."

"Yeah, but we can't do anything if the stuff we find *kills* us—"

Theo grabbed his sleeve, tugging Kade behind him. Kade wanted to be miffed, but he couldn't help but be touched. Even if it meant Theo thought he was a pathetic, lanky loser who couldn't possibly defend himself from whatever was lurking in the house. Theo still wanted to protect him.

"Something's moving," Theo reported. "It's…in the living room? How can it be in the living room, we already checked there."

A low growl echoed from the living room. Kade shuddered.

"Oh shit," Theo slurred, teeth turning to fangs.

Woodchips flew into the hallway. Whatever it was couldn't fit through the living room door.

"Wait here," Theo said. He stepped cautiously into

the hall, eyeing the woodchips spilling out from the living room.

Another dull roar. Then something burst into the hall, the doorway flying off in chunks.

"Oh SHIT," Kade screamed. He grabbed a broom from the kitchen floor and followed Theo into the hall, his heart thudding wildly.

The creature whirled to face them in the narrow hall. It was tall and horribly spindly and *winged*, with white skin pulled taut over its protruding frame. Huge flecks sloughed off its wings, and it took Kade a horrified moment to realize that was skin flakes dripping to the ground. Its ears were huge and ridged, its nose was a giant slit, its eyes liquid black. There were strange black markings on its chest and arms, bunching against its stretched skin.

Its jaw fell open. A hiss scraped up its throat as it crouched down.

Theo turned to Kade. "You need to go!"

The creature sprinted down the hall, blurring with speed. Theo grabbed the broom out of Kade's hands, shoving Kade back into the kitchen.

Kade tumbled into the wall with a yelp, skidding to the floor. He grimaced, looking up just in time to watch the creature pounce on Theo. It roared, shoving him onto the rotting hallway floorboards.

The creature roared. Theo dragged the broom in front of him and the creature's jaw caught on the hard wood, biting, snarling, trying to get past and open Theo's throat.

Kade stumbled up. All his instincts screamed at him to run. The back door was open behind him. He even took a step toward it. Then the broom cracked under the creature's teeth, almost snapping in two, Theo grunting with effort of holding the thing back.

Kade stopped. Theo had pushed him out of the way. He didn't have to, but he did. Kade just found a *clue*, they were in this together—Kade couldn't abandon him now.

"Shit," Kade spat, fumbling with his wallet chain. He unclipped it from his belt and ran at the creature, chain taught between his hands like an assassin with a shitty garrote.

"What are you DOING?" Theo yelled.

"My best!" Kade screamed back, and he wrapped the wallet chain around the creature's throat.

Smoke rose from the creature's skin. It shrieked, rearing back from the splintering broom to claw at the burning brand around its neck.

"SILVER, BITCH," Kade yelled as the creature writhed in agony.

Theo crawled out from under the creature, but not before the creature's long leg struck out, catching Kade in the side.

Kade fell to his knees in the hallway, the wallet chain sliding from the creature's neck. He wheezed, the breath punched out of him, watching through watery eyes as Theo blurred to stand in front of him. No weapons, just bared teeth.

The creature flared its wings and roared. Theo roared back, the noise edged with fear.

Hot, Kade thought hazily, clutching his wallet chain like it could do anything except provide a temporary distraction to the rampaging beast. At least he'd get to watch Theo's back muscles through his terrible basketball shirt while he died.

The creature charged. Theo crouched like he was about to *tackle* an eldritch monster. Kade felt a panicked laugh escape his throat. *I'm going to die in a hallway with Theo "Golden Boy" Fairgood,* he thought, dazed.

Then a flash of silver whizzed down the hallway and lodged in the creature's stomach.

The creature shrieked.

"Holy shit," Kade said weakly.

Theo made a noise of dazed agreement.

They both turned to look behind them.

A man strode through the back door and into the kitchen, a handkerchief tugged high over his face, crossbow raised. The next arrow grazed the creature's side and cracked into the hallway floorboards.

The creature howled, fell against the wall, and righted itself on clumsy limbs. It gave one last screech—neck still smoking from the deep burn scored into its flesh, stomach blistering around the arrow—and then blurred out the back door.

The crossbow man ran after it, coming to a stop on the back steps.

"Shit," he growled, staring out over the empty backyard.

Kade squinted. The man's voice was strangely familiar.

Theo took a tentative step toward him. "Coach *Cheech*? Is that...is that you?"

The man froze. Then sighed, reaching up to tug the handkerchief down to reveal the same mustache, bushy brows, and put-upon expression Kade had stumbled into only a few hours ago.

"Boys," said Coach Cheech. "We need to talk."

BUT COACH CHEECH didn't talk.

He surveyed them both with that weary expression.

"Huh," he grunted.

Then he headed down the hall and stepped through the gaping hole where the living room door had been, slinging the crossbow over his shoulder.

Theo stared after him. "Coach?"

No reply. Theo turned to Kade, listening to his heart race as the adrenaline wore off.

"Mate, I have no idea," Kade whispered.

They followed Coach Cheech into the living room to find the man crouched down in front of the bookcase. At least, where the bookcase used to be. It had been shoved aside to reveal a set of stairs.

Kade gasped.

"Don't," Theo warned as Coach Cheech started down the mysterious steps.

But it was too late: Kade made a high-pitched noise that genuinely hurt Theo's ears.

"Secret room," Kade chanted. "Secret room. *Secret room*!"

"Stop," Theo sighed. "Just follow Coach."

Kade darted down the stairs after Coach Cheech.

Theo followed, telling himself he wasn't endeared even a little bit by Kade's enthusiasm.

At the bottom of the stairs was a small dark room, its contents absolutely destroyed: books shredded on the floor, chairs in pieces, glass smashed against the wall. Whatever was in here, the creature hadn't wanted anyone to see it. Claws marks scored the wood, flecks of thick white skin mixing with the shredded paper.

Theo's gaze fell on a fleck of white skin stuck to Kade's leather jacket.

Theo picked it off. "Monster skin," he explained when Kade and Coach Cheech gave him a curious look.

"*Monster skin*. Need to put that on a T-shirt," Kade said, dazed, staring around the room. He bent down to pick up a shredded book, sifting carefully through the ruined pages.

Coach Cheech sucked on his mustache. The crossbow hung near his hip, gleaming silver. Theo eyed it, only tearing his gaze away when Kade motioned in his direction.

Theo walked over. "What?"

Kade flicked the tattered book. The pages were half ribbons—but only half. There was still writing, scribbles so messy that Theo couldn't tell whether it was English. Every few pages the scribbles were interrupted by a sketch of a woman's face. A shard of a chin, an arched neck, a curved eyebrow.

"This is the only one I can find with her full face," Kade whispered, turning to a page that was almost intact.

A chill ran up Theo's spine. Sharp cheekbones, red plait tied tight around her head, much like a crown. Her eyes were dark and shrewd. She was snarling, her full lips parted to reveal a mouth full of fangs.

Kade whispered, "Cyth?"

Theo shrugged.

Kade rubbed the woman's razor cheekbone. "Maybe Lemmings was her lover. Like Hawthorn talked about. Still trying to free her after all this time."

Coach Cheech sighed. "You know I can *hear* you, right?"

"Sorry," Theo said, automatic. He turned, but not before he spotted Kade ripping the paper out of the book and stuffing it into his back pocket.

Coach Cheech watched them warily. For a second Theo thought he would finally explain what was going on. Then Coach Cheech sighed and dug a pack of cigarettes out of his jacket.

"*Coach*," said Theo, scandalized.

Coach Cheech ignored him and lit up. He paused, then tilted the pack toward Kade.

Kade took one eagerly.

Theo asked, "Coach, what the hell is going on? What *was* that?"

Coach Cheech blew a plume of smoke through his nostrils, surveying the cramped room around them. Theo looked at his thick necklace, the end of it hidden in his shirt. Who *was* this man Theo had known his whole life?

"You first," Coach Cheech told them, muffled around the cigarette. "What the hell were you two doing in this house? What do you know about Cyth? Since when does Lock's golden boy hang out with Monster?"

"Drug deal," Kade said instantly, meeting Theo's gaze in badly disguised panic. *How much are we telling this guy?*

Coach Cheech snorted. "Theo Fairgood doesn't do drugs. Lie better, jackass."

"Uhhh..." Kade gave Theo another despairing look.

Coach Cheech scratched his hairy neck. The handkerchief was bunched under it, still tied. His clothes were dark; he was wearing cargo pants. Theo had never not seen him in shorts before, even in the dead of winter.

"Lemmings only ate animals. Only reason we didn't stake him decades ago. But he's dead, and we're still finding drained deer in the woods. Funny, huh?" Coach Cheech took another drag from his cigarette and turned to face them. He was blocking the staircase.

"You jumped stupid high in the game today, kid. *Stupid* high."

Theo went still. He didn't dare look down at the crossbow dangling from Coach Cheech's hand, the next arrow already loaded. He didn't look past Coach Cheech, the narrow stairs waiting behind him.

Next to Theo, Kade's breath hitched. His nervous sweat overpowered the smell of smoke. Theo could probably shove Coach Cheech out of the way and make a break for it, but what about Kade? He'd meant what he said in the car—Kade *was* a good guy when he wasn't barking at people. He was weird and guarded and annoying, but he was also smart and—if Theo was honest with himself—kind of sweet. Theo couldn't let him get hurt.

"I'm sorry I walked out of the game," Theo tried. "I...there's no excuse—"

"I don't know, I think we should all be pretty glad you didn't stick around and start biting." Coach Cheech let out a mouthful of smoke. "Relax. I'm not gonna kill you."

Kade let out a smoky breath.

Theo tried to think of an appropriate response. "Thank you."

Kade gave him an incredulous look. Theo glared back, then asked, "Did you, uh, kill Lemmings?"

Coach Cheech coughed. He thumped on his chest, smoke jolting out of him. "What? No! Like I said, as long as he kept his fangs out of people, we left him alone. Some of us weren't happy with it, but we put up with it."

"Who put up with it?" Kade asked, fast and excited. "Who are the other hunters? Which families?"

His cigarette vibrated between his slender fingers, jumping on the balls of his feet. Theo had to stop himself from reaching out and stilling him.

Coach Cheech rubbed his lined forehead. "I shouldn't be telling you this shit."

"Why? We're involved!" Kade slapped Theo's shoulder, lost in excitement, then flinched like he'd forgotten the whole No Touching thing. Luckily his hand had only come into contact with Theo's shirt.

"Was that a vampire?" Kade continued. "Did it turn Theo? Is Theo gonna turn into that big spindly thing?"

"Yes, it's a vamp. No clue if it turned Theo. No, Theo won't turn into that. Probably."

"Probably," Theo repeated. "Wait, who else in town is a vampire?"

"Lemmings was the only one we confirmed. The others are in hiding. Could be goddamned anybody." Coach Cheech kicked at the mess on the floor, shoe catching on paper, dust, shed skin. "Ugh. Don't pull that super jump shit again, Fairgood. No super speed, no showing off your new vamp strength. Keep that shit under lock and key. Whoever turned you did it for a *reason*." He twisted toward Kade. "You still haven't told me why the town freak is here."

"I've kind of been...feeding off of him." Theo said

reluctantly. "It was an accident, the first time. Then he had a bad reaction after we stopped, so I figured we better keep doing it."

"What, like..." Coach Cheech made a face. "Jesus, Fairgood, how often did you bite the kid? Can't go into venom withdrawal *that* fast. Any case I've heard of takes *months* of consistent biting."

"Great," Kade said flatly. "Nice to know I'm special. That's not the only weird thing, look."

He reached out a hand, looking toward Theo expectantly. No nail polish today, Theo noticed. Just short nails, bitten ragged.

Theo hesitated. Then he reached out, pressing the tip of his thumb into the back of Kade's hand. Kade winced, the sound of sizzling flesh filling the small room.

Coach Cheech jumped, ash spilling down his shirt. "Jesus shit!"

Kade pulled his hand away, waggling his slender fingers. "*Weird*, right? And look, watch—"

He tilted his hand toward Theo again. Theo pressed his thumb back into place and concentrated, ignoring Kade's gasp and the resumed sizzle. His thumb tingled, the blister shrinking underneath it. As he pulled back, the burn turned to smooth skin.

"So I'm guessing that's not typical," Kade said, shaking his newly healed hand. "Like, he doesn't burn anyone else. Just me. So what's the deal with Cyth, is..."

He trailed off. Coach Cheech was staring at them

like Theo had just buried a knife in Kade's chest. His cigarette burned dangerously close to his fingers, forgotten.

"Uh," Theo said. "Coach?"

"Christ," Coach Cheech muttered. He gave the cigarette one last suck and dropped it on the floor. Then he turned, heading up the stairs toward the living room.

Theo looked at Kade. Kade looked back cluelessly.

"Coach," Theo repeated.

Coach Cheech stumbled on the rickety steps and swore, grabbing at the peeling walls. "I...shit. I need to make some calls. Get out of here and shove the book-case back before you leave, alright?"

"Got it," Theo said slowly, stomach sinking into his sneakers.

Coach Cheech's cigarette was still smoking, dangerously close to all that paper and old skin littering the floor. Theo stomped it out. He didn't have to ask if Kade had the same sinking feeling he did: he could see it on Kade's face, how he was gnawing his lower lip.

Something bad had happened. They just didn't know *what* yet.

"Didn't even ask if we wanted a ride home," Kade bitched as he slid into the passenger seat of Theo's Lexus. "Asshole."

Theo took his half-smoked cigarette and threw it out the window.

"Hey!"

"Not in my car," Theo told him. He adjusted his letterman jacket. Lemmings's succulent sat in his pocket, sufficiently hidden unless Kade looked too closely. He'd slipped it into his jacket after he pushed the bookcase aside. Alone, of course. Kade had offered to help, but he'd said it in that slick tone that usually meant a joke, so he'd turned Kade down before he could go *psych*! or *you really thought I'd help when I had a super-powered jock right here? Go on, blood boy.* Or something. Imaginary Kade was never as eloquent as real life Kade, who could disarm Theo with a few well-placed words.

Kade scratched his black blouse. There were no words today, just a bleached skull and lace at the throat. He also had a spiky wristband that Theo hadn't seen in months. Not that he kept track of Kade's fashion sense—he just noticed that kind of thing. Kade put on such a spectacle all the time, he had to be doing it so people would notice.

"Seriously, are you hungry again?"

Theo startled. "What?"

"You're staring," Kade said. "I have to assume that means you're snacky."

"Not snacky," Theo said, tearing his gaze away from the dull glint of Kade's wristband and starting the car. "You shouldn't have told him about the burning thing."

"Excuse the hell out of me for wanting answers! We

were finally talking to someone who knows stuff, *first-hand*, no myths or books needed. Of *course* I told him. It's not *my* fault he freaked out."

Kade bit at his cuticles. Theo was about to tell him to stop it before he made himself bleed when Kade spoke up again.

"Turn on your lights, blood boy. Not all of us can see in the dark."

"Shit." Theo clicked on his headlights.

Kade was quiet for a long moment. "Thanks, by the way."

"For what?"

"Saving me back there." Kade twisted his hands together. His cuticles were raw and pink, but there was no blood yet.

Theo shrugged. "You saved me back."

"Right. Sure." Kade reached up, hand flickering next to his ear for a moment like he'd forgotten he didn't have hair anymore.

Theo made sure Kade wasn't looking. Then he reached down to his pocket, reaching in to touch the succulent. It was already going wrinkly. He'd water it when he got home.

"What happens when you eat human food?"

Theo yanked his hand out of his pocket. "Huh?"

"Earlier, you said—"

"Right," Theo said, tone going bone-dry. "Thanks for asking, Kade. I puke, Kade. Lots of disgusting black stuff, Kade. Which I never would've found out if you didn't put the idea in my head, KADE."

Kade laughed, sharp and shrill. "When did I put *any* ideas in your head?"

"In the funeral home, when you were talking about puke and you asked if I could eat human food anymore!"

"Oh. I...didn't expect you to listen to me."

Theo frowned. "Why? I don't have anyone *else* to listen to about this."

"Right," Kade said cautiously. "We're...trapped together."

"Trapped together," Theo agreed.

The silence stretched. Theo waited for Kade to make a joke, maybe burn him with one of his silver earrings again. But nothing came. Theo looked over just in time for Kade to look away, fast, like he'd been caught doing something he shouldn't.

Kade cleared his throat. "We would've told Cheech about the burning thing eventually, I was just speeding up the process. Really, you should be thanking me."

"Wow," Theo said dryly. "Thanks—oh, shit."

"What?"

Theo swore again. "Car's coming our way."

"So?"

"So *duck*, they can't see you in the car with me!"

"Bloody hell and Mary too," Kade grumbled, and ducked.

The car glided past. Theo smiled tightly at the

driver, a groan leaking out of his teeth when he realized it was the Fletchers. Mrs. Fletcher powdering her nose, Aaron scowling in the backseat. Mr. Fletcher peered at him, head twisting to watch him for a moment longer before he was forced to look back at the road. The star player walking out mid-game—it would be the talk of the town.

Theo's hands tightened around the wheel, plastic cracking under his grip.

His parents were going to be *so* pissed.

THEO WAS SO ENGROSSED in trimming the rose bushes he didn't hear the gardener until a throat cleared behind him.

Theo spun, clutching the shears guiltily in one hand. "Russel! You're early."

Russel gave him an amused look, his tool bag bumping against his hip.

"Says the teenager up before six a.m.," Russel said. He nodded at the half-trimmed rose bush behind him. "Stress gardening again?"

"No stress. Just gardening."

He held out the shears. Russel didn't take them.

"I heard about the game," he said, mouth scrunching apologetically.

Theo sighed. "Awesome. You know there are towns where no one cares about the high school basketball team?"

"Sure. Towns that have more than one high school." Russel shifted his tool bag to the other hip. The material was getting thin on the bottom, even with the patches holding it together. "At least they're rescheduling. That's pretty good luck."

"Uh-huh," said Theo. *Good luck, and somebody bribing or threatening the other school.* He wouldn't put it past his parents to do either. His mom was better at bribes, his dad with threats.

"They said you looked pretty rough," Russel said. "Are you feeling alright now?"

"Yeah. Feeling great." Theo held out the shears again.

Russel shook his head, dropping down to sit on the grass. "You keep at it. Gotta get that stress-gardening done before your parents get up."

Theo let out an awkward laugh and turned back to the bush. They'd done this more when he was younger and didn't know what he was doing. He'd wake up early and meet him outside, and he'd show Theo hands-on stuff the YouTube tutorials never went into.

"Hope your parents didn't give you a tough time," Russel said as he continued to trim the rose bushes. "Not like you could do anything about being sick. What did they want you to do, throw up on the court?"

Theo laughed again.

Yes, was the honest answer. His parents had been waiting for him when he came home last night. He'd opened the door to find them sitting in the front hall.

They'd taken chairs out of the kitchen so there was no pause between opening it and meeting their carefully cool gazes.

Fairgoods don't give up, Victor had said, his hand a tight fist in Theo's hair. *If you have to puke on the other team, fine. But you finish the game.*

You just had *to lose against the Wayside Hawks*, Carol had added with a shudder. *Honestly, vomit would have been too good for them.*

They hadn't brought up his impossible jump. Theo wasn't sure if he was disappointed or relieved. He was just glad they didn't notice the succulent tucked in his pocket and that they let him go to bed when he faked needing to puke for long enough. For a while he thought they were going to keep him there in the front hall all night, Victor gripping his hair so hard it hurt. But they'd let him go. It almost made Theo feel worse—they had to be planning something. There was no way he would screw up *that* bad and not have any consequences when he got home.

"Well," Russel continued. "I hope you're taking it easy today."

"You know it," Theo lied. He was studying, then hunting, then studying some more. Felicity had texted him a few times to ask if he was alright—she knew how his parents could get. She'd even asked if he wanted to get a coffee. Theo had been touched, but the idea of pretending to drink coffee with her made him so tired he'd told her no. He'd see her tonight anyway.

"We're heading over to the Fletchers' for dinner," he said. "It was supposed to be a celebration dinner, but..."

He dropped the shears on top of Russel's gardening bag. "Anyway, I'm gonna go inside. Before they wake up."

"Right," Russel said. He had this look he got sometimes, like he was worried but didn't want to say anything. It was sweet. Theo liked it when people worried about him, even if it made his stomach squirm in mortification and a strange sense of danger. Like if anybody found out that Theo wasn't doing *great* every minute of every day, he'd be in trouble.

He puffed his chest out, making his smile extra cocky. "See you, Russ. Remember to put the wire back over the tomatoes when you're done this time."

Russel snorted as he left. Theo pretended not to hear it. There were only two people who could make him feel like a little kid: his parents, and Russel. He didn't need to feel any smaller. Not with what was waiting for him in that house.

Theo sat in his room, waiting for his parents to come up and tell him his punishment. He listened to them bustle around the kitchen, talk about work, take phone calls. They sounded...normal. Theo even heard them laugh and dance around the living room, his dad humming along to a song Theo didn't recognize.

By midday Theo thought he might be safe to go on a

trip. They hadn't forbidden him from leaving the house yet. He wouldn't be breaking any rules. Technically he'd be breaking their family motto—*Fairgoods are vicious*—which he was leaving the house to deliberately disobey, but they didn't have to know that. You couldn't be vicious *all* the time, he told himself as he tucked a new pair of knitting needles tucked into his backpack. Even his *parents* weren't vicious all the time. They were known around town as stand-up people who you didn't want to get on the bad side of. And they were lovely to each other. They were lovely to *Theo*, when he was behaving. Viciousness was just...a reaction for when things weren't going their way.

Theo knew how they would want him to act with Kade "Monster" Renfield, who lived on the poor side of town and got arrested and snarled at teachers. They would want him to hold the venom over his head as leverage, ignore the fact that he needed Kade even more than Kade needed him. Turn it into a power play. Never talk to Kade more than he had to. Ignore him in the hallways.

They wouldn't want him to *apologize*. Especially not with new knitting needles to replace the ones Theo broke in class. But Theo couldn't help it. He'd put Kade through enough. The guy deserved *something* from him.

Theo considered his bedroom window. It was safer than going through the house. He took two steps toward it and froze.

Footsteps were coming down the hall. There was nothing this way except his bedroom.

He had time. He could blur out the window and be on the ground outside before they reached the door. But fear rooted him to the spot. He yanked off his backpack and slung it under his bed just in time for the door to open.

Victor nodded at him. "Theo?"

"Yes, Dad?" Theo looked him straight in the eyes, like he was taught. Even though everything in him wanted to stare at the ground and cower.

Victor leaned on the doorframe. It was uncharacteristically casual of him. Theo wondered what the game was. Should he get on his knees? They liked that sometimes. Other times they claimed he was making fun of them, and he got punished with another hour awake. So he usually waited until they told him to do it.

"I'll stay up tonight," Theo started, one of his parents' favorite punishments. "I know I messed up. I really was sick—"

Victor sighed. "I believe you."

Theo's jaw snapped shut.

"I want to say we took pity on you last night," Victor continued. "But honestly, one of us would've needed to stay up to check you were fulfilling your whole punishment, and neither of us could be bothered. Especially if you were throwing up."

Theo nodded fervently. "That's fair. I'm sorry."

"I believe you," Victor repeated softly. "Now that

we've had time to cool down…we talked about it. You didn't want to throw up in front of everybody like you did on that aquarium trip, right? You couldn't lift your arms over your head the next day. Nobody would want a repeat of that."

Theo nodded some more, hands shaking at his sides. He'd forgotten about that aquarium trip. He tried not to think about the rest of that day, his parents making him hold his arms up until they went numb.

"But you can't focus on your fear," Victor continued, striding forward. "You have to think about what will take down your opponent. If you have to projectile vomit on somebody, go for it. We won't count that as you making us look bad."

"Okay," Theo whispered. He cleared his throat, trying to get rid of the terror squirming in his stomach. He wasn't worried about physical punishments anymore. He could lift weights the whole night and not break a sweat. Their disappointment, though—he felt *that* like a knife. All they had to do was look at him wrong and he was a little kid again, begging for forgiveness.

"So I'm not embarrassing us if I'm vicious," Theo said. He always wanted to know the rules. Some of them made sense—get good grades, be a good athlete—and others he could never figure out, like their hatred of athletics-enhancing drugs. They'd let him have a party at the house where everyone else got wasted, but god forbid *he* have a drop to drink. He could live with their rules, he just wished they would be *consistent*.

Victor nodded. "We'll accept a lot if you're doing it for the right reasons."

He reached up. Theo tensed, waiting for a hand to clench in his hair. But Victor's hand settled on his shoulder, squeezing hard.

"I worry about you sometimes," he admitted. "That you're...I don't know. Putting on a show. That it's not in you, deep down."

"It is," Theo said, rushed. "I swear. I'll be better, Dad."

"I know you will." Victor reached up further, ruffling the blond curls they shared. He did it with a smile, but Theo could see the threat behind it: even the loosest hand could turn into a fist.

Theo ran to Kade's place through the woods. Yesterday someone had asked him why they'd seen his car parked on this side of town. He'd never been more grateful he'd parked a few blocks away from Kade's house when he dropped him off.

He stared through Kade's bedroom window. Kade was on his bed, flicking through a magazine. His shirt rode up, exposing a pale sliver of his hip.

Theo tore his gaze away and knocked on the window.

Kade flailed so hard he almost fell off the bed. He

looked around wildly, and Theo thought of rabbits in tall grass. Then Kade's gaze landed on him, his bony shoulders tensing.

Theo waved impatiently. His hands were still shaking from his talk with Victor. He clenched them hard around his backpack straps.

Kade bolted over to the window and jerked it up. "Did I miss a text?"

"No." Theo dug the knitting needles out of his backpack and shoved them at Kade. "Here."

"What's...?" Realization dawned on Kade's pinched face. His lips parted.

He looked so different with his guard down. Like you could never cut yourself on him. Like he'd never launched himself at a classmate in the cafeteria or got arrested for shoplifting. In that moment, looking at those knitting needles like they were something precious, he looked...soft.

Theo swallowed back the startling heat surging through his cold chest.

"Just take them," he said, shooting another nervous look around. He'd be able to hear someone walking up, but he couldn't help feeling like he was being watched.

"You got me knitting needles," Kade said disbelievingly. He reached out and touched a pointy tip with one gentle finger, and Theo stupidly thought of Sleeping Beauty. Kade had that fairytale savageness. But he'd be a fae or some half-human creature, not the princess who got saved at the end.

"Yes," Theo snapped. "Take them already!"

Kade stared at him. "Why?"

"Because I broke your other ones, obviously!" Theo twisted again to look. Just a barren lawn opening into the forest. It didn't stop the skin crawling at the back of his neck. "I shouldn't even be here. Just *take* them."

He shoved them at Kade's chest, careful to only touch his shirt.

Kade took a step back. Some of that guardedness was coming back, that soft boy becoming sharp once more.

"Is this your way of making up for doing something nice? You have to be an asshole while you do it?"

Theo groaned, frustrated. His hands were still shaking. He couldn't make them stop.

"I'm not trying to be an asshole," he snapped. He sucked in a breath, hoping for calm. It didn't help being assaulted by Kade's hungry scent, which was strangely familiar after spending so little time with it.

Theo had imagined this going differently. A few jokes to ease the tension. Kade would say something witty and Theo would come up with something witty to say back, for once. Theo wanted to make him laugh. Properly, openly, not the jagged bitter thing he heard in school.

"I do try," Theo realized. "I try really hard, actually. I...my parents, they..."

Immediately the panic swarmed in, tense and overwhelming. He checked over his shoulder. Still no one.

Still that looming sense of doom, *your parents will know you're being bad, you're going to get in so much trouble.*

"Never mind," Theo said hastily. "Yeah, I'm a jerk sometimes. Everyone knows that."

Kade gave him an unreadable expression. That softness was back, but there was something underneath it that would have made Theo sweat, if he still could. A terrible understanding.

"Your parents are assholes?" Kade asked.

"What? No." Theo scowled. "My parents are great. Why would you say that?"

Kade snorted quietly. Finally, *finally*, he took the knitting needles, careful not to touch Theo's hand.

"Lucky you," Kade said slowly. "My parents were... let's say they were *complicated*."

Theo tried not to let his dread show. Was Kade an orphan? He remembered making some Orphan Annie jokes to him in freshman year. Kade had looked like he was going to maul him right there in Homeroom. Now Theo thought he should've.

He swallowed. "I'm sorry. I'm trying to be...less of an asshole. Don't tell anyone."

Kade sniggered, twirling one of the knitting needles in a way that reminded him of Felicity making coins dance over her knuckles.

"That you're secretly being nice to Monster? No one would believe me, golden boy."

Theo shoved his shaking hands in his pockets.

"You're not the monster, Kade. Pretty sure I got that one in the bag."

Kade hummed. "You're not *that* bad, mate. Monsters don't bring their food knitting needles."

Theo decided to let that *food* comment slide. He looked past Kade into the bedroom he'd once climbed into. It was cleaner than before—fewer clothes piled on the floor, fewer mugs scattered on every available surface. There was a desk in the corner heaped with scraps of fabric and what looked like a half-covered sewing machine. Was this a *thing* for Kade?

Kade asked, "Does this mean you're going to let me sit in the passenger seat now?"

"No."

Kade groaned loud enough that Theo panicked, watching the door for someone to come in. No one did.

"It's for your safety too," Theo tried. "If the vampires know you're in on this, they might—"

"What, come after me?" Kade rolled his eyes. "Keep telling yourself that, blood boy."

Theo pushed down a surge of bitterness at the nickname and tried to think what somebody who wasn't an asshole would say. "So you knit?"

"Nope," Kade said instantly, still spinning the needles between his long fingers. "They're for defensive purposes."

"A knife might work better."

"I don't know." Kade leaned over and started

rummaging through one of his leather jackets, which was draped over a chair. He came out with a broken half a knitting needle. "I think I can do some damage with this."

Theo stared at the spiky end. "You kept it?"

"Sure. Fun to fiddle with." Kade gave it a little spin and tucked it back into his jacket pocket. "Still going to the Fletchers tonight?"

Theo nodded.

Kade gave Theo's knitting needles another spin. The stainless steel caught the dim light of Kade's bedroom, making Kade's gray eyes light up like a solar flare.

Theo swallowed. "Any advice?"

"Sure," Kade said. "Don't get staked."

CHAPTER
SIXTEEN

THE FAIRGOODS SHOWED up at the Fletcher house at seven on the dot.

Fairgoods are only ever late on purpose, Theo's dad liked to say. *To show them we don't give a shit about them. If you're ever late, it has to be a 'screw you.' Not because you got stuck in traffic.*

Everybody was already inside, sitting around their too-big dinner table. Felicity was seated next to Aaron, makeup at its normal level for the first time in days. It looked like she'd finally gotten enough sleep.

Theo immediately made a beeline for her as his parents exchanged the usual boring pleasantries with Mr. and Mrs. Fletcher.

"Hi, asshole," he whispered as he slid into the seat beside Felicity, letting relief bleed into his voice: he needed as many people on his side as he could get tonight.

"Bitch," she replied. Her hair was up in a sleek, pale ponytail, like it always was around Aaron's family. They preferred her with it up.

He raised his eyebrows expectantly. *How bad is it?*

The side of Felicity's full, pink mouth twitched down. *Bad. Good luck.*

Theo held back a groan as his parents sat down across from him.

Aaron leaned around Felicity, snapping his fingers at him. "Hi, Theo. I'm here too, Theo."

"Hi, Aaron," Theo said, trying to keep the wariness out of his tone. He might be closer with Aaron than Felicity these days, but if Aaron's parents had decided to be pissed off at Theo this week, that meant Aaron would follow suit.

Theo tried not to think about what that would mean if they were hunters. If they figured out Theo was a vampire. He wanted to believe Aaron would choose him over his family, if it came down to it. He just didn't know if he could.

Mr. Fletcher sat down after the obligatory back-slapping hug from Victor. "Thank god. We've been staring at this food for ten minutes. Didn't my wife do a good job?"

Mrs. Fletcher preened. Everybody said she was the reason Mr. Fletcher stopped being so reserved in his late teens—she was a free spirit, always throwing parties and hosting fundraisers and making connections. Whenever they went out, Mrs. Fletcher would get side-tracked talking to people. Aaron joked that they had to allow an extra half hour before a movie so she had time to catch up with the person who owned the theater.

"It looks wonderful," Carol told her.

"It's great," Theo agreed, looking over the table—a platter of fish stuffed with herbs, shiny potatoes, salad gleaming with creamy dressing, bread buns still steaming from the oven. A few weeks ago he would've been excited—they didn't do family meals at the Fairgood house anymore, and Theo had gotten used to dinners that required the least amount of effort after finishing his homework—but now, he felt nothing. The salad was just leaves. The fish was dead, artificially warm from the oven.

As everybody passed around the food, Mr. Fletcher said, "We were just talking about Felicity jumping back into gymnastics. Isn't that great?"

Felicity paused. The look on her face meant that they hadn't been discussing anything close to that, but she caught herself easily, sending the table a tight smile. "It's really not that big of a deal. I won't be competing or anything. And modeling still comes first. I have that sparkling water ad coming up and my agent says it's going to be very big."

She said the last part forcefully, as if she could make it true if she said it loud enough. *Modeling comes first.* Theo wondered what her mom thought of that. Theo still remembered Mrs. Beverly Sloan—who still insisted on being called *Mrs.* even though her husband had died when Felicity was small—showing up to a sleepover and demanding Felicity come home and practice her tumbling. They didn't even have a competition coming up. *It's about the discipline,* she had insisted as she dragged Felicity out the door.

"Still," Mrs. Fletcher said, raising a glass of white wine. "Our very own rising star. We're so glad our boy finally snapped you up."

"It was a very smart choice," Carol agreed. She tossed a look at Theo, widening her eyes pointedly.

Theo ignored her, spooning two small potatoes onto his plate. He'd tried explaining to his parents that he was genuinely happy his friends were dating each other, even though, yes, he used to have a crush on Felicity.

You two would have made a powerful duo, Carol had said dismissively. *But you waited too long. Aaron will hold onto that girl, mark my words. He knows what's good for him.*

Carol kneaded her forehead.

Mr. Fletcher frowned. "Are you alright, Carol? Are you feeling faint?"

"I'm fine," Carol said, as she always did. "I just need more of this wonderful fish. I was too busy for lunch today."

Theo watched her anxiously. Carol insisted she was fine through all her dizzy spells. Even when Theo was nine and found her crawling to the kitchen. He'd had to bring her a peanut butter sandwich and a chocolate bar, watching her eat them both as her eyes drooped. Victor carried emergency chocolate in the pockets of his slacks after that, just in case his wife's blood pressure tanked. *A sweet for my sweet,* Theo heard him say once, pressing a kiss and then a chocolate to her grinning mouth.

Theo's phone vibrated in his pocket. He snuck a look.

It was Kade. *good luck infiltrating fletchers. remember to ask questions but BE SUBTLE ABOUT IT BLOOD BOIIIIII.*

Theo rolled his eyes. *Infiltrating.* Like Theo wasn't over at this house once a week hanging out with Aaron. At least Theo had deleted all the emojis Kade had put after his name when he'd keyed his number into Theo's phone.

"What are you looking at?"

Theo looked up guiltily. Victor stared at him from across the table. He'd picked the seat directly in front of Theo, probably so he could stare the most effectively. It reminded Theo of that time Victor scared off a barking dog just by glaring at it.

"Nothing," Theo said, stuffing his phone back in his pocket. "That funeral was today, right? The Lemmings guy?"

"Bet it was *packed*," Aaron muttered.

Felicity laughed, a beat too late. She sucked a pea off her fork, spinning her knife in her other hand.

"Hey now," Mrs. Fletcher said warningly. But she was smiling, that small smile that meant she agreed with every word her son said.

Mr. Fletcher said, "I'm just glad that house can

finally get bulldozed. That old fag did nothing to fix it up for decades."

Victor clicked his tongue disapprovingly. "None of that. We're in the twenty-first century, if you haven't heard."

Theo stared down at his plate with the same deep focus as his friends next to him: three bisexual teens hoping the adults didn't notice that they got suspiciously quiet whenever the subject of queerness came up.

"Right," Mr. Fletcher said, smiling tightly. "Sorry. Anyway, you know we tried to convince him! I heard people used to sneak in to mow his lawn. Maybe that's how he died—he finally caught 'em and he took horrible offense to someone trying to fix up that pigsty. They stabbed him in self-defense."

He slapped Victor's back, laughing heartily. He was one of the only people allowed to touch Victor beyond a handshake, and even then there were times when Victor went stiff under his hand. Like now—still smiling, even laughing a little. But he looked at Mr. Fletcher like he'd better drop his hand, and Mr. Fletcher did.

Carol shuddered. "Ugh, let's talk about something more pleasant. I can't stand to think about that man or that place. It's awful, what happened."

"Awful," Mr. Fletcher echoed. He coughed into his meaty fist. "No, you're right. Let's change the subject. So, the game got rescheduled! How'd you pull that off?"

"Nothing you can make us admit to," Victor said,

slicing his portion of fish into pieces. He always did that: small cuts until everything was in tiny bits. Only then would he eat.

Mr. Fletcher let out a booming laugh. He went to slap Victor's back again. Then he thought better of it, hand coming back to smooth his own gelled hair back. "Well, even if Theo did let us all down, that was one hell of a jump! All that training really paid off. You should've seen him a few days ago on our court, he was running rings around our boy, wasn't he, son?"

Aaron grunted. "It's all the steroids."

"Ha ha ha," Theo said, too loud. He sent a nervous glance at his parents. The one and only time Theo joked about being on steroids, they made him lift weights until he cried. It wouldn't be so bad now, with his newfound vampire strength, but he couldn't take the humiliation again. They had sat there the whole time, giving him heavier and heavier weights as his arms shook and sweat soaked his clothes.

I thought you wanted me to win at any cost, Theo had croaked later, trembling in a bathtub full of ice cubes.

His father had given him a tired look. *If you need drugs to win, you don't deserve to win at all*, he'd said. Then he'd emptied another bag of ice into the bath.

Theo still didn't understand—his parents were fine with lying, cheating and stealing their way to the top, but they drew their line at drugs?—but he wasn't going to ask questions. He didn't dare.

Victor sliced through a fish eye. He always took the

head. "Theo knows what we'll do to him if he ever does anything harder than whiskey."

Everybody laughed. Theo laughed along with them, slowly realizing he could never get drunk again. That was disappointing. He liked drinking, even though he liked it as a once-every-few-months activity rather than a several-times-a-week activity like some of his classmates.

He wondered how much Kade drank. He was always wasted when he showed up to parties, and Felicity had mentioned that Kade was her most loyal customer when it came to her mom's booze stash. Definitely more of a several-times-a-week guy.

"He really was something," Mrs. Fletcher said, jolting Theo out of his thoughts. "Right up there— whoosh! Even cleared the backboard!"

"Aaron said it was like he flew," Felicity agreed, pointy chin in her hand. She was still twirling her butter knife in her hand.

Theo picked at his potatoes anxiously, eyeing the potential hunters. Mr. and Mrs. Fletcher didn't look suspicious, like he'd worried about. They just looked jazzed about the star player. Aaron looked annoyed, but the normal kind, the kind he always got when it became obvious that Theo was better at basketball than him. No murder on his mind. No *ridding the world of the vampire scourge*, or whatever hunters believed.

"Here's hoping he can bring that same energy to that same game next Friday," Victor said mildly.

"Strangest thing—Coach wanted to push it back another week."

Theo put his fork down. "What? Why?"

"I don't know. He got really worked up about it." Victor popped the other fish eye into his mouth, ignoring his wife when she looked away in disgust. "I never liked that man. He doesn't care enough about his job. Whatever you do, you have to go all in."

Theo hummed in agreement, distracted. He didn't hear his dad's utensils stop until it was too late.

"Why aren't you eating?"

Theo looked up. Victor was staring at him again. It was never, ever good when Victor stared at him. It could be something small—an offhand comment, or a warning—or it could be big, like making him lift weights until he cried or stand in one place overnight, no sleep, legs trembling with effort of staying upright.

"I'm still not feeling great," Theo tried.

Carol frowned. "Really? It's been all day."

"Yeah, but..."

"The Fletchers made you a wonderful meal," Victor said, voice low. "You aren't going to eat it?"

Felicity started, "Sir, if he's not feeling well—"

"Maybe just a little," Mr. Fletcher said over her. "Settle your stomach."

He gave Theo a broad smile. Theo smiled back, thinking of that small fry and all the black vomit it had produced. He looked down at his plate—a small handful of potatoes, a lump of fish, a single bread roll, and a few limp leaves of lettuce.

Aaron leaned behind Felicity and tapped Theo on the shoulder.

Theo looked over.

Aaron motioned at the bread. *Easy*, he mouthed. He'd gotten sick with the flu last summer. Theo spent most of that week in Aaron's room watching the wrestling channel and eating plain bread with broth while Felicity lounged across their legs, painting, cleaning, and then repainting her toenails.

Theo lifted the bread to his mouth and chewed. It tasted like sludge. He ate slowly, letting the conversation continue without him, and by the time he finished the roll he hoped it was over. But as soon as he swallowed the last bite, his dad looked expectantly at the rest of his plate.

Theo kept eating.

CHAPTER
SEVENTEEN

KADE SMILED the whole way to first-period gym on Monday.

Listening to everyone bitch about Theo losing the game was the best for two reasons: one, it was always a good time when the rich jocks got dunked on. Two: only Kade knew the truth. The important part, anyway. The part everyone was groaning about in Homeroom, trading gossip while the teacher ignored them: diet pills, overtraining, food poisoning, *actual* poisoning courtesy of the Westside Hawks. That it wasn't sickness at all, it was a panic attack. That someone from Westside bribed Theo to throw the game.

It's way worse, Kade wanted to tell them. *He ran off the court because it was either bite me in the bathrooms or sink his big ol' vampire fangs into the other team in front of the school and his parents and God and everyone. And the coach is a hunter! But he didn't kill Theo! The story keeps unfolding!*

He wanted to yell it in their faces. But he also wanted to hold it close to his chest—he was one of a select few chosen to be in this weird, dark story. Kade had always been an outsider, but this was the first time it felt good. *Properly* good, not good like scratching an itch and looking down to realize you've torn through your skin.

Kade was still smiling as he walked through the swinging gym doors. Then he heard a low gasp from Delilah Emmerson, the student body president who had promised better water fountains and never delivered.

"Oh wow," Delilah murmured. "Golden boy looks bad. I guess he *was* sick."

Kade followed her gaze as casually as he could and had to hold back a swear.

Gone were the shiny curls of Friday night. Gone was the healthy skin and alert eyes. Theo looked like he'd spent the whole weekend curled miserably over a toilet bowl, and he was not a good enough actor to fake it.

Kade sighed. He considered waiting it out and texting him later. Then he watched Theo push a lank curl behind his ear, fumbling it with weak fingers.

Kade sighed louder. He turned toward the gym hallway and whispered: "Meet me in the disabled bathroom, blood boy."

He didn't check if Theo had heard him. He didn't have to.

. . .

When Theo showed up a minute later, Kade was balancing on top of the lidless toilet, holding his lit cigarette out the window.

Theo wrinkled his nose. "Come on, man."

"You don't even *breathe*," Kade sneered. He took another drag, taking in Theo's pitiful appearance. "When did this happen?"

Theo shrugged with tired shoulders. "Dinner party, remember? I had to eat."

"So?"

"So I don't just throw up the *food*," Theo said, like Kade was being an idiot.

Kade cocked his head. "Thought you were trying to be less of an asshole."

He mostly said it to piss him off, but that got a reaction: Theo's shoulders hunched, head ducking like he was actually ashamed. He still scowled while he did it, but there was genuine guilt there.

Kade tapped ash on the windowsill. "Why didn't you call me?"

Theo shrugged again. This one was slower, like he had something to say but didn't want to say it. He looked Kade up and down: a black tee with a red heart sewn into the middle; tight black pants, combat boots.

"Why do you never bring your gym gear?"

Kade snorted. "Screw uniforms."

"It's not a uniform, it's *gym clothes*," Theo said, flat and exhausted. "Though I guess you don't have to worry about sweating. What's your excuse today, acute foot-hurt-itis?"

"Maybe I'll join in for once." Kade sucked hard, blowing a plume of smoke into Theo's face. "Seen the coach yet?"

"No." Theo folded his arms over his wide chest. "Not like I can ask him anything during class. I gotta corner him after. Or something."

Just the idea of it made him look even more tired.

Kade stubbed the cigarette out on the windowsill. "We should break into his house. See what *else* that guy's hiding."

"What? No!"

"What, we can break into a dead guy's house but not your coach's?" Kade snorted. "Did you find out anything at Aaron's place?"

"Not really."

"Did you *ask?*"

"*Yes*. God. I even broke into their mysterious greenhouse, okay?"

Kade blinked. "Their what?"

"It's a locked greenhouse out back that no one's allowed into, me and Aaron always joked there were bodies in there. I broke in, and guess what? It's just dirt! And Aaron's parents found out and bitched him out because they think *he* did it, so I got him in trouble for nothing." Theo folded his arms tightly over his chest. "I still think you're wrong. *Maybe* Aaron's family is involved—and that's a *big* maybe—but I don't think Aaron is."

Kade scoffed. "He's going to stab you in the back, and you'll just walk into the knife! *Oops, what's that pain in my spine? Oh, shit, hi Aaron! What're you doing back there? You know what? Not my problem.*"

He climbed off the toilet, catching his knee on a spare toilet paper roll and sending it careening off the toilet tank. He pulled his shirt down, exposing his neck.

"Because I'm *nice*," Kade told him, ignoring how Theo's gaze followed the rolling toilet paper as it trekked across the ties, "I won't make you beg."

Theo gave him a look that would've been unimpressed if he wasn't so obviously aching for Kade's neck, eyes half-lidded and hungry.

Kade suppressed a shiver. *This isn't hot,* he told himself. It was a losing argument. Even if Theo was an asshole, even if they were trapped together in this situation neither of them would choose—an attractive boy staring at him with such hunger would always be hot. Kade had never been *needed* like this. Even if the venom did nothing but hurt, there was something addicting about Theo looking at him like he was starving and Kade was the only one who could give him what he needed.

Kade tilted his head. "Come on, blood boy. You get yours, I get mine."

Theo nodded, distracted as his fangs formed. He reached up like he was going to grip Kade's arm, then his hand stuttered sideways to tangle in Kade's shirt. The sewed-on heart folded dangerously in his grip.

"Careful," Kade mumbled. "It's, um, not sewed on right."

Theo paused. "What?"

"The heart," Kade said, feeling stupid. "It's not..." He'd sewn on the heart last night, clumsy and vibrating with leftover adrenaline. He did a lot of craft when he couldn't sleep.

Theo moved his hand down, clutching the fabric over Kade's flat stomach. His fingers twitched, like he wanted to pull. Then he stepped in and sunk his fangs into the curve of Kade's neck.

Kade bit his tongue to stop a pained gasp from slipping out. He was determined not to make any embarrassing noises this time. Then that sweet venom bled through his system, killing the burn and sharpness, and determination died with them. A happy moan trickled from his slack mouth as Theo fed from him, but Kade was only distantly aware of it. The venom was so powerful, Theo was so close. No one got this close to him unless they were going to hurt him.

Too soon, Theo pulled back. He brushed his fingers over the wound, still humming with venom, and Kade shivered as the bite closed up and the burns faded.

"Cool," he croaked. He tapped Theo's sleeve. "Good game."

Theo stepped back, uncurling his hand from Kade's

shirt like he wasn't sure if Kade would fall over without support. "You good?"

"I'm *great.*"

"You're shaking."

"I'm a shaky guy," Kade rasped. He grinned loosely. "Hey, at least now I got a real excuse to get out of gym class. Not supposed to exercise after you give blood."

"When do you ever do what you're supposed to?" Theo said, a beat too late. He glanced at the door. "I'll go out first. People will actually notice if I'm missing."

Kade made a noise like he was mortally wounded, clutching his chest.

Theo scratched his mouth, hiding a smile. It straightened out fast, a strange look replacing it. The same expression from when he'd showed up to Kade's house with knitting needles. Like he was worried someone was listening in.

"Next time this happens," Theo asked. "Should I call you?"

Kade nodded. "Trapped together, remember?"

"Right," Theo mumbled. His hand flexed at his side.

Kade looked down just in time to watch Theo wipe a red speck on his gym shorts. The heart patch had left a shred of glitter on Theo's hand.

Kade gave it two minutes. He spent most of that drinking water right from the tap, peeing, and staring at himself in the mirror trying to make himself look normal. His pupils were huge, his cheeks flushed despite the blood he lost. He looked tired, but *wired*. Like he'd just been to a concert, spilling onto the night streets with the music still in his veins.

The bell rang.

Kade slapped his red cheeks.

"Be normal," he told himself, and laughed. *Good luck, Monster.*

He strolled back into the gym, hands in his jeans pockets. They were still shaking.

Coach Cheech was dividing the class into two groups. Dodgeball, Kade guessed. Good to know he'd miss a session of people throwing things at his head as hard as they could.

"Renfield," Coach Cheech said, not even a pause before the name. Like he didn't save their asses from a monster and then bounce. "Team two."

"I actually can't do it today," Kade said. "Sorry, Coach."

He'd expected Coach Cheech to give him this. He had ditched them and ran off suspiciously, after all. But Coach Cheech didn't even bat an eyelid.

"Do you have a note?" he asked. Like this was just another day at the office and he'd never shot a winged vampire in front of a student.

"Uh," Kade said. "No."

"Then get the hell in your team. And take off the boots, don't scuff my floor."

Kade couldn't stop himself—he glanced over at

Theo, who had of course been chosen as head of team two. Theo's face was tight and worried, more than it should be. Then Theo's head jerked pointedly toward Aaron standing next to him, and Kade's blood ran cold.

Aaron was staring straight at Kade. His head was cocked, suspicion clear in his sharp face. Had he seen them go into the bathroom together?

Kade kicked his shoes off, wincing as they bounced on the wall. Monster didn't care about shoes, but *Kade* sure did. He'd polish them later to make up for it.

Felicity bounced from foot to foot as he came back around. Her shorts showed off a massive bruise all down her leg, and her knuckles were freshly swollen once again.

"It must suck not being able to use your teeth on the other team," she told him "Dodgeball rules are so boring."

Kade bared her teeth at her half-heartedly. She bared hers back, blunt and chemical-white. Then she crouched in a way that reminded him she used to be very, very fit.

He took a ball and lined up with his team, cursing silently as Aaron made an immediate beeline to stand in front of him.

"Hope you're ready to die, Monster."

"Back at you," Kade snapped. Not his best work. But he was stressed and dehydrated and *very* annoyed at Coach Cheech for relying on old teacher-student dynamics and not people-dragged-into-a-secret-deadly-world dynamics, which would've meant Kade could go to the nurse's office and *maybe* get filled in on what the hell was going on.

Coach Cheech blew the whistle.

Kade threw his ball. Aaron ducked as it sailed harmlessly past his head.

Kade swore, preparing for the inevitable return. But Aaron just stood there, ball in one hand, green eyes drilling into him. Someone behind Aaron aimed a ball at Kade, then immediately diverted his target once he saw Aaron marking his territory.

"Nice shirt," Aaron said. "Is that a heart?"

"Is that a zit?" Kade replied. He went to step back.

Aaron stopped him, reaching his hand out to grab the heart sewn shoddily into Kade's shirt.

"You gotta remember your place, you cockney shit," Aaron whispered. He was obviously trying for his usual brand of unaffected cool, like he was going to ruin Kade's day without breaking a sweat, then go back to his life—but there was something burning behind his green eyes.

His nail dug further into the red fabric, prying under the clumsy stitches.

Kade snarled. "Hey!"

Theo called out from the other side of the court. "Aaron! Cut it out!"

Aaron shot him a confused look and tugged. The heart stretched out from Kade's shirt, stitches popping.

One more yank and the heart snapped off, dangling from Aaron's loathsome hand.

Kade's head rang. Some of it was weakness from Theo's bite. But most of it was *rage*, pure and simple. Righteous fury. It would feel so *good* to drive his fist into Aaron's smug face. Good like putting his fist through a window during a house party. Good like stealing something in full view of the store owner, knowing he'd chase Kade down the street.

"Aaron," Felicity called. "That *no biting* rule is for you, too, babe."

Aaron ignored her, leaning forward. He tapped the heart against Kade's nose.

"Whatcha gonna do?" he whispered. "Monster."

Kade tackled him. Aaron hit the ground with a grunt, lifting his arms to protect his face.

A gasp went up. Shoes squeaked to a stop all around the gym.

Felicity let out a shocked laugh. "Okay, *here* we go."

"*Guys*," Theo snapped. Kade couldn't tell who he was more annoyed with, Kade or Aaron or even Felicity for laughing along.

Blood roared in Kade's ears. He could hardly make out Aaron's words as he whaled on his arms, trying to get to his face. It felt *great*. Like scratching an itch. Like tearing a hole in your skin.

Someone started barking, a fun thing people did now when Kade started a fight.

"You're a goddamn animal," Aaron said through

gritted teeth, as people yelled, cameras flashed, and Coach Cheech screamed for them to get the hell off each other. "Somebody should put you down."

Kade sat back and punched him in the stomach. "Rabbit-killing shit!"

Aaron curled over protectively, breath knocked out of him. He stared up at Kade, his confused face slowly going red.

"*What?*" he wheezed.

Arms closed around his shoulders. Kade struggled, but the grip was iron. One of them, anyway. He turned to find Theo gripping one arm, Coach Cheech on the other. Kade considered headbutting Cheech in the face. Then he went stiff, letting them haul him up.

"Alright," Mr. Cheech yelled at everybody taking photos. "Everybody sit down and shut up. I better not hear anything while I take care of this. Aaron—you hurt?"

"Not for lack of trying," Aaron replied stiffly, pushing himself up off the floorboards. He stared at Theo, who let go of Kade's sleeve like it burned him.

"Great," Coach Cheech barked. He let go of Kade and sucked hard on his mustache. "Renfield, go take a walk."

Kade looked over at him, surprised. He was expecting the principal's office. Maybe a suspension. *Detention*, at least.

"What? You said you can't do gym today, go have a free goddamn period."

Kade glanced at Theo. Theo stared back, confused, as Coach Cheech marched off.

The gym filled with murmurs. *Nobody* let Kade off scot-free. The last time Kade acted up in gym, Coach Cheech made him run laps until a hungover Kade puked on the floor. Then he made him mop up the puke.

"Cheech," Kade yelled after him. "What's the catch?"

Coach Cheech turned. "Get. *Out.*"

Kade shrank back, turning his flinch into a shrug. "*Fine*. Should've just let me go at the start, save everybody the trouble."

His gaze caught on something red and glittery. The heart patch had flown out of Aaron's hand when Kade punched him. Kade bent down and scooped it up as he skulked toward his boots. He tucked the patch into his pocket and ignored all the whispers behind him, no one daring to look directly at him lest he launch himself at them next.

He stood up and swore. Felicity Sloan stood next to his shoulder, gaze wary but aimed straight at him.

Kade sneered. "What?"

She shook her head. Her gaze dipped toward his pocket.

Kade shuddered with mortification at the idea she might've seen him pick up his stupid glittery heart.

"You need to move," Kade snarled, "Or you're gonna have to call your modeling agency and tell them you can't do that sparkling water job with a busted nose."

Felicity's pink lips curved up. She was rarely scared of him. Shocked, sure. *Amused*, even. But he hadn't gotten an inch of real fear from her in all the years he'd been in Lock.

"*You're* going to break my nose, Renfield?"

"Maybe," Kade spat, feeling like an idiot. They both knew he wouldn't hit her. Not unless she hit him first. And fistfights didn't seem like Felicity's style. She cut with words, not with her polished nails. Even if she looked like she wanted to take a swing at him right now, bright with sweat and adrenaline. She'd been lobbing dodgeballs like her life depended on it, smiling through a snarl.

Kade shouldered past her, the heart burning a hole in his pocket.

She called after him, Forrest Gump style. "*Run, Monster, run.*"

Don't look back, he told himself. He didn't want to see his classmates whispering about what a freak he was, Aaron sulking over his bruised arms, Theo joking to try and make it better.

Don't do it, he told himself as he pushed open the door. *Don't—*

He glanced back. Felicity was adjusting her ponytail as she ran back to her boys. Cheech had his phone out, texting furiously and barking at everyone to shut up and get back in their lines. Aaron had a dodgeball in his hand, spinning it like a basketball and getting annoyed when it spun onto the ground.

Theo held out a sneakered foot. The ball rolled to a stop under it. He was watching Cheech text, his blond brows furrowed. Then, just as Kade was about to let the door swing shut between them—he looked up. Right at Kade.

It lasted maybe a second. But as the door swung closed, Kade knew:

They were going to break into Cheech's house.

EIGHTEEN

THEO SPED out of the gym changing rooms and almost ran down Felicity, who was checking her eye makeup in her phone reflection.

"Watch it," she told him as he steadied her. "You—oh."

She gave him a surprised look. He'd yanked her up too easily.

"You've been *lifting*," she said, squeezing his arms. "Has Aaron gotten snippy yet?"

Theo glanced nervously at the changing rooms behind them. "No, and he's not going to get the chance. Move."

She stopped and stood in front of him, twirling a strand of wet hair around her fingers. She hadn't even taken the time to blow-dry it. She'd been dripping with exertion by the end of class, sprinting laps like she was being chased. Bruises showed under her gym shorts, dark purple and vomit-yellow.

My body's not used to it anymore, Felicity had sighed when Theo asked her about it. *It'll stop bruising so much when it remembers.*

He walked past her, pulling her down the hallway. She leaned back, resisting.

"Come *on*," Theo hissed. "It's the only class we have without him! It's my one chance!"

"Sure," Felicity said, all faux sweetness. "He'll *totally* forget by lunch. So what the hell is going on with you and Kade Renfield?"

Theo shushed her. More students were piling out of the changing rooms, wisely stepping out of their way. You didn't just ask Theo Fairgood and Felicity Sloan to *move*.

"There's nothing *going on*, I just stopped the guy from beating Aaron to a pulp."

His phone vibrated in his pocket. He dug it out. It was a text from Kade: *yeah he's not gonna tell us SHIT we gotta take this into our own hands. meet me after school u WIMP*

Felicity swayed forward. "What's got you all worried?"

"Nothing. Shut up," Theo said, holding the phone away from her prying eyes. "What's with *you* lately? Huh? Why are you suddenly throwing yourself into gymnastics like your life depends on it?"

"It might," Felicity said, laughing like she was an

unwilling participant in someone else's inside joke. "I told you, it'll calm down once my body gets used to hitting a mat again."

She lunged for his phone. Theo held it higher.

"Good luck stealing my phone again," Theo spat. "I changed the passcode."

He stopped as the phone was swiped unceremoniously from his hands. Theo turned to find Aaron, damp-haired, face dangerously blank, looking down at the text.

"Hey," Theo barked. He swiped the phone back, panicked, but it was too late.

Aaron stared at him. "You're...you're actually *hanging out* with Monster?"

"No," Theo said. He stuffed his phone deep in his pocket like that would cancel out what Aaron had seen. "Guys, it's not like that."

"I thought Tommy H's girlfriend was lying for attention when she said she'd seen you guys driving around," Aaron said. "But you're *actually* hanging out."

"It's for drugs," Theo said. He winced, looking around, but no one was close enough to hear.

"You don't *do*—" Aaron bit the inside of his cheek, nodding to himself. He was rigid, a muscle twitching in his cheek. Felicity sauntered up next to him and put a hesitant hand on his arm. He twitched like he was going to hold it. Then at the last second he pushed it off.

"You were...weird, in class. With him." Aaron said. "Are you guys hooking up? You can tell us."

"No!" Theo cleared his throat. "With *him?* God, no. Why would I ever...he's...no."

Aaron nodded again, sharper than before. "Right. Cool. Lie to my face."

"I'm not lying! Look," Theo said, desperate to stop this before it got ugly. "I know I've been...distant, this week. But Kade's nothing! You really think it could be anything else?" He hesitated, meeting Felicity's gaze. Felicity just stared back at him, tired and wired, like she had a hundred other things to worry about that had nothing to do with Theo's boy troubles.

Theo cautiously touched Aaron's arm. Aaron twitched again, but didn't shove it off.

"Come on," Theo said softly. "It's you and me and Liss. Always."

He met Felicity's gaze again, pleading. Curiosity burned behind her clear blue eyes. She wanted to know. But today, she took pity on him. She slid an arm around Aaron's hips, holding him fast when he stiffened. She didn't have muscles like back when she did gymnastics, but she could still dig her nails in.

"Come on, babe," she said, resting her sharp chin on his shoulder. "Quit needling our boy and let us get to class. Ms. Day told me if I'm ever on time after gym, she'll pee herself from happiness. Don't you want me and Theo to see her pee?"

Aaron finally looked at her. She dug her chin in harder. It had to hurt. Theo didn't get them sometimes, all their pulling away, slapping each other's hands.

Sometimes they pinched each other hard enough to leave marks.

Love and hurt always go together, dumbass, Felicity told him the only time he asked about it. She'd even given him a funny look, like she was surprised he was asking.

Aaron's jaw flexed. Felicity let up the pressure: showing a reaction meant you lost. At least, it did for Aaron.

"My parents want to have dinner with us again. They've been weirdly pushy about it. You especially," he told Theo. "Dad wants to talk about your training regime. Mom wants to talk about..." He frowned. "Your uniform, or something."

"We can have a celebration dinner after the make-up game," Theo offered. "After we win."

The bell rang.

Felicity sighed. "Guess nobody's seeing Ms. Day pee."

"Stand behind her and scream," Aaron suggested darkly, and turned toward the gym doors.

Felicity sauntered after him. Theo eyed her jeans, remembering the giant bruises on her thighs as she ran relentless laps around the gym.

It was a quiet drive to Coach Cheech's after school. Mostly because Kade spent the ride crouching low in the backseat so nobody could see him.

"You said somebody already spotted me," Kade

called, muffled. His mouth was pressed into his knees. "Surely we can just—"

"There's a lot of talk in this car with just me in it," Theo said.

Kade flipped him off.

"This is what you get for being a hothead idiot," Theo told him.

Kade made a noise against his legs. It sounded like *takes one to know one,* so reminiscent of Felicity that Theo huffed a laugh. If those two ever became friends, the world would tremble.

Theo thought about asking if Cheech caught up with him after class and gave him detention. Asking him how Kade could do something so stupid, especially if he was convinced Aaron was involved in all this.

He sighed instead. "You okay?"

Kade let out a startled laugh. "I've had worse, golden boy. Don't trouble your pretty head about it."

Theo paused, Kade's words rolling over in his head. "Did you call me pretty?"

"No," Kade said, too fast. "I was mocking you."

"Oh," Theo said. "Here I thought we were being nice."

"We can do both," Kade said, the words muffled against torn denim.

Theo's mouth twitched in a reluctant smile. He chewed his cheek until it went away.

· · ·

Coach Cheech's house was nice, until you looked closer. Faded paint, chips in the wood. Rot creeping up the foundations. It had been in his family for generations, two stories tucked one road over from the only supermarket in town.

"He doesn't let anybody in to clean it," Theo told Kade as they crept into the backyard. "I just hope it's better than the Lemmings place. Cheech doesn't seem like much of a cleaner."

Kade made a dubious noise, looking around. The grass was long and brown, the flowerbeds long empty. Old garden stakes protruded from the dirt. Cheech's parents had kept tomatoes before they died and left him the house.

"You're *sure* he won't be home?" Kade asked as they headed up the concrete steps to the back door.

"He's at his bowling club," Theo replied. He reached for the shiny doorknob. "Do you think he's the kind of guy who locks his back—ow!"

He leapt back with a yelp as pain flared through his hand.

Kade let out a shocked laugh. "Holy shit! Is it—?"

"Silver," Theo said through gritted teeth. He shook his seared hand hopefully. The burn stayed. He sighed and stepped back. "You try it."

Kade slipped past him. His hand hovered over the doorknob.

Theo rolled his eyes. "Come on."

Kade grabbed the doorknob and jerked, a pained gasp spilling from his throat.

"What?" Theo reached for his shirt, ready to yank him back. But before he could—

"Psych." Kade turned, holding up an unscathed hand.

If Theo had a heartbeat, it would be thundering.

"Asshole," he spat. "Don't yell when you're breaking into someone's house!"

"I didn't *yell*," Kade mumbled. He took the doorknob and rattled it. "Locked."

It took only two minutes of searching to come up with a key. Theo floated a few inches above the ground and caught sight of a silver flash tucked above the doorframe.

He grabbed it and hissed. The key clattered onto the steps, Theo shaking his burned fingers.

Kade cackled. "He got you again! This is hilarious, mate. I bet everything in there's lined with silver."

Theo took his burned fingers out of his cool mouth. "Shut up and grab the key."

Kade bowed, like an asshole. "Of course, your undead majesty."

Theo hid a snort and floated down to the bottom step. When his feet hit the concrete, the door was still closed. Theo found Kade watching him with a goofy little grin that made Theo's mouth twitch unwillingly.

"What?"

"Nothing," Kade said, too fast. He scratched his face to hide his smile. "'S cool you can fly, is all. Didn't really appreciate it when you had me shoved against my own ceiling."

The door clicked. Kade swung it open, gesturing with a flourish. He did that a lot, Theo was noticing—little flourishes. Like an actor in a play.

"The adventure continues," Kade said.

"Great," Theo replied. "Let's get this little vampire adventure over with."

He pushed past Kade, ignoring Kade's annoyed grumble.

It *was* better than the Lemmings house. No stink of decay, just neglect. Everything was sparse, long hallways of dusty family photographs and bedrooms that hadn't been used in a decade, woodwork falling into disrepair.

The kitchen was the first room they found that looked lived in: a fruit bowl full of bananas and oranges, empty cans of Bud Lite, and a dehydrator on the bench with dried fruits waiting inside. Then the living room, which had no family photographs on the walls. Instead there were framed movie posters and a calligraphy that said, I'M NOT RACIST—I HATE EVERYONE EQUALLY!

"Yikes," Kade said.

Theo nodded. He couldn't help thinking of the Lemmings house, where they'd rooted around for ages and come up with nothing. Theo had thought they were wasting their time. Then that monster had lurched in out of nowhere, making the trip not useless after all.

He turned to Kade. "If this was some stupid monster story, where would he hide something important?"

Kade stared at him, parting his chapped lips in surprise.

Theo sighed. "I don't want to spend my time rooting through old sci-fi books or going through his laundry for nothing. If you have any ideas, now's the time."

Kade considered. His gaze skimmed the room—the expensive couch covered in Cheeto dust, the bookcase stuffed with yellowing sci-fi tomes from the eighties.

"I don't know about you," he said, "But I'm betting on another secret room."

Theo groaned. "Just because Lemmings had one—"

"You can't say it's not realistic—"

"Lemmings was a vampire, Coach Cheech is a hunter!"

"Exactly! Cheech is from a long line of hunters, and this is the family home, there should be a *ton* of weird secrets hidden away in a—holy SHIT!"

"What?"

Kade ignored him, running over to the bookcase so fast and gesturing at the books. Theo was about to ask him again when he noticed what Kade was pointing at: amid all the old paperbacks sat a big, black leather book with a golden sun on the spine.

"Holy shit," Theo echoed.

"Right?" Kade giggled. Theo had never heard him

giggle before. It was weirdly cute. "Now, if I know my stories…"

Kade pulled the book out. Something clicked behind it. The bookcase creaked out from the wall.

Theo stared. "No way."

"YES way," Kade hissed joyously. "Secret room part two, baby!"

He jumped up and down on the spot. Theo couldn't help it: he grinned. He tried to stop it as soon as he felt it, but Kade didn't see, too busy pulling the bookcase all the way out to reveal the room behind it.

Theo's grin faded when he stepped into the dark room.

Weapons lined one wall. Crossbows, axes, one huge sword that looked like it would burn Theo to a crisp if he even went near it. Family photographs lined another wall. There were fancy clothes, like the photographs in the hall. Except the fine clothes in *these* photographs were dressed in dirt and blood. Generations of Cheeches lifting silver crossbows and axes. They got less bloody with each decade: by the time Theo spotted a young Cheech, they looked like they were posing. Like their hunting gear were props. Nothing like the older photos—in the oldest one, a beaming toddler was holding a severed head.

"Jesus," Theo whispered. He lifted a hand and wiped away the dust. *Everything* in this room was covered in dust—the white wallpaper, the display case holding an old scroll unfolded to show unintelligible writing, the wooden floor. The only thing that looked used was a desk and chair tucked in the corner.

Theo started toward it.

"God, you must suck at video games," Kade told him. His gaze was glued to the glass case and the scroll displayed inside. "*Everything* in this room points to this. Might as well be a giant spotlight going THIS WILL PROGRESS THE PLOT."

"Or we could check the only place in the room he actually bothers going," Theo replied, walking over to the desk. "Just a thought."

Kade grunted, distracted. He chewed his thumbnail, scraping blue polish with his teeth. Theo tore his gaze away from Kade's mouth and turned toward the desk. It looked like it had been stolen out of the older classrooms at the high school. Same off-brown color, same bored doodles scratched into the wood. Papers were strewn across it. Some of the sheets were torn, like a pen had been pushed into it with such force it met the wood on the other side.

Most of the pages were crossed out. Only one thing remained: a date, written huge and circled twice.

Theo touched the numbers. "There's a date here. That's next Friday...and then it just says *dark*? So, night-time, I guess?"

"Awesome," Kade said, still hovering around the glass case like he was checking for booby traps. "Anything else?"

Theo sifted through the papers. There was a

strange, gnarled tree doodled in the margins of most of them. That same tree was carved into the table, branches twisted and spindly. Theo touched the divots in the wood. He'd seen it before, a long time ago. Maybe in a dream.

He slid a finger down the etched trunk and shivered.

"What?"

"Uh, nothing." Theo pulled his hand away. "Hey—that date."

"Yeah?"

"That's the game."

Kade looked at him blankly.

"The game that got rescheduled," Theo explained. "Coach tried to talk them into making it a different day. He was yelling and everything. My dad told me."

"Coach does love to yell," Kade said slowly. He tapped the glass case thoughtfully. "Shit. Guess something's going down on Friday."

Far away, something clicked. Theo froze.

Kade's hand stilled on the glass case. "What is it?"

Theo shook his head, listening hard. There—the creak of a door opening.

"He's here."

CHAPTER
NINETEEN

KADE STARED. "You said he was bowling!"

"He *was*," Theo insisted. "Every Monday night, his bowling club goes—"

Kade shushed him, heart pounding. This was one of those story moments where everything came down to what he decided to do in the next few minutes. Unfortunately—like all story moments he'd lived through—the part of his brain that told him what would logically come next in a story was drowned out by blind panic.

Kade shoved the glass case open. Before he could grab the scroll, Theo blurred over and grabbed his sleeve.

"What are you *doing*?" Theo hissed. "He'll notice it's gone!"

"What's he gonna do, shoot you?"

Theo gestured at the weapons and bloody family photographs lining the wall. "Maybe!"

Kade winced. He hadn't noticed the photo of the toddler holding the decapitated head.

He dropped the glass case back into place and wrestled his phone out of his pocket.

Theo glanced anxiously at the living room. "He's coming."

"Then shut up!" Kade aimed his camera at the scroll, trying to stop his hands from shaking.

Theo jerked his sleeve. "Take the goddamn picture!"

"I'm trying," Kade snapped. "My hands—"

Theo grabbed the phone off him and took five photos in rapid succession. He shoved the phone back at Kade and then dragged him into the living room, only letting his sleeve go to push the bookcase back into place.

Kade started, "Where—?"

They both went still as Cheech's humming drifted down the hallway.

Theo swore, grabbing Kade's sleeve again.

Thank god this man has such a stupid big house, Kade thought as Theo yanked him behind the couch. The only thing behind the Renfield couch was the wall. *This* couch had another half of the room behind it, complete with a chest of drawers, an angel statue nudging into Kade's foot, and a whole other couch that looked like it had been last sat on in 1983.

The humming came closer.

"What's the plan?" Kade whispered.

Theo stared at him, blank and panicked.

Kade winced. "Shit."

He fell silent as Coach Cheech walked in. There was the familiar *crack* of a beer can being opened. The humming faded into a weary sigh as Coach Cheech dropped onto the couch.

"Crap," Coach Cheech said. The TV flicked on.

Kade's knees ached with how hard he was clutching them. He squeezed even harder as Cheech changed the channel to an old *MASH* rerun. If Cheech was anything like Aunt Sundance, they could be stuck here for hours.

Kade squirmed. The angel statue pressed hard against his jeans, and there was no room to move over. Its arms were outstretched. If Kade were a religious man, he might've taken that as a sign everything was going to be okay.

Kade was not a religious man. Historically, very few things turned out okay for him.

Pain burst in his thumb. Theo had leaned too close and touched it, skin-on-skin.

Kade gasped, jerking sideways into the angel statue.

Something cracked.

Theo blurred with speed, reaching past Kade to steady the angel statue and catch the tip of its wing, which had broken off when Kade bumped it.

Kade cowered with his burned thumb in his mouth. Was this how he died? Squished between a statue, a couch, and a boy who was trying very hard not to touch his bare skin?

The TV turned off.

Shit, Kade chanted silently. *Shitshitshit. Please don't shoot us. This is the part of the story where we get away. A daring escape, come on, I know my life has sucked so far but that's all underdog setup, right?*

For a moment, nothing moved. Then there was a slow creak of floorboards supporting Cheech's weight as he stood. He didn't call out or ask if anybody was there. He just stood there, listening. Then he murmured something, so low Kade couldn't hear it.

Kade's gaze darted desperately to Theo. Theo stared back at him, his perfect hair falling down his forehead. The tip of the angel's wing sat in his outstretched hand, gray and dusty.

Kade wet his chapped lips. *Throw it,* he mouthed.

Theo frowned at him.

Kade nodded to the broken stone in Theo's hand. *Throw it!*

Theo's expression smoothed out. He leaned around the side of the couch and slung the stone.

Kade squeezed his eyes shut, listening. The stone zapped into the hallway, bouncing along the walls. Theo had thrown it *hard*.

Cheech took off. Kade waited until his footsteps hit the hall, then grabbed Theo's letterman jacket.

"Grab me and run," he whispered. "Fast as you—"

He didn't finish. Theo had already scooped him up, rushing into the next room. Wind rushed past Kade's buzzed scalp. The world blurred past. Kade squeezed his eyes shut. If he wasn't putting all his effort into forcing himself to be quiet, he would've yelled. It was the most alive he'd ever felt since Theo put his teeth in his neck.

When Kade opened his eyes, Theo was propping him up next to the car and telling him to get in.

Kade folded himself into the backseat, ignoring his wobbly legs. Theo tore out of the street like there were people after them. Kade risked a look out the back window—no one. He patted himself down—everything was where it should be, including his wallet, wallet chain, and the pointy end of the broken knitting needle Theo had stepped on in class. For fidgeting purposes, he told himself. Or maybe he really could use it to defend himself one day.

"So," he started. "Bowling, huh?"

"He does it every *week*," Theo said. His nails split on the steering wheel. Theo swore, pushing at it like he could glue it back into place if he pushed hard enough. His hand was still burned from the silver, but the skin had already faded pink.

Kade pressed his head harder into his knees. His burned thumb throbbed. "So we just send Milly the picture? Ask for a translation, lie about where we found it?"

"Looks like."

"Did you take a picture of his desk?"

Silence.

Kade groaned. "Come *on*, mate!"

"We got the date and *kind of* the time," Theo said over him. "That's what's important."

Kade sighed, leaning with the car as they sped around a corner. He couldn't see the windows when he was hunched over like this, but Cheech's place wasn't far from home. And Theo parked a block away from his place, anyway.

"Right," Kade said. "We'll just follow Cheech."

"He'll be at the game."

Kade lifted his head. "No he's not. You saw that mess all over his desk, he'll find a way to weasel out of the game if it's THAT important."

Theo glanced in the rear-view mirror. Kade only caught a sliver of his expression, but it was enough.

"Oh my GOD," Kade said. "You want to be at the game!"

"I have to! I let everyone down!"

"The vampire hunter hand-feeds us a date and time, but noooo, you need to prove to everyone you're still the town golden boy!"

"We don't know what Cheech meant," Theo argued. "It could be anything! It might not have anything to do with us!"

Kade laughed, loud and spiteful. It cut off when the car turned, making Kade veer sideways and bang his head on the car door. "Ow! Bloody hell, Fairgood!"

"You can walk from here," Theo announced.

Kade rolled his eyes, trying to hide the wet sheen. His thumb was bad enough, but now his head stung.

"I can't believe I'm stuck with you," he told Theo as he un-pretzeled himself from the backseat. He dug in his pocket, pushing a cigarette between his teeth.

Theo made a warning noise. "Not in the car."

"I'm getting out!" Kade reached for the car door, hissing when it caught on his burned thumb. "*Ow*. I was actually having a good time for five seconds back there, and then you ruin it by being a jock asshole. What happened to all that shit you said with the knitting needles, huh? God forbid you miss the big game that had to get rescheduled because *you* messed up the first time—"

Kade's words died in his throat as he opened the door to find Theo standing there, palm held out. Kade stared at it.

Theo swallowed. He had the gall to actually look hurt by the stuff Kade had said.

"Just let me heal you so you can stop bitching," Theo said, voice low.

Kade scoffed, unlit cigarette still clamped between his teeth. "When did I bitch?"

Theo's jaw worked. He grabbed Kade's hand. Kade hissed reflexively, pain blooming around Theo's grip. But tingling followed it, those burns sucking back into his skin along with the burn on his thumb.

Theo let him go, looking guilty. "There. You can shut up now."

Kade flexed his newly healed hand. "So you have to focus."

"What?"

"To heal me. You gotta focus. Doesn't just happen automatically."

"I guess." Theo frowned, like he didn't understand why it was important to know these things. If *Kade* was turned into a vampire, he'd want to know everything about every ability he could get his hands on. He'd buy a cool notebook and a fancy pen and write everything down.

Kade got out of the car, pulling a plastic lighter out of his pocket. He waited for Theo to move out of the way. But Theo just stood there, watching Kade dig his cigarettes out.

"I expected something fancier," Theo told him. "Like...silver. Engraved. Got a coffin on it."

"We can't all afford engraved lighters," Kade drawled, lighting up. He sucked in a breath, shoulders already relaxing. "Are you going to let me go home or are you just gonna stand there?"

"You know that's disgusting," Theo said. "Right?"

Kade grinned around the cigarette. "Secondhand smoke can't hurt *you*. Right, dead boy?"

Theo tilted his head. Kade lifted his hand, worried Theo would snatch the cigarette right out of his mouth.

"Alright," Theo said instead. "Gimme one."

Kade raised his eyebrows. Theo held out a hand,

index and middle finger parted. Waiting for Kade to slot a cigarette in.

Kade fumbled for his cigarette pack and handed it over.

"Thanks," Theo said, placing the end in his mouth.

"Oooh, even got the correct end," Kade muttered, pulling his lighter back out. He flicked the trigger, watching it crackle and then fade out. "Breaking and entering. Now he's *smoking*. Watch out, Lock, there's a new bad boy in…"

He trailed off. Theo was ignoring the faulty lighter still unlit in Kade's hand, opting instead to lean in and press the tip of his cigarette to Kade's. He breathed in, long and steady, gaze never dropping.

Kade watched him, frozen. His lips slackened around his cigarette. Then he realized he had to help this along and sucked in a tight breath.

Their cigarettes flared: first Kade's, then Theo's. Catching the spark.

"Thanks," Theo said again, leaning back all casual, like he hadn't launched Kade into a full gay freakout.

Kade nodded, hoping like hell Theo wasn't paying attention to his wild heartbeat just then. Or his burning cheeks. He couldn't help it. Not a lot of guys wanted to get that close to Kade "Monster" Renfield unless they were beating the crap out of him.

"Do you even breathe anymore?" Kade asked, desperately trying to claw back some semblance of dignity. "Like, normally?"

"I try to," Theo said. "Have to keep my image."

He gave the cigarette a considering look. Then he brought it to his lips and sucked, grimacing as the breath went on inhumanly long. When he finally breathed out, the entire cigarette was ash.

"Great party trick," Kade croaked, still stuck on how intense Theo's eyes had been when he leaned in. All pupil. Like he was hungry.

"Thanks," Theo repeated, quieter than last time. He thumped his chest. "God. Like licking a fire pit."

"Don't knock it," Kade said faintly.

Theo nodded. He watched Kade smoke for a few seconds longer, like he wanted to say something more. He looked almost...nervous. Then he turned to get back in the car.

"See you next time you need a bite," Kade told him, voice thin.

"Right. If you need..." Theo turned back, face twisting. "Venom? Uh, let me know."

"I think we sync up." Kade grinned. He tried to make it sharp, the kind he gave to teachers who pissed him off, but he was still shaky with adrenaline. The smile slid into something soft, almost teasing, the kind of goofy smile he gave his aunt when she caught him on a good day.

Theo blinked. But before Kade could reign his smile in, Theo's mouth twitched. Like he was going to smile back.

"Hey," Kade said, to save himself the embarrassment

of a vampire overhearing his heart do something stupid under the force of a slightly soft Theo smile. "Did you hear what Cheech said? When we were shitting ourselves and waiting to see if he'd discover us?"

Theo paused. He reached out and touched the hood of his car, tapping a beat along the shining paint job.

"No," he said. "Your heart was beating so *loud*. It was hard to hear anything else."

Kade tried to think of something to say to that. He couldn't stop staring at Theo's hands, those hands which had been tucked under Kade's knees and braced along his back, carrying him to safety. Couldn't stop thinking about his stupid heartbeat acting up when Theo had leaned in with that cigarette, cherry glow reflecting in those big brown eyes.

Kade managed a grin. "Sorry for my loud heart."

"THEO," Mr. Hawthorn called. "Could I talk to you for a minute?"

Theo paused in the middle of sliding his pencil case into his bag.

"Sure," he said. He kept his head down as he zipped up his bag. He felt his classmates' gazes on him as they filed out, Felicity and Aaron among them. But also Kade.

Theo knew he should have looked at his friends. But for one stupid, knee-jerk moment, Theo's head started turning toward Kade.

It was a slip they couldn't afford. Not with Aaron 'probably a hunter' Fletcher watching, *definitely* not with their classmates watching. There was no reason, in the reality everybody else lived in, for the golden boy to look anywhere near Kade "Monster" Renfield unless it was to trip him in the halls. They were good at not looking at each other, for the most part. But it was getting harder. Theo would find his gaze dragging over to the rough stubble of Kade's scalp, watching Kade flip a pencil or jiggle his leg or carve something into the table when the teacher wasn't watching.

It was hunger, Theo told himself. Or boredom. It was the way you stare at anyone who hadn't texted you back yet, even if the text was *has M texted you about the photo*, which was still a no every time Theo asked. It was the uncomfortable thrill of a secret: walking around like Theo had never had his mouth against Kade's neck, making him bleed and then healing the wounds. Theo could smell him from halfway across the school, metal and softness and, on some days, the bitter stench of booze. The scent was still in the room when Aaron's hair gel and eucalyptus drifted into the hall after his girlfriend.

Mr. Hawthorn made an impressed noise from the front of the class. "Great jacket today, Kade!"

"Uh," came Kade's uncertain voice. "Thanks, Mr. H."

Theo couldn't help it: he looked up.

Kade's pale scalp vanished into the hall. Theo told himself he wasn't disappointed, then pulled up a polite smile and headed to the front of the class where Mr. Hawthorn was waiting.

"What's up?"

Mr. Hawthorn leaned back against the board, adjusting his glasses. He had that look that meant he needed to say something a student wasn't going to like, but goddamn he was going to be nice about it.

"You're distracted," he said.

"I'm turning in homework," Theo replied. "I'm kinda participating in class discussions. Sort of."

Mr. Hawthorn waved him down. "Your grades aren't taking a hit. Yet, anyway. I just wanted to remind you that you can talk to me. I won't send you to the counselor, I know how that went last time."

"What do you mean?"

Mr. Hawthorn held back a smile. He pushed his chest out, tossing his hand through his hair and making his voice deep in a way that was, Theo was embarrassed to realize, a pretty good imitation of him. "*I'm fine. Everything's fine. I wasn't crying in class because of the venus flytrap documentary, I have allergies.*"

"I do," Theo protested. He cleared his throat. His voice had squeaked on the lie. "I *am* fine. I'm...going through some personal shit. I mean, stuff. But things are looking up. I promise I'll stop looking out the window during class, or whatever. I'm *fine*," he repeated as Mr. Hawthorn opened his mouth.

"But you do know," Mr. Hawthorn said over him. "That you *can* talk to me."

"I gotta go," Theo called as he backed out the door. "I have a thing. Thank you, bye!"

. . .

Kade was balancing on the lidless disabled toilet when Theo walked into the bathroom the next day. A freshly crushed cigarette butt sat on the windowsill, smoke still hanging in the air.

"Smoking kills," Theo told him.

"Oooh. Tell me more, dead boy." Kade jumped down from the toilet and stretched. Today's shirt was a silky black button-down with see-through sleeves. Theo had never worn anything so sleek. He wondered how the buttery material felt against Kade's bare chest.

Kade strode forward. "Didn't wear a necklace today. You're welcome."

"You usually don't," Theo told him.

Kade raised his dark brows. "I'm sorry, did you just say you pay attention to my accessorizing?"

"It's hard not to," Theo said. His voice was flat, but his smile betrayed him. For all Kade annoyed him, it was impossible not to be charmed. Even before all this, Theo would have to stop himself from smiling at Kade's biting remarks in class.

For a moment Kade just blinked, mouth slack. Then he smiled back, surprised and pleased. His cheeks flushed.

Hunger rose in Theo's gut, huge and powerful.

He grabbed Kade's shirt. Kade's breath caught as Theo tugged him forward, making sure not to rub the silky fabric. It felt just as smooth as it looked.

"Right to business," Kade said. "Alright." He tilted his head to the side to expose the long line of his neck.

Theo stared at it. Something about touching Kade's shirt made him remember another shirt, days before.

"Did you find your heart?"

Kade blinked. His pupils were already swelling with anticipation. "My...huh? My loud heart?"

"What? No, the one Aaron ripped off. During dodgeball," he added when Kade just looked more confused.

"Oh." Kade blinked again. Theo wondered about those long lashes, if they, like the shirt, would feel as soft as they looked. Not that Theo would ever find out. Putting his fingers near Kade's eyes sounded like a recipe for an ER trip.

"Yeah," Kade said. "I found it before Cheech sent me out. I'll sew it back on later."

"You sew, then? Not just knit?"

Kade leaned back to give him a look. "Who says I knit?"

"Right," Theo said. "Defensive knitting needles."

Kade crossed his arms guardedly. "*Everybody* can sew."

"I can't."

"I'm shocked," Kade drawled. Then his gaze dropped. He scuffed a boot against the floor. "Just get your teeth in me already, blood boy. I have places to be."

Theo ignored the disappointment curdling in his stomach and leaned in. It was nice to drink when he wasn't starving, for once. It made it easier to notice

Kade's happy sigh, feel the warmth of his skin to offset the incredible heat of his blood.

Kade swayed when Theo drew back. Theo put a hand on his neck, burning and healing and steadying all at once.

"Milly texted," Kade slurred. He shook his head hard. "Shit. Sorry, still coming down. Milly texted, the translation's done. What she could get off that blurry picture, anyway."

Theo sagged in relief. "Just in time. The game's in a few days."

"The game that you'll be at," Kade agreed dryly. "Because golden boy's basketball game matters more than our little vampire adventure."

"Yeah, yeah, shut up," Theo told him. He watched Kade head for the door, fiddling with his wallet chain. "I thought you had places to be?"

"I do," Kade said after a moment. "Milly's place."

Milly had them meet her at her house.

"Sorry," she said as she ushered them into the tiny living room. "I had to close early today. I have Dungeons & Dragons tonight, I have to make snacks and finish off some DM prep. Do either of you want a drink? I have juice and soda."

"I'll have juice," said Kade.

Milly went to the kitchen. Theo sat down on the couch she'd pointed them at and looked around the living room: knitted shawls tossed over the couches, homemade carvings and odd ornaments stacked along windowsills. Where there weren't knick-knacks there were photographs: well-dusted group photos of people tangled together in a hug or crowded around a dinner table.

Theo leaned over and picked the closest one off a shelf. Milly looked around twenty in this photo, hair shorter, face unscarred, wrist uninked, overwhelmed but happy. She was tucked in the middle of a group of teens crouched at the end of a dinner table: on one side stood a large, giggling girl with a deeply 2000s-era denim dress, hugging a girl with dark skin and a shy smile. On her other side stood two boys, one lanky with glasses, the other short and stocky. They were arguing, and from the looks of it they were enjoying it immensely. All of them had friendship bracelets. The bracelet colors varied, but one thing stayed the same: each had a tiny skull knotted into it.

Those same people showed up in almost every photo: dinners, bowling, graduation, picnics. One photo in a hospital waiting room where they were all splattered in dirt and blood, which was...concerning. Was one of them missing an *arm*?

"Looks like a fun gang," Theo said, placing the dinner table photo back as Milly came back into the room. "Your D&D group?"

Milly laughed as she set a glass of juice down in front of Kade. "No. I had one campaign with those guys, but it ended ages ago. We see each other on holidays, mostly. Are you sure you don't want a drink?"

"I'm fine." Theo smiled politely. "Thanks again for doing this for us."

Milly sat down on the couch opposite them. It was one of three crammed into the tiny room. It was surprising, learning Milly had so many people in her life. Theo had assumed she was a loner. She seemed the type.

"Well, thank you for waiting. I hope I'm not coming close to any deadlines."

Theo shook his head. "This is actually going beyond the project now," he said. "We're just super interested in town lore."

"*So* interested," Kade echoed. He downed his juice in three large gulps.

Milly nodded, distracted. She pulled a journal out of her pocket, brown leather with a clip holding it closed.

"Cool," Kade muttered.

"Thank you," Milly replied, looking genuinely pleased. She flipped it open, turning to the latest page to reveal neat writing that had been corrected, crossed out, and rewritten below. Notes jumbled in the margins.

"So," Milly started. "Before I start—*where* did you find this? I see a glass case, does somebody have a collection they haven't made available to the public?"

"It's private," Theo said hastily. They'd agreed on this lie in the car. "Huge history buff. We can't tell you whose it is."

"Alright." Milly gave them a sly look that implied she knew full well they weren't allowed to show her the scroll in the first place, then continued: "From what I can see—and keep in mind I can only see about a third, thanks to the photo quality—it looks like some sort of prophecy."

Kade sat up straighter than Theo had ever seen. "Prophecy?"

Theo shot him a warning look. *Calm down.*

Prophecy, Kade mouthed. His knee jittered up and down. Theo supposed he was lucky he wasn't jumping on the spot.

Milly cleared her throat. "It speaks of a vampire. A boy. The phrasing they use implies he's a youth. Uh, young. He'll be given a special title, and unique assets. Including a...*beast*, of some sort. And he will set the trapped vampire of Lock free from her burning prison, and help her bring her flame to the doomed town."

Theo sat there, frozen. He wanted to laugh. He wanted to pick Milly up and shake her until the answers fell out. He wanted to drive to Cheech's house, to Aaron's, and scream in their faces until someone told him what the *hell* was going on—

His panic spiral was interrupted by a gleeful whoop.

"Holy shit," Kade said, grinning like a kid in a candy factory. "The plot thickens! Mate, this is *so*—"

"Thank you," Theo said through gritted teeth. "This was...helpful. You're very helpful."

"You're welcome," Milly told him. "Do you want me to keep translating the other book?"

"Yes," Theo said, and stood. "We have to go."

"What? Now? But—" Kade's grin gave way as he caught Theo's expression. "Right. Let's go."

Theo thought seriously about making Kade walk home. He thought about it right until Kade climbed in the backseat and curled over wordlessly. Not even a cutting quip.

Theo drove to the nearest backroad and pulled over, putting his head in his hands.

Kade sat up cautiously. "*Now* did you bring me out here to kill me?"

"Please just shut up," Theo said. He rubbed his eyes. "You get this isn't a story, right? This is my *life*."

Kade hummed. "Do you think that's what the Friday thing is about? Does Cheech think you're gonna bring about the end of the town tomorrow?"

"Why would I...?" Theo shoved his head against the steering wheel, forehead smearing the peeling plastic. "I don't...no one's...*why* would I do that?"

"At least you get a beast," Kade said. "*That's* cool. I hope it's a three-headed dog."

Theo laughed miserably. "Yeah, that'd make up for destroying the town."

Kade climbed into the passenger seat. He didn't even open the door to do it, just clambered with his long legs smacking the seats, boot squeaking on the window. Theo glared at him, but Kade didn't stop until he was settled in the passenger seat next to him.

"Tell me the truth," Kade said gravely. "Do you need me to slap you?"

"Just try it," Theo said weakly. He wanted to go to sleep so *badly*. He wasn't tired, not after feeding this morning, but he wanted to lie down and go away from the world. It was too heavy. Too horrifying.

"Maybe prophecies are bullshit," Kade tried.

"What, like *vampires* are bullshit? Like…like flying, and sires, and a monster locked under the town for centuries?" Theo laughed again. It came out embarrassingly watery. "The murderous vampire under the town is real and *I'm* going to let her out? Why would I *do* that?"

Theo sniffed back more tears. He hated crying in front of people. One good thing about crying black, oily tears—it meant he'd never be able to cry in front of anyone again. *Cry and they'll find out you're a monster* was a much more convincing deterrent than Theo's usual *cry and they'll know you're a loser who gets emotional over venus flytraps.*

"This is so *stupid*," he spat. "What the hell is going on? What does that date mean, why won't Cheech tell us anything? He helped us, then he clams up and leaves the second I burn you? What does the burning mean? Why just you? Are you, like, *part* of this?"

"I mean, yeah," Kade said. "*Now* I am. Wait, you

mean...like, am I a secret agent planning on double-crossing you?"

"You have to tell me," Theo snarled, voice breaking. "I'll...I'll..."

Kade held up his hands. "You know everything I know, jackass! Remember all the screaming in the Lemmings house? That wasn't for show. You heard my heartbeat at Cheech's place. Probably sounded like a spark in a firework warehouse."

Theo's eyes burned. He wiped them furiously, hand coming away streaked in black. He couldn't cry in front of anybody ever again—except Kade.

"Ooookay," Kade said, sounding very uncomfortable. "You know what you need?"

Theo looked over. Kade had the neck of his shirt pulled down, beaming nervously.

"Blood junkie," Theo rasped. He cleared his throat. He didn't want to say *junkie*. It made him feel like the latest update in Kade's endless list of things he used to mess him up. Kade was annoyingly sweet when he wasn't barking at you.

Before Theo could apologize, Kade stiffened and barked, "Hey, I'm helping you *out*. Excuse the hell out of me if *your* stress relief is awesome for me, too. You're not the only one who had a shitty day."

"How was *your* day shitty? You were having a *great* time in there."

Kade shrugged. "You didn't see the usual barrage of shit that happened before you hit me up in that bathroom. Newsflash: most of my days are shitty. Are you going to bite me or not?"

Theo knew he should say no. Two bites in one day couldn't be healthy. But Kade was offering. He knew his own limits. Right?

Kade sighed, sitting back in the passenger's seat. "Well, shit, if you're not hungry..."

"I'm hungry," Theo said quietly. "I'm always hungry."

It would quieten after Kade let him feed, but it didn't go away. It never went away except for those sparse moments after he leaned back from Kade, full and satisfied and finally warm. He wanted to forget about his hunger, about the threat carved in the dead man's chest, about prophecies, one best friend drifting away from him and the other best friend maybe planning to kill him along with their coach. He wanted to forget about anything that wasn't Kade's warm neck.

Theo leaned in. Kade's heartbeat picked up, head tilting almost unconsciously as Theo got closer.

The mole on his neck was so dark on his pale skin. Theo moved toward it like a planet orbiting a black hole, teeth sharpening in his mouth as he imagined pressing his thumb against it.

You'll burn him, Theo reminded himself through the rising haze of bloodlust. *Don't hurt him anymore than you have to.*

"Go on," Kade prompted when Theo hesitated. "Just a little. I'll say when to stop."

He leaned in. Kade let out a groan, first of pain and

then of slow ecstasy as the venom bled into his bloodstream. Theo pushed as much of it into Kade as he could, jaw buzzing, head full of nothing but Kade's taste and scent, all metal and sweetness and softness. Kade's shirt twisted in his grip as he pulled him closer.

"*There* we go," Kade moaned. His hand came up to the back of Theo's head, not touching skin, just gripping Theo's hair. The pressure was good. Grounding. Theo made a muffled noise into Kade's neck as he sucked more and more blood into his mouth.

Just a little. Theo pulled back reluctantly, licking blood from his lips.

Kade whined. He pulled at Theo's hair, willing him back in.

"You said just a little," Theo reminded him. "We already—"

"I had a crazy big lunch," Kade slurred. "'N water. *So* hydrated right now. Go for it, blood boy."

He was slurring. His smile was hazy, like he was on something. Later, Theo would curse himself for leaning back in. But in that moment, all he could see was Kade's eyes, a thin line of gray around his huge pupil, the ring of blood and burn on his neck. That small mole.

Beautiful, Theo thought. "Promise you're okay?"

Kade nodded like a bobblehead.

Theo leaned back in.

Kade let out a happy sigh. There was no pain, Theo realized. He was still under the venom's spell.

Theo drank. Each pull of blood was like finding

water in the desert, rich chocolate after a lifetime of gruel. He was so deep he almost didn't notice when Kade's hand went slack on the back of his head. Then it dropped.

Theo pulled back. Kade was limp in his arms. Theo shook him. Kade's head lolled in the car seat. His eyelids didn't even flutter.

"Oh," Theo said, voice cracking. "*Crap*."

TWENTY-ONE

THERE WAS a soft pressure around Kade's hand. The room stunk of cleaning fluids. Something was beeping.

Wait. Kade recognized that beeping.

He cracked an eye open and groaned. He'd landed himself in hospital again. Great.

The pressure vanished from his hand. Kade looked down and saw Theo pulling his sleeve back up. He'd been holding Kade's hand, he realized numbly. He'd pulled the sleeve over his fingers so he wouldn't burn him.

Kade had no idea how to handle that. He decided not to.

"Whassappened?" he slurred.

"What happened is you're an *idiot*," Theo snapped. "Who the hell—?"

He fell silent as a doctor and a nurse came into the room.

"Mr. Renfield," the doctor said. He had half-moon glasses and his voice was shockingly deep, like an opera singer. "I'm Dr. Gupta. This is Nurse Rain. How are you feeling?"

"Fine," Kade said automatically, watching the nurse walk around his bed to examine a machine next to it.

Dr. Gupta nodded. "And your arm?"

Kade looked down. The arm that didn't have an IV in it had a thick bandage around it.

"Uhhhh," Kade said. "It's...also fine."

He looked to Theo for help. Theo was busy staring up at the doctor with his best I'm-innocent-Officer expression, which didn't make Kade feel any more secure.

"Any dizziness?"

Kade shook his head.

"Headache?"

Kade shook his head again. When did he cut his arm? The last thing he remembered, he was passing out in Theo's embrace while riding the best high he'd ever felt. It had happened so fast he hadn't realized what was happening. He liked to think he would've made Theo stop.

Dr. Gupta clicked his pen off. "Well! I'd say you're in the clear. Right now we're just waiting on your aunt to get back to us so she can pick you up."

Kade grimaced. He'd promised he wouldn't land himself in hospital this year.

Nurse Rain unstuck the tape from Kade's arm. "Little pinch," she warned.

Kade winced as she pulled out the IV. She was gentle about it, unlike some of the Lock doctors Kade had dealt with. They must've already known Kade by reputation, because they'd already seemed annoyed or wary of him.

"I hope I don't see you again, Mr. Renfield. No strenuous activity for the next couple of days. Drink plenty of water and don't fall on any more rocks." Dr. Gupta gave Theo a lingering look, his face carefully blank. Kade's heart sank. The doctor didn't buy it. But whatever Gupta's suspicions were, he didn't voice them. He just gave them both a tight smile and left, Nurse Rain trailing behind him.

Kade waited for the door to close. Then he turned to Theo, rubbing the spot where the IV had stuck him. "A rock? I have fabric scissors! Just say I fell on them!"

"I just said the first thing that came to mind!" Theo spat. Then he frowned. "You have fabric scissors?"

Kade busied himself with prodding at the bandage on his arm. His neck didn't hurt, so Theo had healed that, at least. "Why'd you cut me?"

"I couldn't exactly drag you into the hospital with a bite in your neck!"

"So you *cut* me?" Kade pressed down on the bandage. It throbbed.

Theo grabbed his sleeve, jerking his hand away. "Quit it! You needed stitches."

Kade groaned, flopping back against the plasticky hospital sheets. "My aunt is going to freak out. I promised her no more hospital visits."

Theo dropped a plastic bag full of Kade's clothes, still dotted with blood. "Get up. I'm driving you home."

Kade lifted his head hopefully. "Really? You'd sneak me out?"

"If you get up in the next thirty seconds, then yes. Otherwise I'm leaving you behind."

Kade scrambled to grab his clothes.

It didn't make sense.

That's what Kade heard the nurses whispering when he went to find a vending machine.

The cut was deep, sure, but it didn't hit an artery, so it wasn't enough to explain the blood loss Kade had experienced. But from what they could find, it was the only cut on his body.

"From what they could *find*," Kade whispered to Theo. "What did they do, strip me naked?"

"No, they just checked artery sites!"

"So my groin."

"No! I don't know, it's pretty obvious if you've been bleeding really bad from—" Theo cut himself off with a frustrated groan. "Just get your chocolate and get out of here. I'll be in the parking lot."

"Sure, wouldn't want to be seen with Monster," Kade snapped as Theo stalked down the hospital corridor, head down, like it would stop anyone from recognizing Lock's golden boy.

Kade watched him go with a flicker of irritation. If they weren't technically sneaking out of the hospital, he would yell something after him. *Really* make people look.

Instead, he turned back to the vending machine. He'd have a big dinner when he got home, but before that, he needed some good old-fashioned sugar. He fished in his jacket pocket for his wallet and pulled out the pointy end of the knitting needle Theo had stepped on. He gave it a quick spin, relieved that the hospital staff had let him keep it. He wouldn't put it past them to classify it as a weapon. Especially with him involved.

The break room was right next to the vending machine. Voices drifted out as Kade typed in the numbers for a Snickers bar.

"It's been a weird day," said a nurse. "First Renfield and his mystery blood loss, now this? What the hell is happening this week?"

Kade's finger paused on the button pad. *Now this?*

"I'm just glad she came into the ER and not the morgue," Nurse Rain replied in a hushed whisper.

Kade froze. The *morgue?*

"Two murders in one week would be depressing," Nurse Rain continued. "Was it the guy who killed Jeremiah Lemming? Like, do we know?"

"She just said it was fast. I mean, him. *He* was fast." A nervous giggle that reminded him of Felicity Sloan, but with less acid. "He *bit* her. Like, better than stabbing, I guess?"

"I'd take a bite over a stab any day," came Nurse Rain's reply. "As long as I get my rabies shot afterward—"

Kade didn't hear the rest. He was too busy running down the hall, stuffing the Snickers bar into his mouth as he went.

Theo leaned against his car, head tilted. He snapped to attention when Kade sprinted up, concentration fading into an annoyed frown.

"Dude, they just *said* don't do any strenuous activity."

"We need to get back in there," Kade said, garbled. He swallowed his too-big mouthful with a wince. "Were you listening?"

"What?"

"You can hear the break room from here, right?"

Theo looked caught out. "You mean the staff room? Maybe. I don't know. There's a game on in the waiting room."

"Jesus, save me from super-hearing Yankee jocks." Kade swallowed the last of the chocolate and wiped his hands, ignoring that he was getting stains on his best jeans. "Somebody else got *attacked*, Sherlock."

Theo's eyes widened. "What? Where? Are they alive?"

"She's alive. Let's go tune in your super hearing to something that isn't the big game."

Kade took off, ignoring how his head swam. The chocolate would take care of it. He was so busy running he almost missed Theo's mutter of, *it's not the BIG game,* before he caught up. Not feigning behind, or walking ahead pretending not to notice him. Theo stuck right to Kade's side, falling into step beside him. Apparently panic made him forget that he used to get Kade to walk on the other side of the street. His shoulder brushed Kade's, and Kade told himself the shiver it induced was just blood loss.

It was easy finding out what hospital room someone was in when your partner in crime had super hearing. It just involved a lot of standing in the hallway, waiting for someone to say something relevant.

"We could just start going into rooms," Kade suggested. "It's not a big hospital."

"Sure," Theo said, faux brightly. "Hello, did you get attacked by a mysterious creature? No? Sorry to bother you, have a great day. Not suspicious at *all*."

"You *just* ate. You shouldn't be this bitchy after—" Kade cut off as Theo's head shot up like a bloodhound scenting a rabbit. Or a duck. A deer? Kade didn't know what bloodhounds tracked. Whatever they wanted, right? Could they track people?

"Can bloodhounds track people?" Kade asked.

"What?" Theo said, distracted. "Of course they can, they have sniffer dogs finding bodies. She's down this way. It's Skeeter Bass."

"Skeeter *Bass*," Kade repeated, loud enough that a receptionist glanced up from her desk.

Theo shushed him and led Kade down a corridor. Then another one. They got to the room Kade was just in, a nurse already stripping the bed free of its Kade-stained sheets and Dr. Gupta talking to her in a low, concerned voice.

"Oops," Kade whispered.

They hurried to the next door and knocked.

"Um..." came a familiar voice. "Come in?"

They pushed the door open. Skeeter Bass sat propped up in the bed, her neck thick with bandages. Her braces-heavy smile faded into confusion as she realized who it was.

Skeeter was head of the debate club. One time she got so mad at losing a War On Drugs debate she picked up the microphone and started hitting her opponent with it. It would be enough for Kade to think she was cool, if he only knew which side she'd been gunning for.

Theo waved. "Hi, Skeeter. How are you feeling?"

"Um, fine?" Skeeter's gaze flickered between them, trying to make sense of Theo Fairgood and Kade Renfield coming to see her. *Together*, no less.

"I really am sorry about your shoes," she told Theo.

Theo gave her a blank look. "Oh! Don't worry about it. Seriously. They got even more ruined later."

"Are you still sick?" she asked. "I heard about the game. Must've been *really* bad if you made us lose to the Wayside Hawks. My mom kept going on about how you let us all down, but I think if you're sick, it's alright. And Stacey J. said you looked *super* bad this morning, so—"

"The game got rescheduled," Theo said flatly, smile rictus stiff. "We're still going to win it."

"Oh," Skeeter said. "Um. Great."

Kade hid a snicker. "He's my reluctant ride to the hospital," he explained, lifting his bandaged arm. "We heard what happened. Thought we'd drop in and see how bad the damage is."

Skeeter scratched the bandage on her neck. "It's... fine."

"You sure? Looks pretty gnarly." Kade gestured at the heavy layer of bandages pushing into her chin. "Messed up thing to do to someone. What'd he look like?"

"If you want to talk about it," Theo added. "It sounds like a lot."

Kade glanced over at him, surprised. Theo's voice was strangely soft, if a little awkward. Then Kade remembered Theo had been through his own version of this and wanted to smack himself. Of *course* he'd know it was a lot. He'd been hoisted into the air, feasted on, and dropped in a lake. He'd probably have nightmares, if he could sleep.

"It's not *not* a lot," Skeeter said with a breathy laugh. She flushed, dark freckles turning splotchy. "Um, I already told the cops everything. It...*he* was too fast."

"He bit you," Kade said. "Thought you'd at least get a glance."

Skeeter's flush darkened. "Has anyone ever bit you in the neck? There's not a lot of—" She stopped, chewing her cheek. "Sorry."

"No," Kade said, faintly impressed. "Go off. Like, you can totally tell me to piss off if you want. But we kinda need—we really want to know about him. Anything you can remember. Was he tall? Thin? What color was his hair? Did he smell like anything?"

"I...don't know." Skeeter fumbled at the cross on her neck. "He was so strong. And it hurt so much. He was... tall? He had to bend down. Or maybe my...my feet lifted up? I didn't see his hair or anything. He was *on* me."

"How'd you get away?" Theo asked.

"I don't..." Skeeter sighed. "I pushed him. It didn't do anything. And then he jerked back. I heard something burning, it smelled like milk when it boils over? And I pushed him again, and he dropped me. I don't know why, I wasn't pushing hard, he was so *strong*. I..."

She glanced at a plastic bag on a chair next to her bed.

Kade stepped toward it, only stopping when Theo shot his hand out to grab him by the back of his shirt.

"What?" Theo said. "You can tell us, we won't think you're crazy."

"Did he have wings?" Kade blurted.

Theo trod on his foot.

She gave him a strange look. "Did he have what?"

"Nothing," Kade said. "Joking. What were you saying?"

She hunched uncertainly. "I was gardening. I still had a plant in my hand. He only let me go when I touched him with it."

WEAKNESS, Kade wanted to shout. *THE MONSTER HAS A WEAKNESS! THE PLOT THICKENS!*

"What plant?" he and Theo asked as one.

She held out a hand. Theo let Kade go, and he shot over to hand her the bag. She unfolded the bloody overalls with a grimace, digging into the deep pockets. She uncovered a spiky weed Kade had never seen before in his life. Red thorns and tiny black flowers clung to the stem.

Skeeter started, "It's—"

"Fire eye," Theo finished for her, sounding way too excited. "It only grows on this side of the country, near tree roots. It—"

He cut off, the bright interest in his face turning guarded. A sensible response, Kade thought, to having two people stare at you like you've grown another head.

"What? I read about it somewhere," Theo said

defensively. "So you think he stopped because of the fire eye?"

"No, that's insane. I just—I don't know why he pulled back. Or why it...burned him. I definitely smelled something burning." Skeeter winced, tugging at her mousy brown hair. "That's crazy. I sound *crazy*."

Kade laughed. "Mate, this doesn't even make the top five craziest things to happen this week." He pointed at the strange, spindly plant. "Can I take this?"

She hesitated. Then she nodded and dropped it into his waiting palm.

Kade twisted it in his fingers, pressing his nail into one of the bigger spikes. He knew exactly what he was going to do with this.

TWENTY-TWO

"KADE, I swear to god, if you burn me one more time—"

Theo cut off with a yelp as Kade shoved the point of the stalk into his neck. The car swerved. Kade cackled, falling against the passenger door. The fire eye fell with him, and Theo sat back up with a scowl.

"Quit it! You're such a baby!"

"Vengeance," Kade hissed. Any threat underneath it was ruined by laughter. It was almost a *giggle* now, weirdly sweet and croaky, cheeks creasing with the force of it.

A small *crack* made Theo look back at the road. He'd dug his fingers through the steering wheel again, through the leather right into the plastic.

"Oooh," Kade crooned. "Careful. Daddy won't like what you're doing to his Lexus."

"It's *my* Lexus," Theo protested, twisting uncomfortably in his seat. His dad *wouldn't* like what he was doing to the car. Theo would have to ask for money and then pay someone under the table to replace the steering wheel. Maybe it cost less to just replace the plastic?

He sucked in a calming breath, then grimaced as Kade's soft, metallic scent washed over him. Maybe it was a Pavlovian thing, but Kade's scent made his mouth water like no one else's.

"We need to corner Cheech," Theo said. "Force him to tell us what's going on. If he won't, then we get him to tell us who will—"

Kade slung his legs up on the dashboard.

Theo swatted his boots. "Get off! I let you sit up front and *this* is how you thank me?"

Kade put a big show into bowing. "Holy shit, you're right, thank you for letting me sit up the front like a *person*."

"We're gonna find out what the hell is up with this prophecy," Theo continued, ignoring him. "We'll find out what this burning shit is about—"

"Win the big game," Kade added, twisting the fire eye around his long fingers.

"Obviously," Theo replied, turning them down the road that would take them to Kade's house. "I'll feed on you right before. We can't take any chances. No going feral on the other team, no letting my powers slip out—"

Kade let out another croaky laugh. Something twisted in Theo's stomach, huge and hungry.

"I was JOKING," Kade exclaimed. "Seriously, screw the big game! You just got told you might release a hoard of hungry vamps who go on to *burn down the town* and you're like *whatever, go Nightfowls?*"

"You heard Skeeter. I let the whole town down."

"That's on them for getting invested in *high school basketball*," Kade said with a shudder. "Do you even *like* it?"

It was such a strange question Theo turned to stare at him. "*Obviously*. I'm the best."

"Uh-huh." Kade's tone turned bitter. "For a second I thought you might be a three-dimensional person instead of an asshole jock out of an eighties movie. My bad."

Asshole jock out of an eighties movie? The steering wheel creaked in Theo's grip as he pulled up outside Kade's house. Had Kade's image of him not changed at all in the past week? They'd snuck into a morgue together. Broke into two houses together. They'd almost *died*. Theo had seen Kade's shocked expression when Theo put his body between him and the monster, not to mention when Theo gave him knitting needles. They'd shared that cigarette, had a few laughs in between the horrors. And he still thought Theo was an eighties movie jock?

"Wow," Kade said. "Pulling up right next to my house. People will *talk*, you know."

He reached for the door handle. There was something flat and oddly disappointed in his face.

"Look," Theo said hastily. "I'm...I'm sorry. Okay?"

Kade paused. He watched Theo cautiously. It reminded Theo of a stray cat that used to hang around the back door. Theo had left dinner scraps out for it until it finally let him close enough to pat it. Then one night Theo woke up to a cat yowling, and he never saw it again.

"If I never bit you," Theo continued, "you wouldn't be, like...holding out for my venom. I kinda screwed you over. Like, I know it's a good high, and you get to tag along on my *little vampire adventure* or whatever, but this hasn't been that exciting, man. It's scary and it sucks. I'm sorry for trapping you in this."

Kade rubbed the door handle. Even his thumb was gangly, stroking an anxious line into the plastic.

"It does *suck*," he said slowly. He raised his thin brows pointedly.

"What?" Then it clicked. Theo sighed. "Vampire, sucking, ha, ha. Sorry for trying to be *nice*."

Theo's phone vibrated. He checked it—a text from Felicity. *wanna get mcdonalds tonight? my treat. mom's being SUPER annoying tonight.*

He frowned. Yet another invite from Felicity, who until recently hadn't tried to hang one-on-one for years. *Something* was going on, and it looked like she was even ready to talk about it. He *knew* it had something to do with her mom.

Theo started to write out a reply. Then he stopped.

Kade hadn't moved. He was the stillest Theo had

ever seen him, watching Theo with that stray-cat expression again. Like he was waiting for an excuse to run.

Kade paused. "Why'd you take the succulent?"

Theo froze. "What?"

"From the Lemmings place," Kade said. "What'd you do with it?"

Theo looked away. In middle school their teacher had come up and slapped a book on a distracted Kade's desk. *Do I have your full attention?*

You can't handle my full attention, Kade had snarled back.

And it was true. Everybody knew it: if Kade "Monster" Renfield was giving you his full attention, you'd have a bad time. He'd either be kicking your ass or slamming you with an insult.

And here he was, pinning Theo with his defiant gray eyes. Theo wanted to hide. Theo wanted Kade to keep looking at him forever. Theo wanted, stupidly, to touch his jaw. Feel the bone shift under his skin. Let his touch drift sideways and touch his chapped lips.

He imagined Kade's skin scorching and winced.

"Nothing," he lied.

"Come on."

Theo thought about telling him to get out again. But Kade's voice was oddly soft under its usual intensity, and anyway, who would he tell? Who'd believe him, even if he did?

"It's in my room," Theo admitted. He tucked his phone away. He'd answer Felicity later.

"Why?"

"I don't know," Theo said honestly. "It would've died."

"So? Let it die. It's a plant." Kade cracked his neck, the loud snap of his joints making Theo wince. "You've had no problem tripping me in the hall for the last six years—"

"I've tripped you *twice*." *And the second time was an accident*, Theo thought.

"And making fun of everyone, and making Gertrude from maths class cry—"

"It's *math*," Theo said. "And how was I supposed to know she has a lazy eye?"

"But you can't let a plant die," Kade finished.

Theo swallowed. "I like plants."

Kade nodded. His chapped lips twitched. "*Any* plants?"

"Not, like, *flowers*," Theo tried. It was a lie, but he was confident he could pull it off. "Cannibal plants with venom and shit. And, um. Fungi."

"Mushrooms?"

"Mushrooms are cool," Theo argued, "and not even technically a plant! We only know a really small amount about mushrooms. Like, ninety-seven percent of the information is still undiscovered."

"Wow," Kade said. "Tell me more about mushrooms."

Theo glared. He'd actually thought Kade might be cool about this.

"Shut up."

"No, really." Kade jumped in his seat, settling into it like a kid eager to hear a bedtime story. His smile only looked a little mocking. Mostly, it looked delighted. "Regale me with the three percent of information we have about fungi, golden boy."

Theo stared at him. He was ninety percent sure Kade wasn't making fun of him.

"You can't tell anybody," he said cautiously.

Kade rolled his eyes. "I'll add it to our ever-growing list of secrets."

Kade's smile softened. How had Theo never noticed how vulnerable his shaved head made him look, all that pale scalp under that dark stubble? He'd spent so many years watching Kade snarl and hunch into his shoulders, he never knew how beautiful the boy could be when he wasn't baring his teeth.

Kade raised his eyebrows expectantly. What were they talking about? Right. Mushrooms.

"So there are these mushrooms that glow in the dark," Theo started. There was a flash of movement over Kade's shoulder, and Theo froze. "Shit."

"What?" Kade whirled around just in time for a woman to knock on the window. "Oh, shit."

The woman glared at them, face lined with worry. Her dark graying hair frizzed around her head like Kade's used to. Her work uniform had a logo on it from the metal mill. He could picture her there perfectly, her stance sure and solid as she operated machines ten times her size. She looked like the kind of person you wanted on your side in a barfight.

Theo pulled up his politest smile and hoped he didn't look as panicked as he felt.

"Hello! Hi! I'm Theo. Uh, Fairgood. You must be Mrs. Renfield. Miss?"

"Sundance is fine," she said, her British accent so faded Theo barely noticed it.

Sundance gave Kade a pointed look, tilting her head almost imperceptibly at Theo.

Kade shook his head. Whatever that meant, it made some of the worry leave Sundance's lined face.

"I found him in the woods," Theo said. "I'm the one...I, uh, got him to the hospital."

"And got him out," Sundance said slowly. She leaned on the car door, sizing him up. "*Without* parental consent."

"Come on, Aunt Sundance," Kade sighed. "You know how bored I get in hospitals."

She grunted. "So you needled him into it? *And* got him to drive you home?"

"What can I say? Theo's a generous guy," Kade said sardonically. It was such a departure from the soft delight he'd had about Theo's mushrooms that Theo's cold heart clenched.

You're not friends, he told himself, trying to make the

sting of betrayal go away. *You're trapped together. Who cares if he doesn't like you? You don't like him.*

It felt flimsy. Kade was surly, sure. Annoying. A bit of an asshole. But Theo couldn't *not* like him after the crazy shit they'd been through. Not after Kade showed him glimpses of softness under his spikes. Not after he'd had Kade's skin open under his teeth. Not after the knitting needles or the cigarette or every time Theo had to hide a laugh about Kade's dumb antics.

He *did* like Kade Renfield. He liked him so much it scared the shit out of him.

Kade slapped Theo's shoulder. Theo jumped reflexively. It didn't hurt, but any contact made him hyperaware of how Theo could burn him with one clumsy mistake.

"Well, thanks for the ride, Fairgood!" Kade announced. "I should—"

Sundance cut him off. "Would you like to stay for dinner?"

Kade glared at her. Sundance ignored him, gray eyes drilling into Theo.

"Uhhhh," Theo said. He looked at Kade helplessly. He should say no, right? Kade didn't exactly look eager. It was late, it would make sense if Theo had already eaten. And he still had that text from Felicity inviting him out to McDonald's and probably an important talk about whatever the hell had been going on with her for the past few weeks.

"Theo just ate," Kade blurted. He scratched his neck, and Theo had to fight a stupid urge to laugh.

"A drink, then. I got water, juice, tea." Sundance knocked on the doorframe. "Come on, gotta thank you somehow for bringing my kid home to me. Even if you signed him out without me."

Kade ducked his head. He lifted his hand to his jaw, skimming empty air before dropping it. He used to play with his hair, Theo remembered. Sometimes he looked like he was hiding behind it.

Theo watched him fidget and realized with no small surprise that he wanted to take Sundance up on her offer. He'd never seen the Renfield house when he wasn't freaking out over Kade dying of blood loss.

Sensing the silence had gone on too long, Kade looked over at him. His dark brows were furrowed, like he was waiting for Theo to come up with an excuse. *I have somewhere to be. A dinner. A date. Anywhere but here.*

"Alright," Theo said instead.

TWENTY-THREE

"YOU HAVE A LOVELY HOME," Theo told Sundance as she slid a tray of fish sticks onto the kitchen table.

Kade snorted, twirling a fork in his hand. It was hard not to feel defensive as rich kid Theo looked around their tiny kitchen: ratty tea towels, plastic countertops, old burns above the stove from Kade leaving a pot of pasta so long it dried out and caught fire. Everything smelled faintly of ketchup for reasons Kade had never been able to identify.

"What?" Theo gave Kade a pointed look. "It's homey."

Kade surveyed him for signs of sarcasm. There were none. He'd forgotten about Theo's polite, almost bashful act he could put up around certain adults. He usually only saw it around Mr. Hawthorn in history class.

Sundance sat heavily in her seat. They'd had to drag an extra one out from the laundry room, a plastic chair that Sundance had insisted on taking.

"Dig in," she said.

Kade speared the crispiest stick. "I thought you had to pull more shifts."

"I do." She eyed his bruised knuckles. "I took off when I heard my kid was in the hospital."

"Sorry," Kade muttered. Sundance reached over and cupped his face. Kade rolled his eyes, but leaned into it. It wasn't long before he pulled away, shooting a nervous look over at Theo. Theo's gaze instantly darted back to his glass of water, pressing the rim to his mouth and faking a sip.

"Theo," Sundance said. "You said your last name was Fairgood?"

"That's me, ma'am." He gave her a winning smile. Kade rolled his eyes.

Sundance reached for another fish stick. "Dropped my shopping bags in the parking lot once. Your daddy helped me pick it up. Nice fella, for a lawyer."

"He is," Theo agreed. "He's great. They're both great. My mom plays tennis, do you ever play?"

Kade sniggered.

"I don't have a lot of time for that sort of thing," Sundance said blandly, instead of laughing in his face. "And I do enough running around at work. You hang out with my kid often, Fairgood?"

Kade traded a panicked look with Theo. They couldn't go with the drugs cover story to his *aunt*. She knew he didn't sell drugs.

"Not until recently," Theo said.

"He just found me in the woods," Kade said over him. "We don't..."

He trailed off. Theo's answer had shot his own in the foot.

"We only started hanging out last week," Theo tried. "We don't share the same friend groups, but we, uh... bonded. At the Founder's Day party. We talked about..."

He looked beseechingly at Kade.

"Fashion," Kade supplied. "He wants to experiment with his aesthetic. Jock isn't really cutting it anymore."

"My aesthetic isn't just *jock*," Theo argued.

"You're literally wearing your letterman jacket right now!"

Sundance interrupted them. "Why don't you show him that shirt you're working on, Kade? Broaden those fashion horizons."

The kitchen went silent. Theo paused in the middle of pretending to take a sip of juice. It pooled at his lips, spilling over the glass.

"God," he said, wiping his face. "Sorry—"

"Theo doesn't want to see my shirt." Kade smiled, sharp and warning.

Sundance ignored it and arched a dark brow, looking expectantly at Theo.

Theo opened his mouth.

Don't, Kade thought.

"Kade's working on a shirt?"

Kade groaned.

Sundance nodded. "Gonna be a world famous designer one day."

"Okay, shut up." Kade fended off her gentle nudge with a fish stick, scattering crumbs down both of them. Theo watched them scatter to the floor with a weirdly nervous expression, like he was waiting for Sundance to start yelling about the carpet. He looked surprised when she turned to him and continued, "He's a genius. He has to be, with all the practice he's got under his belt. Last summer he made one piece of clothing a *day*."

"Nothing *else* to do," Kade muttered, slouching back in his seat. "It was that or start joyriding. And I don't have a car."

"Carjacking," Theo suggested

Sundance smiled reluctantly, leaning over to Kade. "What was that one I liked? The one with the tassels, what was it?"

"Tassels," Theo repeated. "Goths can wear tassels? Can *I* see the tassels?"

"Boy wants to see the tassels," Sundance said flatly.

Kade gave her a seething look. She stared steadily back, munching her fish stick.

"You're not being a very good host," Theo told him.

"Oh my *god*," Kade said, and stood up so fast the chair screeched.

. . .

Kade forced himself not to check Theo's reaction to his room—well-loved posters, piles of dirty laundry, fashion books, stray mugs, mouthwash on the nightstand—as he got on his knees in front of a dresser. The lowest drawer was full of fabric scraps. The next one was jeans in various forms of tatter, ties, hats, and yarn. The next was full-length shirts, a pincushion, jackets, and loose stencils. Nothing was folded.

"This is stressing me out," Theo told him, frowning down at his phone. "You don't have a better organizing system? This is it?"

"It *is* organized," Kade said. He nodded at Theo's phone. "Trouble?"

"What?" Theo's expression cleared. He shoved his phone back into his pocket. "Just Liss. I'll talk to her later."

Kade was half tempted to ask what the hell was going on with Felicity these past few weeks—rumors were flying about an abusive mom, abusive boyfriend, fight clubs, money trouble that only gymnastic competitions would solve, as if her teen modeling career wasn't going perfectly fine—but something had caught his eye. A pair of knitted gloves sat at the bottom of the accessories drawer, partially obscured by some truly unfortunate belts. He tugged the gloves out. They were dark yellow and wonky, stitches missing every few rows. He hadn't seen them in years.

"What's that?"

"Hmm? Nothing." Kade clutched them to his chest protectively.

Theo tugged the gloves from him, ignoring Kade's protests. "I *knew* you were lying about the defensive knitting needles. Did you make these?"

"They're the first ones I ever made." Kade crossed his arms tight over his chest, fighting the urge to grab them back and hiss. "Give them back."

"Oh." Theo hesitated. Kade waited for him to hold them over his head and tell him to jump, but Theo just handed them back and scratched his head sheepishly. "Are they, like...special?"

"No." Kade paused. "Sort of. We had...my mum had this thing. The first time you make something, you give it away."

"And you still have these because...what, they suck? They're not *that* bad. Better than anything I could do."

"Yeah, no shit." Kade's grip tightened around the clumsy yellow wool. "They're too big for my aunt. And I don't..."

He trailed off. *I don't have anyone to give them to* was too pathetic to say to anyone, let alone to Theo Fairgood. Even if they were stuck together now, a jock was a jock. Even if he was trying to be *nice*, with his stupid new knitting needles and asking if Kade was *okay*. Like it didn't make Kade's traitorous heart spasm every time.

Theo shrugged. "I'll take them."

Kade looked up in surprise.

"What? I'm doing you a favor. You get yours, I get mine, right? Now gimme my gloves."

Kade handed them over warily. Theo tucked them in his pocket, and Kade waited for Theo to shove him and say *psych,* or start barking at him, or something equally stupid. But Theo just waited, and Kade stood there dumbly until Theo raised his pale brows and Kade remembered what he was supposed to be doing.

He whirled back, rummaging through the drawers and throwing shirts out at random. Black Dolly Parton shirt, black button-down, black cravat, black shirt with wonky red stitching spelling out *I AM SO FUCKING LONELY* that Kade didn't even remember making.

"Whoops," Kade mumbled, stuffing that shirt back into the drawer, without checking whether Theo had seen it. He made a faint noise of triumph when he grabbed a familiar crop top.

It was black, of course, with a crackle of gold in the middle. Tassels dangled from the hem. There were little white pins on the ends, like shooting stars.

Theo touched one of the pins. "Cool."

"Yeah. Sure. It's not very goth."

"It's black."

Kade sneered. "*Black* doesn't automatically mean *goth*."

"Right," Theo said dubiously. "Remind me the difference between goth and emo?"

"After I went on a whole spiel to Felicity last year? You *were* there."

"Yeah, but I didn't *listen*. Tell me again."

Kade narrowed his eyes. Theo kept standing there all weird and half-smiley, like they were *friends* or something. A big part of Kade wanted to snarl at him and run. Another part of him wanted to take what he could until this was inevitably over. Like that shirt said—he *was* so fucking lonely. And Theo was surprisingly fun to hang out with, when he got over himself.

"Emos are depressing," Kade started. "Their fashion sense is too casual to be interesting. They're broody and they think everything sucks."

"Goths don't think everything sucks?"

"No. Goths are..." Kade squirmed. "We're *passionate*. The world is a dark place, but there's beauty in the darkness. You know? We're all about hope. No hope with emos. They're all nihilists. It's boring."

Kade reached back into the drawer. He picked up a belt with a snake skull on the end, poking the fangs so he had something to look at that wasn't Theo and his piercing brown eyes.

"Could've fooled me," Theo said.

Kade looked up reluctantly from the snake belt. "What?"

Theo shrugged. "All your partying. Getting into fights. Doing stupid shit that could get you killed. It's very nihilistic."

"Um," said Kade, for once trying to find a way not to take that as an insult. "I guess."

He twisted the belt in his hands. He desperately

wanted to say something else, keep the conversation going, but he couldn't think of anything.

"We should go find the tree," Theo blurted. "Cheech's tree, the one he doodled in his secret room... thingy."

"Why? You gonna ditch the big game after all?"

Theo snorted, like the idea of ditching a basketball game for something that might decide the fate of the town was the most ridiculous thing he'd ever heard.

"*No*. Just—we can check it out. Look for clues, or whatever. After school tomorrow?"

"I'll see if I can fit that into my busy schedule," Kade said dryly.

Theo nodded. The conversation dripped to another stop. Kade waited for Theo to make an excuse to leave, but he just stood there, rubbing his own pockets.

"Hey," Theo said finally. "I always wanted to ask..."

Kade tensed, waiting for a hundred different horrible questions.

"Why'd you cut your hair? I always thought you loved that monster of split ends hanging around your head."

Kade laughed sharply. "I *loved* it. 'S why I shaved it off."

Theo frowned. "You got rid of it...because you loved it? I don't get it."

"Yeah," Kade said. "You wouldn't."

He could see the next question forming behind Theo's mouth.

Don't ask, Kade thought. If Theo pressed him about it, Kade was guaranteed to ruin their perfectly nice night. And he was sick of ruining things.

Theo took a breath.

Kade braced himself.

"See you tomorrow," Theo said quietly, and left.

CHAPTER
TWENTY-FOUR

KADE STOOD at the mouth of the forest for a long time, staring back at the cliff next to Theo's house. He looked uncomfortable.

Theo could relate. His bedroom overlooked that cliff, and he'd taken to closing the curtains whenever he could. If he looked at that cliff too long, he remembered the terrifying lift into the air, that cold mouth pressing against his neck. *I'll see you soon, Cyth.*

Kade squirmed, scraping his boot against the grass. He'd been crying when Theo confronted him on the cliff, eyeliner dripping down his cheeks. Theo had forgotten about that in all the mess that followed. Should he ask about it? Maybe he'd get a razor-sharp response. Or maybe he'd get something strangely vulnerable, like what Kade had shared with him in the Lemmings house.

Couldn't face it, Kade had admitted. *The world. Life.*

Then he'd changed the subject, the regret obvious in his forced-casual tone. Maybe he wouldn't have, if Theo had said something. He'd wanted to. He just couldn't think of a response. No one had said anything so vulnerable to him before.

Theo whistled. "Hey! We've got a lot of ground to cover, and it's going to rain soon."

Kade spun. "Did you just *whistle* at me? I'm not a dog."

"Could've fooled me," Theo told him. He bared his teeth and barked. He meant it jokingly, the mean-spirited joke he'd share with Felicity or Aaron.

But Kade looked hurt. He flipped Theo off and charged past him, into the woods.

Theo followed, watching the back of Kade's head and trying not to feel disappointed in himself.

"I was *joking*," he said. "Since when do you care about that kind of stuff? You *love* all that Monster shit."

Kade gave him a guarded look. He looked...oddly betrayed. Then he covered it, a mean smirk twisting his thin mouth.

"I *do* wear it well," he said, baring his teeth. "Better than your *golden boy* title, anyway."

He didn't like being Monster, Theo realized. All that snarling and barking and growling, and Kade...didn't like it? Why put all that effort into a costume if you hated wearing it?

Kade's smirk dropped fast. He plodded along dejectedly, like Theo was supposed to already know that

Kade didn't like the persona he'd been playing into for years.

Theo thought about getting defensive. Telling Kade he was being stupid. Getting *vicious*, like his parents wanted. But he'd promised to be nicer. He actually *liked* being nicer, especially to Kade. Every time he made Kade smile—not snarl, but *smile*, all soft and surprised—Theo felt like he'd just won a prize.

"Okay, jeez," Theo huffed. "I won't bark at you again. Could've just *told* me you don't like it."

Kade blinked. His lips parted like he wanted to say something. Then he fell quiet, all the while Theo tried to come up with something better to say.

They walked in silence for several minutes. Into the woods, not along the cliffs. Getting deeper and deeper.

Kade stared at the sky, which was growing dangerously cloudy above the trees. "You're sure it was around here?"

"It has to be," Theo replied, relieved they were talking again. "My dad used to take me on walks through these woods. Always near our house. Not long —about an hour. And we still had to get back, so the tree will be half an hour in any direction."

Kade gave him a dubious look. He was an expert at dubious looks. He did them differently than Theo— Theo's were high and mighty, condescending to the max. Built to make the person receiving them feel small and get out of the way. *Kade's* were jagged and dangerous, built to make the other person's neck prickle and make them call him Monster. It was hard to believe this was the same boy who had stayed in bed for weeks, unable to force himself out the front door. The same boy who knitted gloves and loved his aunt and seemed genuinely excited that Theo wanted to tell him about mushrooms.

"Are you sure it wasn't—oh, I don't know—any other part of the massive amounts of woods around town?" Kade threw his skinny arms out at the vast expanse of trees surrounding them. "Come on. I've lived here for six years and I've seen a lot of these woods. Parties. Finding a quiet place to drink. Boredom walks! Our tree could be on the other side of town."

Theo shook his head. "It was so vivid. I must've seen it a lot. Had to be on one of these walks."

Kade groaned. He kicked a loose rock in front of him with one lanky leg as he walked. "So we just keep walking?"

"I'll know it when I see it," Theo said.

Kade gave him another withering look. His next kick sent the rock spiraling off into a clearing. Kade swore and ran after it.

"Look," Theo called after him. "I'm not saying it'll be quick—"

Kade yelped and fell forward. He hit the dirt chin-first, and his pained groan wasn't finished in his throat by the time Theo blurred into the clearing after him.

"Stupid roots," Kade spat, getting his elbows up underneath him. "Lost my rock."

"Dude, watch where you're going!" Theo held out a hand.

Kade stared at it pointedly.

"Crap," Theo said. "Right. Sorry, I..."

He trailed off, stuffing his useless hands in his pockets. The root Kade had tripped over was small, almost hidden in the dirt. It got thicker as it went along, bending at odd angles until it finally reached a tree trunk.

Something itched at the back of Theo's head when he looked up. The tree was tall and gnarled, knotted branches reaching out like they wanted to grab something.

"This is it," he announced.

Kade eased himself up, brushing dirt off his ripped jeans. "Seriously?"

Theo nodded, reaching out. The bark was rough and unexpectedly warm under his fingers. That itch at the back of his head was still there, an animal scratching at a door.

Theo shivered.

"Seriously," Kade repeated.

"Yes! I'm sure. This is it."

Kade immediately straightened, bouncing on the spot like somebody had poured a whole pot of coffee down his throat. "Why aren't you excited by any of this shit? This could be, like, the KEY! Can you see any symbols? Maybe we push something and a secret passageway opens up!"

He circled the trunk, jabbing at knots in the bark. That gleeful look was back again, the look he'd gotten in Milly's bookshop and when the room had opened up in Coach Cheech's bookcase. It was the complete opposite of the dubious look Theo had seen so many times before: that look was sharp and guarded. This was soft and open, smile loose in a way Theo had only gotten glimpses of. He looked like a little kid. Theo almost forgot about the horrible dread, watching him.

"So we have the time, the date and the place," Kade continued. "I don't care if golden boy's playing basketball, I know where *I'm* gonna be. Right here, watching whatever the hell is going down."

Theo didn't reply.

Kade looked up. The gleeful smile faded. "What?"

"I don't know," Theo said. "I just...thought it'd take longer. Finding it."

"Okay, well, *I'm* happy we didn't have to walk aimlessly for hours—"

Theo cut him off. "It was too easy. I..."

He stopped. That itch burrowed away in the back of his head. He looked around the trees, almost expecting to find someone looking back. Theo stilled, listening for breathing, shoes shuffling in the dirt. But it was just him and Kade in the clearing, summer leaves swaying in the wind, bugs crawling around the roots.

"Maybe it's fate," Kade suggested. "The story unfolds."

"Shut up about stories for five seconds, okay? I'm

not getting, like...getting *pushed* toward something. *I'm in control of my own life.*" Theo shifted uncomfortably, scratching the spot where the vampire had ripped open his neck. "If this is a story, then we have no say in anything. And what if it has a sad ending?"

Kade didn't respond. Theo looked over, expecting him to be prodding at knobs in the tree for trapdoors, maybe trying to climb a low branch. But Kade was staring at Theo, skin even paler than usual.

"What?" Theo asked. "You seriously never considered it?"

"'Course. I'd be an idiot not to consider it." Kade chewed on his chapped lips. "I just...I hoped..."

A gunshot rang out.

Theo whirled just in time to watch the bullet whiz above Kade and into a tree on the far side, showering Kade with bark.

"WHAT THE SHIT," Kade shrieked, hands coming up to shield himself.

Theo blurred across, putting himself between Kade and the voices that were coming ever closer through the forest.

"...have to pay somebody's family because you killed their kid, it's coming out of *your* trust fund," said a familiar voice.

"But you *said*—" Aaron stopped, stumbling to a halt in the clearing. His dad followed, blinking in the overcast light. They were dressed in their hunting gear, with rifles strapped over their shoulders and high-visibility orange caps so people could see them easier. If Theo were paying attention, he'd be able to spot them from half a mile away.

He took a careful step away from Kade. Like they were two strangers who had run into each other in the woods, and Theo hadn't just been shielding Kade with his body.

Mr. Fletcher whacked his son in the back of the head. "You almost hit your best friend! What'd I say, huh?"

Aaron rocked with the impact, scowling. "You said *deer*!"

"I said *wait*," Mr. Fletcher growled. He sent Theo a friendly smile. "Sorry about that, boys! No harm done. No thanks to some of us."

Aaron rubbed the back of his head. His cheeks were ruddy with embarrassment, his eyes alight with panic. He looked genuinely confused to see Kade there. Theo was ninety-five percent sure he hadn't shot at him on purpose.

Mr. Fletcher held out a large, gloved hand at Kade. "Renfield, right? Your aunt works at the scrap warehouse."

"That's me," Kade said slowly, eyeing Mr. Fletcher's outstretched hand like it might explode on contact. Nobody was lining up to shake hands with Kade Renfield. When he did finally take it, he did so gingerly, jumping when Mr. Fletcher squeezed his knuckles.

"What are you doing?" Theo asked Aaron, who was

busy staring at his dad like he'd grown a second head. "I thought rabbit season isn't for a while."

"It isn't. This is target practice." Aaron hunched, glaring guiltily at Kade. "I didn't get you, right?"

Kade startled. "Uh, yeah. It didn't get me."

"Okay." Aaron deflated fast, rubbing his face. "Shit. That would've been embarrassing."

"Sorry, kid," Mr. Fletcher told Kade. "For a moment we thought you were a prey animal. Sure are wiry enough."

He let out a booming laugh and tapped Kade's skinny arms, then turned to Theo. "Excited for the big game tomorrow? My wife's been talking about that celebration dinner all week. What do you want, fish?"

"Steak," Theo said, stomach sinking as he realized he'd have to puke black bile all Saturday.

"You got it. Rare, like always. Bloodier the better, right?" Mr. Fletcher laughed again, teeth gleaming in the gray light.

When Theo was eight, the school had Mr. Fletcher play Santa in the Christmas play. He suited it. Mr. Fletcher was warm and welcoming in ways Theo's own father never was, even with those strange flashes of burning fury. For a long time, Theo had believed Mr. Fletcher would die before hurting him.

He didn't know if he believed that now.

Mr. Fletcher pointed between Theo and Kade, standing a safe distance apart in front of the tree. "Since when do you two hang out? Renfield isn't a new part of the group, is he?"

"No," Aaron said, so incredulous that his father turned to him to chuckle.

"Right, he knocked you one last year, didn't he? Bashed one of your teeth out. Vicious!" Mr. Fletcher tapped Kade's shoulder again, oblivious to how Kade's shoulders climbed up to meet his ears in response.

"I was on a walk," Theo said. "We just ran into each other."

Mr. Fletcher nodded. Aaron just stood there and stared, face still flushed, gripping the strap of his gun so hard his knuckles went white.

Above them, thunder rolled.

"Looks like a big one's coming our way," Mr. Fletcher said, squinting at the sky. "Renfield, you going to the game?"

Kade shook his head, backing away until he was leaning, faux-casual, against the twisted tree trunk. "No. I have better things..."

He trailed off. A frown dented his dark brows. His eyelids fluttered. Then he wobbled, knees giving out underneath him.

Theo couldn't stop himself from jerking forward as Kade steadied himself against the tree with a pained gasp.

"Whoa, hey, are you alright?" He hovered his hands uselessly over Kade's bare arms. He was shocked by how badly he wanted to touch them. The best he could do was touch his back, feeling Kade's warmth through his shirt.

Mr. Fletcher laughed. "One too many, kid?"

"'M fine," Kade croaked. He looked up at Theo, gray eyes glazed and full of confusion.

"I remember when *I* used to party it up in these woods," Mr. Fletcher started.

Aaron cut him off. "Dad. Let's *go*."

Mr. Fletcher looked at him in surprise. Aaron rarely used that sharp tone with his parents.

"If we hunt in the rain, you bitch the whole time," Aaron continued, jerking his gun strap higher up his shoulder. "Come *on*. It's getting dark anyway."

Thunder rumbled. Mr. Fletcher glanced up through the trees with a grimace.

"Come *on*," Aaron repeated, and strode off without a reply. He didn't even look at Theo as he headed into the trees.

Mr. Fletcher blinked. He gave them a short nod, gaze lingering on Kade bracing himself against the tree.

"Don't party too hard," he said. Theo couldn't help but wince as Mr. Fletcher followed his son out of the clearing. Aaron would pay for his curt tone later. Just like Theo would pay for spending more time with Kade. Aaron was always harder to deal with after his parents punished him.

As soon as they were out of sight, Theo sighed. "I *told* you to drink more water. Do you need electrolytes? I have sports drinks back at the house."

"Get your nasty sports drinks away from me," Kade slurred. "I'm fine. I...I think I saw something."

Theo waited. Kade kept blinking hard, like he was banishing spots from his eyes. A raindrop dripped into his forehead, curving down his cheek. He wiped it away.

"Something," Theo prompted. "Like...*all that sleep deprivation and binge drinking and blood-giving is catching up to you* something?"

Kade groaned, still braced against the tree for support. "No, asshole, like a vision! What the hell is your freaky vampire venom *doing* to me?"

"What? Why is this *my* fault?"

"What else could it be?" Kade winced again, squeezing the bridge of his thin nose. "Shit, that hurt."

"What did you see?"

Kade blinked some more, long lashes catching on each other. His gaze was unfocused. "It was the woman from the book we found in the Lemmings house. Same killer cheekbones, same haircut, same creepy eyes. She was in this forest, saying stuff. Couldn't make out what it was. *Ow.*"

He pinched his nose again. Theo smelled it before he saw it: a fat drop of blood rolled out of Kade's nose, curving over his upper lip.

Theo averted his eyes, shoving down on the howling hunger that reared up inside him. He gritted his teeth. "Cyth?"

"Don't know who else it'd be." Kade scrubbed the

blood off his face with his jacket sleeve. It didn't go well —leather jackets weren't made for absorption.

Another speck of rain hit Kade's scalp.

Kade sniffed, sucking blood back into his nose. "You know Aaron's going to shoot, right? When his parents tell him to?"

Theo glanced back at the trees where Aaron and his dad had disappeared.

"Maybe you're right," Kade said. "Maybe he *doesn't* know. But he's gonna find out, and they're gonna tell him to shoot, and next time you're gonna be in front of the gun. He *will* do it."

"He won't," Theo argued quietly.

Another roll of thunder. Rain started falling in earnest, a thin sheet catching on the trees and splattering down into the dirt. Theo raised a hand, covering his hair. Kade didn't bother, standing still as rain soaked his shaved head.

Kade sucked in a sharp breath. "I know you think he cares about you—"

"He's my best friend!"

"Just trust me."

"Trust *you*?" Theo let out a hollow laugh.

Kade's shoulders shot up again. *Like a feral dog backed into a corner*, someone told Theo once. He was pretty sure it was Aaron.

"I've been best friends with Aaron my whole *life*," Theo said. "If you didn't get withdrawals, would you still hang around?"

"Maybe," Kade croaked, rain sliding uninterrupted down his pale face. "If you didn't need my blood, would *you?*"

"Maybe," Theo said mockingly.

Kade jeered. "You won't even talk to me in the hallway."

"What am I supposed to do? It isn't—" Theo stopped, ducking his head. A wet lock of blond hair fell over his eyes. "It isn't like we can be friends."

"Right," Kade said bitterly. "Golden boy and Monster, shooting the shit during lunch. That can *never* happen. Monster helping golden boy not pass out during gym, however—"

"Hey, you like it." Theo's face twisted, gaze dropping to Kade's neck, hunger and terror in equal measure as he remembered the limp weight of Kade unconscious in his arms. "You like it so much you'd let it kill you!"

"Like you'd care."

"I would!" Theo's voice rose over the rain. He winced, looking toward the trees the others had walked into. "I *would* care."

Kade blinked furiously. "But we're not friends," he said, hoping the sharpness of his tone canceled out anything soft implied by his watery eyes and shaking frame. "Right? We're trapped together. But we aren't friends."

Theo's jaw worked. He wanted to tell Kade he was wrong. No, he wanted *Kade* to say he was wrong, so Theo didn't have to. Wanted Kade to say, *I'll be your secret. I'll listen to you talk about mushrooms and I won't make fun of you. I'll show you everything I'm making, I'll knit you a scarf if you want. We'll meet in the disabled bathrooms every couple of days and make each other laugh before you sink your teeth into me. I'll always curl up in the back of your car even though it's really uncomfortable, now I think about it.*

Another boom of thunder. Lightning streaked across the sky.

"*Right?*" Kade snarled, demanding an answer he knew he wouldn't like. Reaching for things that hurt him, always. Theo's dead heart twisted as he realized he might be another tally on that list.

"Yes, alright? I can't be friends with you. Even if I..." Theo hesitated. "Even if..."

"Don't." Kade jerked forward, fists curled like he was going to punch him. Theo's mind whirled with images of burned knuckles, but Kade didn't swing. He just stood there, wet and trembling, staring across at him with eyes the color of the sky right before it rained.

"You're going to be at your stupid game tomorrow," Kade continued. "Right?"

"I *have* to," Theo told him. "Are you going to be there?"

"I'm gonna be *here*, when it gets dark." Kade scrubbed at his face. Theo couldn't tell if he was crying. The rain was too thick. "Before that—who knows? I might drop by. Make sure the golden boy's got his energy up for the big game."

With that, he turned on his heel. Theo watched, mystified, as Kade stalked out of the clearing.

"It's raining," Theo called after him. "Let me drive you home!"

Kade didn't look back. "Oh, and drop me off a block away after I spend the whole ride curling up like a pillbug in the backseat? I'll walk."

"You can sit up front—"

"I'll *walk*," Kade repeated, all barbs and venom. The back of his head was a slick curve, set alight when another flash of lightning streaked across the sky. He looked like a boy out of a fairy tale right before he gets eaten.

Later, Theo would curse himself for not chasing after Kade. Slinging him over his shoulder and burlap-sacking him back to the car. But his pride was stung, and Theo wasn't in the business of reaching out. Especially not if the hand was liable to get bitten.

So Theo just stood there and watched the trees swallow him.

TWENTY-FIVE

WATER DRIPPED down Kade's face as he stalked down the street. He let it happen, glad for the excuse. He didn't want any of these jackasses seeing him cry in public.

His socks were wet. There had been a hole in his boot for months now. He knew his fair share about mending clothes, but only for stuff he could sew or patch. He didn't know about *shoe repair*. He'd meant to take it to the shoe place, but he'd put it off like everything else, and now his *socks* were wet. Because he was an idiot who ruined things, like plans and boots and tentative bonds based on mutual need, the closest thing he'd had to a friend in years and he blew it all up, of *course* he did—

A deep honk jerked him out of his thought spiral. He scrubbed his cheeks, shoulders tensing defensively as a car pulled up behind him. Then he paused. He knew this car. It was Mr. Hawthorn's navy blue 2012 Kia Sorento. Kade didn't know anything about the model— he wasn't a car guy. All he knew was that it was sleek and pristine, just like Mr. Hawthorn's pressed clothes and stylish hair and straight white teeth.

Mr. Hawthorn wound the window down. "Kade! Get in!"

Kade wavered. He was drenched and miserable, but there was a sick satisfaction in it. Part of him had reveled in the idea of another half hour of slogging through this torrent. Also, he didn't want to cry in front of his favorite teacher.

"I'm fine," he called. "This is my weekly shower."

Mr. Hawthorn patted the passenger seat. "I can't let you walk home in this. I see your aunt in Yarn World sometimes, I want to be able to look her in the eye."

Kade sniffed. "You go to Yarn World?"

"I do!" Mr. Hawthorn smiled, showing off all those shiny teeth. "I knit scarves. I have wool in the glove box for when I'm waiting in my car. I'm useless, but if you knit the same stitch over and over for long enough, eventually it's a scarf! I always wanted to learn how to do fancy patterns, but...ah, you know how it is. Are you going to get in?"

Kade considered. He wasn't crying anymore, and Mr. Hawthorn didn't seem the type to get mad at someone for dripping on his car seat.

He got in.

"So," Mr. Hawthorn said brightly as they pulled into

the street, "what made you want to rage-walk through a storm?"

"Who says I'm rage-walking?" Kade asked. He made a face at all the water soaking the car seat. "Shit. Sorry."

"It's fine," Mr. Hawthorn assured him. "Bullies?"

"No. For once."

"Love troubles?"

"Ha," Kade spat. "He *wishes*."

Mr. Hawthorn blinked. He looked politely surprised, like he had been last year when Kade was unloading all his love troubles on him. He'd only done it once and he ended up crying in the empty history class, face red with mortification as he made him swear not to say anything about the asshole he was fooling around with. Mr. Hawthorn had offered him a tissue and told him not to go to next period. Kade had spent the next hour in his empty classroom, hunched over in the corner while Mr. Hawthorn read a book about ancient Greeks. It was the nicest thing anyone had ever done for him since his aunt took him in.

"Oookay," Mr. Hawthorn said, eyes on the road. "Well, I'm always here to listen. You know that. Unless you want to talk to your aunt about this one."

"Ha," Kade said again.

They fell silent as rain battered the windshield. Kade shivered. It was kind of nice. Getting out of the rain.

"Um," he said. Exactly how his word-vomit had

started last year. He wouldn't cry this time, he promised himself.

"He hangs out with these assholes," Kade started. "Assholes who have done some really terrible shit to me. But he won't ditch them. Obviously. Because we're not—we're *nothing*. We're a transaction. He gets his, I get mine."

Mr. Hawthorn hummed, too high. Kade winced. He knew how this sounded. He was glad Mr. Hawthorn was watching the road so intently, avoiding his gaze just like Kade needed.

"But you want it to mean something," Mr. Hawthorn said.

"No," Kade spat. He scraped a hand over his damp scalp. The whole walk out of that forest, he couldn't stop picturing Theo's wet hair, those damp, golden curls against his forehead. Kade wanted to yank it. Kade wanted to curl a fist into Theo's hair, even if it blistered his fingers. He wanted to pull Theo's hair like he wanted to drink until he puked or throw himself at someone fist-first. But he also wanted other things, infinitely more embarrassing: he wanted Theo to touch his hand, feather-soft. Brush a thumb over his hollow cheek. He wanted Theo to smile at him, warm and uncomplicated, no strings attached. He wanted those things with the small parts of him that had nothing to do with self-destruction, and thus they were doomed. Kade did not get warm and uncomplicated. He did not get feather-soft. Theo could hold him gently, but only if his fangs were in Kade's neck.

Kade's eyes filled. He ducked his head. "It's stupid. I know it's stupid. But sometimes I get a glimpse of this really cool guy who likes all this dorky shit, and then, oh no, it's asshole time again!"

"It can be hard to let your guard down," Mr. Hawthorn offered, turning down the street that would lead them to Kade's house. Kade blinked. He had never told his teacher where he lived. Then again, he never told anyone where he lived, and people still painted MONSTER on the front door last Halloween.

"Maybe you need to show him you're a safe person to be himself around," Mr. Hawthorn continued.

"I'm *safe*," Kade spat. "I'm...I just...I can't be soft around him. That's suicide."

"Maybe he feels the same about you." Mr. Hawthorn sent him a bemused smile. "You can have a lot of sharp edges, Kade."

Kade flashed him a flimsy smile. "Porcupine rules, Mr. H. I don't wanna get..."

He trailed off. Down in the footwell, next to his boot, was a large white fleck.

Kade nudged it, a chill crawling up his spine as he remembered where he knew it from: this had been all over their clothes after the creature attacked them in the Lemmings house.

Monster skin, Kade had said. *I need to put that on a shirt.*

"Kade? You were saying something?"

Kade looked up. The car had stopped. They were idling in front of his house. Mr. Hawthorn's gaze was steady on his, eyebrows raised politely.

Kade's throat clicked, suddenly dry. "I don't want to get eaten."

Mr. Hawthorn laughed. It was the same pleasant, bright sound Kade had been hearing since middle school, and yet it sent shivers over Kade's skin. There had been a strange dullness to Mr. Hawthorn's eyes as he waited for Kade to finish his sentence. Like he'd been waiting for Kade to say something else entirely.

Kade had to hold back a flinch as Mr. Hawthorn slapped the steering wheel.

"Looks like we made it." He reached past Kade to open the car door. Kade pressed into the seat as hard as he could, but Mr. Hawthorn's sleeve brushed his stomach anyway. Kade tried to tell if there was any warmth radiating from Mr. Hawthorn's arm, but it was impossible through the sleeves, never mind that Kade was already cold from the spring shower. Even luke-warm would feel hot to him.

The car door opened. The noise of rain rushed in, popping their tiny bubble. Kade looked out at his house —maybe ten seconds away, if he ran down the driveway. He stared at the wisteria climbing the door and imag-ined throwing himself on his bed, hopping into the shower, hugging his aunt, calling Theo to tell him his suspicions...

Bitterness rose in Kade's throat. He turned to Mr.

Hawthorn. "I could show you some fancy scarf techniques. If you want."

"Oh! That would be lovely. Are you sure?"

Kade nodded stiffly.

Mr. Hawthorn stared at him. He didn't blink. At first Kade thought he was going to insist Kade scurry on home. Then Mr. Hawthorn reached over again, elbow brushing Kade's damp shirt, and pulled the car door closed.

They pulled back into the street. Sweat dripped down Kade's back, mixing with the rainwater. When he got out of this car seat, he was going to leave a great big stain. Kade really hoped it would just be water and sweat.

Mr. Hawthorn didn't reach for the glove box to get out his wool. He didn't even speak until they were a few roads over.

"You know," he told Kade. "I never saw you as a porcupine. I always thought you were more of a rabbit."

Kade's heart twisted. "Yeah?"

Mr. Hawthorn nodded, tapping a slow beat on the steering wheel. "Cunning. Quick. Flighty."

Kade unstuck his tongue from the roof of his mouth. "If I were a rabbit, I'd be better at running away."

Mr. Hawthorn laughed again. There was something dark in it that Kade had never heard before. *Relief.* Like an old weight had been lifted off his shoulders.

"Right," he said. "A rabbit wouldn't throw itself at Aaron Fletcher when he pisses them off."

Kade reached slowly into his jacket pocket, curling a loose hand around the fire eye Skeeter Bass had given him in the hospital. Thorns bit into his skin. Not quite breaking it—not yet.

Kade gritted his teeth and closed his fist.

Sharp, stinging pain lit up his palm. Kade couldn't stop the gasp that spilled out of him as warm blood trickled into his pocket lining.

Mr. Hawthorn sucked in a breath. His pupils bloomed, black and shiny. His mouth ticked, the slightest hint of an amused smile.

"Well," he said. "I—"

Kade wrenched the fire eye out of his pocket and shoved it into Mr. Hawthorn's cheek.

The car swerved, Mr. Hawthorn belting out a swear. He twisted the fire eye out of Kade's grasp. An angry line burned into his hand as he threw it in the backseat.

Kade reached for the door handle.

Mr. Hawthorn's arm shot out. He pinned Kade easily into the car seat, trapping his arms at his sides.

"*That*," Mr. Hawthorn said, as if there had been no interruption, "was very rude."

Rain crowded the windows, shielding anyone from looking in. A car blurred by, a smeared shape in the glass. Kade watched it with a sinking stomach. *You need to think before you act,* his mother used to say. Which was pretty hypocritical, coming from a high school dropout with a mid-twenties divorce and multiple DUIs under her belt.

Mr. Hawthorn hummed as he drove. "What's the plan now, little rabbit?"

Kade bit him. He bit his teacher's arm so hard his jaw ached, but the skin stayed intact under his blunt, useless teeth.

Mr. Hawthorn sighed, twisting the wheel to lead them down a back road. "I have orders not to do anything with you until the time comes. *That's* the plan. But plans change."

Kade raised his head. "What plan?"

Hawthorn's hand blurred. One second it was holding Kade still, the next it was over Kade's face, smothering him. Kade yanked at it, fighting for air, but it was futile. Mr. Hawthorn's grip was iron and unrelenting, pulling him down into unconsciousness.

Kade heard one last thing as he slipped into the dark. Mr. Hawthorn's voice, a cold spot in the fuzzy static of rain:

"I always told you, Kade. You're destined for great things."

CHAPTER
TWENTY-SIX

THE GYM WAS SO *LOUD*.

Last time Theo stood in the gym waiting for a basketball game to start, he'd had the hunger blotting most of it out. Now, watching everybody file in, chatting and whispering and yelling across the room at people they'd known their whole lives, music blaring from the speakers overhead, Theo had to force himself not to cover his ears.

Perfume pierced the stench of sweat and popcorn. Theo turned to see Felicity sidling up to him, hair swishing behind her.

"You didn't reply to my texts."

Theo blinked blearily. She hadn't brought it up in the last two days. He'd hoped she had forgotten her unanswered McDonald's invite.

"I was busy," Theo said. He looked up at the

bleachers at his parents wedged next to the Fletchers. "We'll catch up tonight, right? Celebration dinner."

She shook her head. She was looking tired again, shoulders slumped with it. Her makeup was thicker than ever, her smile extra sharp to make up for it.

She flipped her not-so-shiny hair over her shoulder. "I have shit to do."

"Practice?" He nodded down at her knuckles, which were swollen again. "Or are you ditching it for a party?"

Felicity gave him an unreadable look. She looked exhausted. The bone-deep kind, not just the gymnastics kind.

Theo sighed. "Look. I *know* something's been up with you. Something's going on with you and your mom, right? I know I've been busy lately, but—"

Felicity laughed. It was her smarmy you-couldn't-possibly-know-what-I'm-going-through laugh, which Theo thought she had grown out of in middle school. It used to come right before Felicity lashing out with whatever she'd been going through lately. Taking her problems and turning them into something to cut you with.

But Felicity just stared at him. Then she squeezed his cheeks, voice taking on a strange desperation. "What are my chances of talking you into ditching that celebration dinner, huh? We can find a party. You'd be the guest of honor."

Theo looked pointedly at the bleachers where his parents were watching.

"No," Felicity said, smile twisting. "Of course not."

She gave him a little shake, a frown forming on her tired face. "You're so cold. What happened to the warm-up?"

"I'll be fine," he told her. "Liss—"

But she was already turning away, heading back toward the bleachers where there was a spot waiting for her next to the Fletchers.

Theo breathed in. Wood polish and sweat. The telltale stink of hair gel and eucalyptus arriving behind him.

"Hi, Aaron," Theo said.

Aaron jogged up, eyes on Felicity's retreating back. "Did she finally say something?"

Theo shook his head, stomach swimming with guilt. She *might* have said something if he'd agreed to ditch his parents later.

Aaron's jaw twitched as he watched Felicity climb the bleachers toward his parents.

"You look distracted as shit," he told Theo waspishly, finally tearing his gaze away. "Cut it out."

"I'm *focused* as shit," Theo corrected him. "Shut up."

"Just saying, people are watching." Aaron aimed a wave at their parents sitting together in the bleachers. "Don't want to disappoint."

Theo watched their parents wave back, all of them smiling wide. They'd bonded over it when they were small: two boys with a weight on their shoulders, placed by their doting parents. They'd never drop it. They wouldn't dare.

"Not to mention Coach," Aaron continued. "He's been pissed off this week. Don't wanna see what he'll do to us if you screw up again. Sorry, if *we* screw up again."

Theo glanced at Coach Cheech, who was watching the crowd with an intensity that made Theo uncomfortable. He swallowed, trying to shake the knot of worry in his gut.

Kade would be here soon. They'd go to the disabled stall, and all the distant noises of the waiting gym would fade away. The stress, the game, the Fletchers, his parents' expectations—all the worry would drain out of him with each pull of Kade's blood, dark and delicious. Maybe he'd get to make Kade laugh again. And on top of that he'd get to gloat: Coach Cheech had showed up to the game after all. Whatever was going down at the tree, it wasn't important enough to miss the big game.

"Which you won't," Aaron said. "Because you're not at *all* distracted—uh, hello, I'm *talking*."

"You always are," Theo said, distracted. He'd just caught a familiar face coming around the corner of the gym hallway. A face that sent a renewed rush of worry through him.

Sundance Renfield waved.

"One second," Theo told Aaron, and jogged over. He pulled Sundance into the hallway, out of sight of the rest of the gym. "Miss Sundance, hi. What's happening? You smell—I mean, you look really stressed."

If she noticed his slip of the tongue, she didn't mention it. She was wearing her work uniform again.

She was out of breath, her sleeve exposing her bra strap, like she'd been running and forgot to pull it back up.

"I'm sorry. I don't have your number, and I don't know who else to ask. Have you seen Kade?"

Theo blinked. The worry in his gut swarmed out to fill the rest of his body, roaring and unstoppable.

"No," he said, proud of how calm his voice sounded. Cocky and assured. Just like normal. "Why?"

Sundance ran a hand through her dark frizzy hair. She smiled, short and nervous, trying to convince herself she was overreacting. "He never came home last night. I wouldn't...I know how Kade can be, alright? I waited, but he *still* isn't home, and he's not answering my texts. I know he can be a mess, but he *always* answers. Eventually."

"What do you think happened?" Theo asked.

She sighed. "When he cut himself in the woods. You *saw* him fall? He didn't just show up covered in blood?"

"No," Theo said automatically. "No, I saw him fall. I —wait. You think he hurt himself?"

She shrugged jerkily. But there was a terrible worry in her eyes, enough to make Theo's stomach sink.

"Wouldn't be the first time," she said, not meeting his eyes. It came out rushed, quiet, like she didn't want him to hear.

Theo nodded, biting his cheek so hard it would've split human skin.

"Okay," he said, voice squeaky. He cleared his throat. "Alright. Have you called the cops?"

Sundance snorted bitterly. "They won't take it as a missing person until it's been forty-eight hours. Probably not even then. Said he was always the running away type."

She said it so flatly, holding onto her elbows. Theo thought back to that tiny kitchen: photographs on the fridge of Kade as a kid holding up a sewing kit, Kade and his aunt standing in a river. Concert stubs to a band Theo had never heard of. Painted magnets spelling out LOVE U AUNTIE. The walls forest green, the overhead light warm and inviting. There was none of the cool emptiness Theo had grown up with. It felt like a kitchen from a childhood movie, one where the parent helped the kid crack an egg in a bowl in the middle of a montage.

Always the running away type, Theo thought. Two weeks ago he would have agreed. Two weeks ago he wouldn't have given a shit Monster's aunt hadn't seen him since yesterday morning. Even now there was a spark of doubt: maybe Kade had charged off into the rain last night and decided, *screw this. Screw this town, screw this jock, withdrawls are better than staying here one more second.*

But he looked at this woman, stout and dark and sturdy, and knew: Kade would never run away from his aunt. Not without telling her first.

"I know you two aren't close," Sundance continued. "And I'm sorry for butting in like this. But I didn't know who else to—"

She stopped as Theo put a hand on her shoulder.

"Go home," Theo said. "Maybe he'll come back. I'll check out some, uh, other places he might be."

She gave him a wary look. "Like where? Kade doesn't go anywhere. Unless you count walks in the woods."

"I know a few places," Theo said reassuringly, hoping he sounded like he knew what the hell he was talking about. "I'll check them out. You just—"

A stony voice piped up behind him. "You can't be serious."

Theo stiffened. He took a quick breath, and there it was: eucalyptus and hair gel. He turned to find Aaron glaring at them, incredulous.

"You better mean you're doing this *after* the game."

Theo avoided his gaze, giving Sundance a strained smile. "I'll go look for him. You go home."

She eyed Aaron warily. "If you're waiting until after the game, I might try those woods."

"I'll look," Theo said quickly. "Seriously, you go home."

"Excuse me?" Aaron's mouth twisted, the barest downward flicker. "You're seriously leaving to go chase your loser hookup? He's not even that good in bed."

"What?" Theo's face twisted in shock. Aaron had to be joking, but why say that in front of Kade's *aunt?*

"I'll get out of your hair," Sundance said hurriedly, giving Aaron another withering look. She touched

Theo's arm. "Thank you. Kade doesn't have many friends, so...*thank* you."

Theo watched her leave. He wanted to say something comforting, something to get that tension out of her shoulders. But he couldn't think of anything.

"Good riddance," Aaron spat, as the door to the parking lot pulled closed at the end of the hallway.

Theo sighed. "Aaron. *Jesus.* You couldn't have saved that shit for after she left?"

"Hey, she knows exactly who her kid is. Don't stand there and pretend..."

Aaron kept talking, but Theo didn't hear it. Aaron had raised a hand to scratch irritatedly at his basketball shirt, and in doing so he shook something loose: several pale flakes, as large and as thick as a thumbnail.

Monster skin, Theo thought with a dull horror.

He stared at it, his stomach churning as the realization set in.

He's going to stab you in the back, Kade had told him. *And you'll just walk into the knife.*

Theo saw red.

Aaron let out a shocked laugh as Theo grabbed him by the shirt. "Whoa, what's—?"

The laugh guttered as Theo yanked him into the disabled bathrooms, shoving him up against the mirror. Aaron's feet dangled half a foot off the ground.

"Ooookay," Aaron said, strained. Still trying to play it cool. To have the upper hand. "You know what, maybe you weren't lying. Maybe you *are* on drugs."

"Where is he?" Theo spat.

Aaron's faux-calm smile slipped. "What?"

"Are your parents in on it? Are you hiding the creature, too?" Theo shook him, banging Aaron's head back into the glass. "Tell me where he is!"

"The *what?* My parents—?" Aaron spluttered. It had been a long time since Theo had seen him so off balance. "Are you ACTUALLY high?"

Theo swiped a flake off Aaron's basketball shirt and held it in his face. "What's this?"

"I...dandruff? I don't—"

"You use anti-dandruff shampoo. You have a *five-step* hair care routine."

"I don't *know!*" Aaron writhed against his grip. He grabbed Theo's wrists, eyes widening when they didn't budge. They went even wider as Theo leaned in until their noses grazed.

"Where. Is. *Kade?*"

Aaron stopped wriggling. A disbelieving smile flinched over his face. "Why do you *care?* He's in a ditch somewhere, sleeping off a bender. Or he talked the wrong person into a fight and finally got what he deserved!"

Theo shook him hard.

Aaron's head banged back against the wall. He groaned in pain, eyes filling.

"He's a *liar,*" Aaron tried. His voice cracked. "You can't listen to anything he says. *Seriously.* Is he telling you we were together?"

"Together," Theo repeated. Every word made sense, but it still took a moment for it to click in his head, it was so ridiculous. *He's not even that good in bed.*

The realization must've shown on his face, because Aaron nodded, pointy chin digging into Theo's hands. "It's a *lie*. He was obsessed with me, I entertained him because it was funny watching him make goo-goo eyes at me. Then he got weird, and I shut it down. He went *crazy*."

Theo shook his head. He couldn't imagine any version of Kade who would get obsessed with Aaron, let alone make *goo-goo eyes* at him. He tried to picture Kade leaning in for a kiss, threading his fingers through Aaron's gelled hair. It didn't work. He tried imagining Aaron thumbing at the base of Kade's stubbled scalp, leaning on Kade's desk as his sewing machine hummed.

His stomach twisted. "You *did* start that fight in the movie theater parking lot."

Aaron spat a desperate laugh. "He tried to kiss me! In *public*. I *had* to. It would've gotten back to my parents, I...I *had* to."

"You beat the crap out of him," Theo whispered. He lowered Aaron to the ground, letting go of his shirt. He didn't want to touch him anymore.

"He beat the crap out of me, too," Aaron protested. "He's called Monster for a reason. He's not a good guy. When did you start thinking he was?"

Theo didn't answer. *Monster* kept circling in his head. Two weeks ago, he'd believed it. How could he not, with all that growling and snarling and launching himself at people in the cafeteria? With his strange black clothes and weird jewelry and head shaved down to the scalp? He filled his workbooks with line after line of dark scribbles—no words, just darkness. He bared his teeth at *teachers*. There were so many rumors about him, and he never denied them when you asked, he just scowled and flipped you off. Or *grinned* and flipped you off, which was even more disconcerting. He showed up to parties already wasted and always ended up in a fight before the night was over. He got arrested and he was constantly in detention and he looked at you like he'd take a chunk out of you if you came any closer.

And it was all bullshit. It was *bullshit*.

Tears gleamed in Aaron's eyes. "Theo—"

"*Don't*," Theo growled, shoving him.

Aaron's shoulder crashed into the mirror. The glass cracked. Theo didn't bother sticking around to listen to Aaron's pained gasp as he spun toward the door and marched out. He stormed into the gym, into all its overwhelming lights and noise, and grabbed Coach Cheech by the back of his shirt.

"*Where is Kade?*" he snarled, low in his ear. "Why aren't you at the tree? What's so important about tonight?"

Coach Cheech whirled to face him, panicked, already sucking on his mustache.

"Don't bullshit me," Theo warned him. "You tell me or I'll break your arm right here."

Coach Cheech rubbed his arm. He didn't look convinced, but he didn't shrug him off, either. He jerked his head, and Theo followed him into a corner that was less full of curious teammates.

"I don't know what you mean about Renfield," Coach Cheech said once they were out of earshot. "And based off that tree comment, I'm betting that it was you two assholes in my house this week. Tonight's the only night of the year when the...when *they* can do the ritual."

He sent an anxious glance around the gym, sucking again on his mustache. He didn't know who all the vampires were, Theo remembered. If any of them were listening in, they'd have to count on all the ambient crowd noise to keep this conversation private.

Theo lowered his voice. "Then why the *hell* are you still here?"

"They won't do the ritual this year. Everything isn't set up yet. If Kade's missing, they probably took him for safekeeping."

"What? Wait—Kade's part of the ritual?"

Coach Cheech nodded seriously.

"I gotta go get him," Theo said, mind racing. "Can we...the Fletchers..."

Coach Cheech grabbed his chin. "Don't *look* at them, dumbass!"

Theo jerked his gaze away from the Fletchers, who were currently leaning over his parents to talk to Felicity. "They're hunters, right? We can ask them for backup!"

"I wouldn't." Coach Cheech's teeth scraped his upper lip. "They're...don't freak out. But they voted on killing you. Alright? Say you're too much of a risk. If we take 'em, they're more likely to kill both of you than risk the ritual going down next year."

Theo's ears rang. *They voted on killing you.*

"Does...does Aaron know?"

"Not yet. But that won't last." Coach Cheech frowned over Theo's shoulder. "Jesus, what'd you say to the kid? Looks like he's gonna burst into tears right here on the court."

Theo turned, catching a glimpse of Aaron looking more upset than Theo had ever seen him in public, before Coach Cheech dragged him back.

"Let's just try and find Renfield," he said. "You can sense him, right?"

Theo stared at him blankly.

Coach Cheech sighed. "The stories always said you'd be able to sense him."

"Stories," Theo repeated, a wave of memories hitting him all at once—Kade gleeful and grinning, *you want me with you on your little vampire adventure, let's unravel this dark little mystery and see where it leads, the plot thickens.* There were *stories* about them. Kade was going to have a shitfit.

Coach Cheech waved him down. "You can tell where he is, right?"

"I can hear his heartbeat louder than anyone else's."

Coach Cheech held a thick finger in front of his face. Theo had had that finger in his face enough times to know it meant *shut up and listen.*

"Focus," Coach Cheech instructed. "Where is Kade?"

Theo looked around amid the music and chatter and people pretending not to watch the coach having a stern talk with the star player.

Coach Cheech slapped him softly in the cheek. "Hey! Where is he?"

"I don't—" Theo clenched his jaw. His eyes slipped shut. Decades of old, stale popcorn, rubber, deodorant. Adults talking, kids yelling over each other. Music making his head throb in time with the beat. Snatches of the Fletchers talking with Felicity (*it's so cute how your mom still packs you snacks for these things*), a snippet of his parents whispering (*what is he doing, should I go down there*), Aaron's breathing, tight and upset near the hallway.

"Go deeper," Coach Cheech told him. Suddenly his voice sounded far away. Something else was creeping on the edges of Theo's senses: a fast thumping. The telltale scent of cheap metal and softness, wool and old liquor, nerves and terror-sweat.

Theo chased it.

"That's it," came Coach Cheech's voice, distorted and faint. "Follow him down."

Theo didn't hear the rest of it. The thunder of

Kade's loud heart was getting closer. Dirt and leaves. Bark against his back. Hands bound, ropes biting his slim wrists, shaking against a warped tree trunk.

Theo's eyes flew open. "Someone has him tied to the tree. We need to go."

Part of him was still stuck with Kade. The din of the gym was muffled, the scents dulled as he turned and walked straight into Victor Fairgood.

"Whoa," Victor said, rocking with the impact. "Save some for the court! Where are you going with that look on your face? The game's about to start."

"Dad," Theo said. He blinked hard. The background chatter of the gym rushed back in, the cloying scent of popcorn drowning out any trace of dirt. It was floorboards under him, not roots. No bark pressed against his back, just his dad's hand, wide and imposing.

Theo swallowed. "I...I need to go."

"Excuse me?" Victor shook his head, smiling stiffly. "You *need* to fix your mistake. Or will our dinner with the Fletchers be another consolation dinner?"

"Right," Theo said distractedly. "I mean, no, it won't. I mean—"

He looked at Coach Cheech beseechingly.

"Uh," Coach Cheech started. "Look, Victor."

"Cheech, do me a favor and hush." Victor reached up and rested a hand in Theo's hair. Loose, almost friendly. Theo had to stop himself from flinching.

"My friend's in trouble," he tried. "I gotta go check on him."

Victor's hand tightened into a fist. "The only thing you need to do right now is get out there and kill those Westside Hawks."

"Dad." Theo glanced around the gym. People were pointing and whispering. Not everybody, but enough. Aaron was watching from the hallway, brow furrowed. He'd seen Victor do this a couple of times, but never in public. Up in the stands, Felicity was trying to smile at whatever the Fletchers were saying, watching him out of the corner of her eye.

Theo tugged gently on Victor's wrist. "*Dad*. People are looking."

"Let them look," Victor replied, staring warily at Theo's hand on his wrist. "I rescheduled this game myself. If you leave *again*, you'll turn this family into a laughingstock. Is that what you want?"

"This isn't about us," Theo whispered.

"Victor," Coach Cheech tried. "This *really* isn't the time."

Victor shushed him, his grip tightening even more. Once his grip was immovable, encompassing Theo's whole head. Now it was thin, flimsy. Theo could yank his hand off as easy as flicking a stray hair away.

Victor leaned in. "Need I remind you who you are? You're a *Fairgood*. We're *vicious*. Are you going to go out there and show everybody, or are you going to *check on your friend?*"

Theo shot another nervous glance around the room. Aaron stood stock-still in the hallway. Up in the bleachers, Felicity was still distracting the Fletchers. She combed her limp hair with her fingers, using the impromptu shield to toss Theo a wide-eyed look: *what's happening?*

Victor sighed. "Whatever you're *actually* dealing with, we'll destroy it. Alright? But right now, you need to—"

Theo yanked out of his grip, staggering back.

Victor stared at him. The hand that had been clenched in Theo's hair spasmed against nothing. More shocked by the audacity than the ease of Theo pushing him off.

A horrible choking noise flooded down from the bleachers. Some of the not-so-subtle stares turned away from Theo to look.

"Oh shit," Aaron yelled, voice scratchy with unshed tears. "My girlfriend's choking! Someone do something!"

Victor twitched toward the yell.

Too little too late guys, Theo thought, and ran.

CHAPTER
TWENTY-SEVEN

KADE'S BUTT was numb on the forest floor.

He squirmed, trying to get away from a root sticking into his spine. "Is this a test? How long can you be quiet until I stop being annoying? Because I can go all night, baby. Feels weird to call a teacher baby, but I'm sure as shit not calling you *mister* after all this."

Hawthorn didn't reply. He stared, unblinking, into the forest. He hadn't moved since he tied Kade to the tree. Kade didn't know how long it had been, but it had been light when Hawthorn carried him here, and now it was dark, moonlight washing the clearing white. His arms ached from being tied behind him, skin scratched from the rough bark.

Kade tried again. "How old are you?"

Hawthorn didn't move. He watched the trees, perfectly still. Even his chest didn't move. He looked like a statue.

"Are the glasses real?" Kade asked. A drop of sweat trickled down his neck. "Am I bait? He won't come. He can find some other blood bag, one he doesn't burn when he bites it."

No reply. Kade thumped his head back against the tree. His scalp stung. He kept waiting for another sickening jolt of a vision, like the one that had hit while Aaron and his dad were prowling around. So far, nothing.

"Am I part of it?" he whispered. "The ritual? The burning, that has to be part of it, right? I'm—what, a sacrifice?"

"You're more than that," Hawthorn said simply. Like he hadn't been ignoring Kade all this time.

Kade gave him a queasy smile. "Are you gonna kill me?"

"*Theo* is going to kill you. When the time comes." Hawthorn cocked his head. Listening, Kade realized. Something must be happening in the forest.

Hawthorn's head snapped back up. He turned on his heel, those same polished boots Kade had seen him wear all through middle school and high school.

"Then again," Hawthorn said, "plans change."

He knelt in front of Kade, reaching up to toy with the gag perched under Kade's chin waiting to be pulled up. His tattoos peeked out of his ever-present sleeves, black tendrils snaking toward his wrist. Gone was the kind, soft-spoken teacher Kade had grown to trust. In its place crouched an animal, watching Kade with a detached interest. Like a lion watching a trapped gazelle. Knowing it was going to eat—but not yet.

Kade tried to laugh defiantly. It came out wet and pleading, all the terror finally catching up to him. "Yeah, well, good luck, asshole. You can't kill me without telling me what I am. I don't—you haven't even told me what I am, you have to tell me, please don't kill me without telling me what I am!"

The words spilled out of him, shaky and uncontrollable. Tears welled in his eyes. Embarrassment was there, even then. But it paled in comparison to that huge, lifelong need to be part of something. He'd spent his whole life as nothing, unwanted, shit on someone's shoe, but now he was *something*. He couldn't die without knowing what.

Hawthorn watched him pant, pupils inhumanly large. Behind him, leaves crunched in the distance. Two sets of footsteps, coming fast.

Kade opened his mouth. Hawthorn slapped a palm over it, then pulled the gag up into his mouth.

"Warn them and I will make you *wish* I killed you," Hawthorn whispered. He patted Kade's cheek and reached down to fiddle with the rope.

Voices drifted through the trees, getting closer.

"...what kind of person eats celery at a basketball game?" said an out-of-breath Coach Cheech.

"She'll eat popcorn at my house, but her mom gets really weird about what she eats in public. She's been getting better about it, but—" Theo stopped when he burst into the clearing, Coach Cheech lagging behind. Coach Cheech wheezed, a crossbow at the ready, a heavy bag slung over his shoulder.

"Mr. Hawthorn," Theo said. "What's going on?"

Mr. Hawthorn looked up, still fumbling with the rope. "Oh thank *god* it's you. I thought one of the bullies was coming back. One of you call the police, quick."

Coach Cheech lowered his crossbow cautiously. "Hawthorn."

"Cheech," Mr. Hawthorn replied. "Call the police. This is *completely* unacceptable. I can't believe someone at *my* school would do this." He swore under his breath, fumbling the rope. "I can't figure out this knot. Theo, come over here, would you?"

Coach Cheech's arm shot out, a line across Theo's chest. "Wait one minute."

"It's fine," Theo told him.

Coach Cheech watched Hawthorn warily. "Sure, but let's—"

"It's *fine*," Theo repeated, jogging over to kneel in front of Kade. He eased the gag out of his mouth, giving Kade a pointed look. He was in his basketball clothes, a twig sticking to his shorts from running through the woods. His perfectly coiffed curls were in disarray. He left the big game to chase after him, Kade realized. A lump formed in his throat, half-touched, half-terror. *Warn them and I will make you wish I killed you.*

Theo raised his brows, a silent question.

Kade sat perfectly still, the gag wet against his chin. He didn't make a sound. He didn't look beside them, where Hawthorn was still fumbling at the rope. He didn't look anywhere but Theo.

Theo's mouth tightened. The start of a realization. Hoping he was wrong, just like Kade had.

Hawthorn cursed again, digging fruitlessly into the rope tethered to the tree.

"I hope your friends aren't involved in this," he told Theo. "I know you boys can be rough sometimes, but I really expected better."

"We're not involved," Theo said slowly. His eyes tracked Kade's face. "You're okay, right, Renfield?"

"Right," Kade rasped. A tear juddered down his cheek. He leaned down to smear it on the shoulder of his jacket. "Prank g-got out of hand."

"Right," Theo echoed.

Behind them, Coach Cheech surveyed the clearing. He eyed the tree line, crossbow at the ready in front of him.

"Nighttime walk in the woods, huh?" he asked Hawthorn.

Hawthorn sighed, sitting back on his heels. "What? Why is no one getting out their phones? Reception isn't *that* spotty in these woods."

"Sure you want us to call somebody, Hawthorn?"

"Why wouldn't I..." Hawthorn trailed off. He stood up slowly. "Fancy crossbow you have there, Coach. I thought you didn't hunt."

"Depends what I'm hunting." The crossbow gleamed in the moonlight. Coach Cheech shifted his grip, and Hawthorn's gaze shifted with it. Following the arrow tip.

Kade shuddered, twisting his hands behind him uselessly. His wrists chafed against the rope. He gave Theo a pleading look, and Theo barely paused a second before reaching out. One firm tug and the rope around the tree snapped, a loud noise that made Kade flinch as it echoed around the clearing.

"Wow," Hawthorn said as Theo broke the ropes around Kade's wrists. "They grow them strong in Lock."

"Damn right." Coach Cheech held the crossbow up, aiming at Hawthorn's heart.

Hawthorn held up his hands. "What the hell are you *doing*?"

"Can it," Coach Cheech barked. He nodded over at Theo. "He got a heartbeat?"

Theo closed his eyes, focusing. When he opened them, his face was twisted in disbelief.

"No," he whispered.

Coach Cheech cocked the crossbow.

"Wait," Hawthorn barked. He looked at Theo and Kade, panicked. "Just hear me out. If it was just you, I wouldn't have needed all the pretense. But I needed to get you away from him first."

Coach Cheech scoffed. "Sure, I bet you—"

Hawthorn blurred toward him. Coach Cheech trailed off in a yell, finger jerking on the crossbow trigger. The arrow made a snicking sound as it skimmed the blur streaking toward him, barely interrupting its sprint.

Kade blinked. Hawthorn stood behind Coach Cheech, neat and unruffled except for the black gash on his shoulder where the arrow had caught him. His hands were tight around Coach Cheech's jaw.

"No," Coach Cheech gasped. "Wait—"

Hawthorn wrenched his head to the side. A shocking *snap* echoed around the clearing. Coach Cheech swayed, his neck bent at an unnatural angle. Then he crumpled, falling back onto his bag of weapons.

Hawthorn heaved a sigh of relief. "You're welcome," he said, voice soft and understanding, like he was telling Kade why he'd failed another test.

Theo shoved Kade behind him, teeth bared. "Get the hell away from us."

Hawthorn gestured at Theo's fangs. "You can put those away. I don't want to fight you."

Kade made an incredulous noise, throat still thick with tears. He'd spent his whole life wanting to be in a story, wanting to be something. Now here he was, and he wanted to go home and put his head under the covers until he stopped shaking.

Hawthorn held out his hands, dark tattoos catching the moonlight. For a moment it looked like they moved, thin strands shifting over his pale skin.

"This must be so disorientating," Hawthorn continued. "And you must be very scared. But you weren't safe with him. I had no other option."

Theo snarled. "Coach wanted to help!"

"Really? A hunter wanted to help a vampire? A vampire who is destined to bring destruction that Lockian hunters have been tasked with stopping for the last two centuries?" Hawthorn sighed. "Come on, Theo. He wasn't your kind."

"I'm not your *kind*, either!"

Hawthorn said, "I'm not one of those crazy creatures trying to unleash hell on the town. I promise. You can trust me. I'm here to keep you safe."

"Like hell," Kade spat. He tugged the back of Theo's basketball shirt. "Mate, he kept me tied up all *day*. He said you were going to kill me."

Theo frowned. "He said what?"

Hawthorn gave Kade a disappointed look, and Kade had to fight not to shrink underneath it. Part of him still reacted to Hawthorn like he was his favorite teacher, even with Coach Cheech's corpse cooling between them.

"I was afraid of this." Hawthorn took off his glasses, cleaning them on his ironed shirt. "Theo—we need to get Kade somewhere safe. There might be more hunters waiting. Rest assured, I truly do want to keep him safe, despite his allegiances."

"Allegiances," Theo repeated. "What allegiances?"

Mr. Hawthorn looked at him pityingly. "You really didn't suspect?"

"Suspect..." Theo's gaze flickered to where Kade was still clutching the back of his basketball shirt. "What do you mean? Kade's not...he's on *my* side."

Kade stood perfectly still, trembling in every limb. A strange feeling of déjà vu washed over him. Like he knew this story already. Like he knew Mr. Hawthorn's words before they left his mouth.

"He's not," Mr. Hawthorn said gently. "He never was. I'm sorry, Theo. He's with the hunters."

TWENTY-EIGHT

THEO SHOOK HIS HEAD, dazed. "No, he's not."

Hawthorn sighed, adjusting his glasses. Theo didn't know why he bothered. The bloody gash in his shoulder was the only thing out of place: his glasses were perfectly straight, hair neat, hands clean despite the dead body on the grass behind him. Coach Cheech lay still and unmoving against the roots of the gnarled tree, crossbow useless in his limp hand. His bag lay under one of his legs, open to display the silver ax Theo had seen in the car on the ride over.

"Theo, you're a smart kid," Hawthorn said matter-of-factly. "You have to *know* you can't trust him. Deep down."

"He's lying," Kade croaked. He looked stunned, hands trembling in Theo's basketball shirt. "He...he *kidnapped* me! He tied me up! I'm not...mate, I *swear* I don't know what the hell is going on—"

Hawthorn cut him off. "Why was he even out there that night? What's the likelihood that he missed all those rocks? Even if he did jump in that lake, he'd never do it without ulterior motives. Why save you? He *hated* you."

"I didn't," Kade whispered. "I don't."

Theo wanted to believe him so badly. But he'd known Hawthorn his whole life. *Trusted* him his whole life. Theo and Kade had their first proper conversation a couple of weeks ago.

Theo asked, "What *were* you doing out there?"

"I..." Kade let out a miserable laugh. He let go of Theo's shirt, hunching into his skinny shoulders. "I was going to jump. I wasn't *really*, I was just drunk and dramatic—I don't *think* I...I'd never do that to my aunt, you know?" A tear rolled down his cheek. He swiped at it, hand missing its target and skating clumsily over his ear.

"Still lying," Hawthorn said. "It's not his fault, he's been manipulated by the hunters."

"What?" Theo said. "He hates the Fletchers."

"You think the Fletchers are the only hunters in town?" Hawthorn fixed Theo with a kind smile. "These past weeks must've been so confusing for you. But you need to know this is the only way. You saw what Cheech tried to do. He won't be the only one who tries to take Kade out of the equation."

"I'll protect him," Theo blurted.

Hawthorn's smile went strained. "That's not how

this story goes. You need to let me take him somewhere safe."

"Yeah? You wanna tie him to another tree?" Theo asked. It felt flimsy. Like he should've asked something else. But there was a part of him, young and desperate, which wanted Hawthorn to say the thing that would make it all make sense. The thing that would make it okay that he killed Coach Cheech and wanted to take Kade away. The thing that would make Kade stop trembling and get rid of the terrible suspicion churning in Theo's gut. The suspicion that made him want to get him and Kade as far away from their history teacher as they could.

"Out of town," Hawthorn replied. "I have friends who can protect him."

"I'm not going anywhere with you," Kade spat. He was still trembling, but his fists were clenched. Like he could do anything with his flimsy human fists. Kade's gaze darted down toward Cheech's bag and that silver ax.

Hawthorn said, "I don't know what those people have told you—"

"Nobody's told me SHIT! Nobody in this shithole town has told me ANYTHING, and they haven't told you anything either!" Kade turned to Theo, another horrified tear spilling down his gaunt cheek. "We're... we're *together* on this! Right?"

It wasn't full of bitter bravado, like back in the bathroom. This was all hope, uncertain and scared. Like he was waiting for Theo to screw him over. Theo wanted to tell him about his dad's expectant face in the gym. How he'd turned away from them, away from the whole town expecting him to make up for his mistake. Not because he wanted to chase some stupid vampire plot, but because he knew Kade was in trouble.

A hand on Theo's shoulder made him jump. Hawthorn had stalked closer without him hearing it.

"Theo," he said, low and even. "I know this must be confusing. But if you just—"

Theo cut him off. "You can't take him."

Kade's breath stuttered. Theo heard it as loud as a foghorn. Everything was so much *louder* with Kade.

Hawthorn paused. "I know this must be difficult. But this is your destiny. Come with me. Meet your people, your *real* people. It was never this town. It was *us*."

Theo stepped back, wrenching his shoulder out of Hawthorn's grip, placing himself back in front of Kade.

Waiting for it to feel like a mistake. But it didn't feel like a mistake. It felt...right. Like plucking a thorn out of his palm.

Mr. Hawthorn stared. One moment he was the kindly teacher Theo had known all his life. Then he nodded, and something in his face changed. The heart seeped out of it, a mask dropping to reveal the cold thing behind it.

"You know what," he said brightly. "Maybe I will kill you."

He rolled up his sleeves. The tattoos along his arms throbbed, black tendrils winding down his wrists like snakes.

"Makes killing Cheech a little useless," he continued, unbuttoning his shirt collar. "But still—that was *fun*. My leader—well. My *temporary* leader never lets us do anything worthwhile. Didn't even let me kill Lemmings."

He shrugged off his shirt. The black tattoo tendrils slithered up his shoulders, down his collarbone. Nestled on his chest sat an inky tree, its branches a mirror of the gnarled tree behind them. Something undulated under his skin, like his bones were trying to escape.

Kade backed away. "What's happening? What's he *doing*?"

Theo didn't answer. He was too busy watching in mute horror as Mr. Hawthorn's limbs stretched. His arms first, then his legs. His torso lengthened until he towered over them. A strange groan ripped out of his throat, his nose melting into one big slit, ears forming into points.

Mr. Hawthorn shuddered. There was a *snap*, like a branch breaking. Wings split from his back, spindly and barbed. His skin was pale and papery, a long fleck sloughing off its wings and into the dirt.

"I'm going to enjoy this," said the creature from the Lemmings house.

Theo turned. "Move!"

"Moving," Kade yelped, running for the crossbow in Cheech's hand.

Hawthorn leapt at him. Theo flung himself between them, braced for impact. It hit him like a freight train, pain bursting over his chest. The world blurred, something cracking behind his back.

Theo opened his eyes. He was on the ground, his basketball shirt in black, wet ribbons. Hawthorn had ripped his chest open and thrown him into a tree.

He looked up just in time to see Kade hit the ground with a pained yell. Hawthorn stood over him, clawed foot pressing hard on Kade's chest. He bent down, fangs bared. Kade whimpered, yanking uselessly at Hawthorn's ankle.

Hawthorn straightened. Kade jerked under him, all that horrible weight pushing down on his narrow chest.

"I'll admit, I was annoyed you got attached," Hawthorn told Theo. His chest flexed, his tree tattoo bright against his pale skin. "Stupid thing to do. Your story was never going to end well. You were always going to kill him."

Theo shook his head. He tried pulling himself up, but his arms collapsed under him. He looked desperately toward Kade, who looked back with agonized tears in his eyes.

"Go," Kade rasped. "Run."

Theo shook his head again. His gaze caught on something red behind his head. Black flowers and spiky stem growing over the tree roots. Theo recognized them. He'd spent so many childhood hours walking through these woods, pretending not to admire the plants.

He reached back, hiding his hands behind him. The fire eye burned his palms as he wrenched it off the tree roots.

"Like hell," he choked, and stumbled up. He ran at Hawthorn, stumbling at first, then blurring. Hawthorn's arm came up again, catching Theo by the throat.

"Come on," he said, almost pitying. "This would be so much easier if you'd just get it over with. Embrace the creature you were always meant to become."

"Screw you," Theo choked, and rammed the vine into Hawthorn's eyes.

Hawthorn screamed, the noise splintering into something horrible and inhuman. Theo gritted his teeth. Smoke rose from his hands as he wrapped the vine around Hawthorn's head. The pain in his lacerated chest was going numb, but the burn in his hands was almost unbearable.

Hawthorn staggered off Kade, clawing at Theo and the vine circling his head. Black blood oozed down his cheeks from the barbs invading his eyes.

Kade sucked in a pained breath as the weight came off his chest, not even waiting one breath before he crawled to the crossbow. Kade gave Cheech a shaky salute as he grabbed the crossbow and turned it toward the two vampires wrestling among the trees.

"Shoot him," Theo yelled. "Shoot—"

He stopped, yelling in agony. Hawthorn had his claws in his back now, trying to tug him off.

Kade cursed, shaking the crossbow desperately. "Son of a bitch isn't loaded!"

"THEN GRAB AN ARROW," Theo screamed. Hawthorn clawed lines into his back. The claws dug and held. Theo gritted his teeth, but the creature was too powerful. Hawthorn wrenched him off, throwing Theo into yet another unlucky tree.

Hawthorn staggered up, eyes punched out by the fire eye barbs. He stood perfectly still, head cocked, waiting.

Kade froze. He was kneeling on the ground next to Cheech's bag, in the middle of reaching for a crossbow bolt. The silver ax gleamed in the dirt beside him.

Theo reached out an unsteady hand. "Don't move."

Hawthorn snarled.

Kade gasped.

Hawthorn ran at him. Kade swore, swinging the useless crossbow out in front. Hawthorn swiped. The crossbow went flying across the clearing.

"Shit," Kade spat. He plunged a hand into his jacket, but it was too late: Hawthorn drove Kade into a tree, his teeth bared and aiming for Kade's throat.

Theo screamed. He surged up, numb chest and burning hands forgotten as he watched Kade get pinned under the creature's bulk.

Then, the impossible: Hawthorn stopped. His dark eyes wavered. Theo looked down. A broken knitting needle stuck out of Hawthorn's chest. Right out of his heart.

Kade's gray eyes met Theo's, defiant and gleaming. His gaze flickered toward the ax on the ground behind Hawthorn.

Theo had to hold back a smile. He bent down and scooped up the ax, careful not to touch the silver blade.

Hawthorn leaned back, dazed. His laughter trailed off into a wounded hiss.

"You stupid little shit," he said to Kade, syrupy slow. "Only...only weak, pissling little vampires die from a stake to the heart. Weaklings like Jeremiah Lemmings, living off of deer blood for decades. You—you can't kill *me* with *this*."

He reached up to tug it out, still laughing weakly.

"Maybe not," Kade said, nodding behind him. "But *that* can."

Hawthorn turned.

Theo brought the ax down. The blade hit Hawthorn's neck, slicing almost all the way through. Gruesome gurgles bubbled out of his torn throat. He fell to the ground, right next to Coach Cheech's twisted body.

Theo straightened, hands shaking around the wooden ax handle. Black blood ran down his face. He couldn't tell if it was his own or Hawthorn's.

Hawthorn made a choking sound. A wizened arm twitched toward Theo's leg.

"Oh, shit," Kade said, dazed. "Almost."

Theo slammed the ax down on Hawthorn's neck. The blade sunk deep into the earth. Hawthorn's detached head rocked once, then stilled.

Wind blew through the trees. The only other noise was Kade, his wet panting and his thundering heartbeat.

Theo turned to him. "Are you alright?"

Kade gagged.

"Okay," Theo said.

Kade bent over, shuddering. Theo hesitated. Then he reached out with a slick hand, laying his fingertips over Kade's dirt-streaked shirt. He sucked in a breath: no cuts. A bruise forming on his forehead and chest, blood pooling under the skin. And mercifully, no vomit.

Theo asked again: "Are you alright?"

"Am I—" Kade straightened, gasping a wet laugh. His cheeks were damp. He smelled like salt and panic. "Mate, you look like *mincemeat*. Gross, black mincemeat…"

He waved at Theo, who grimaced down at his tattered basketball shirt. His back and chest were torn up by Hawthorn's claws. His hands were blistered from the fire eye, red wounds scored deep into his palms.

Kade's hands hovered over the deep cuts in Theo's chest, not daring to touch.

"Poor lefty," Kade whispered.

"What?" Theo looked down and realized that his left nipple had been sliced in half.

"I don't know, my favorite teacher just tried to eat me, I'm in shock." Kade stared at him, tears dripping down his face like an afterthought. He smeared his palms over his cheeks, then fumbled at his neckline.

It still took Theo a second to realize what he was offering. "Kade—"

"You're hurt," Kade snapped. "Just—please. It's bad, Theo. It's *so* bad."

Theo nodded distractedly. He could feel his eyes turning black.

"I'm...I'm really...If I can't stop—"

Kade bent down and yanked the broken knitting needle out of Hawthorn's corpse. He held it up, hand shaking. "I have my stake. And your fire eye is around here, somewhere."

"I'll teach you how to recognize it in the wild," Theo slurred. His teeth were sharpening, black eyes glazing over. "Is that the knitting needle I broke?"

Kade nodded.

"Good. Keep it close." Theo's hands were strong and desperate as he tugged Kade forward by his collar, pulling it down so he could sink his teeth in.

Waves of ecstasy rushed to meet him, but Theo didn't dive in and lose himself. He clung to the small part of him that was still Theo, standing in a forest with the trembling boy who saved his life. Who growled at him in class last month. Who gave him a pair of knitted gloves with a smile so soft Theo couldn't look directly at it.

Theo pulled back. The cuts on his chest were thinner now, already crusting over.

"You're still hurt," Kade said. He fumbled the broken knitting needle back into his jacket and touched Theo's ripped shirt.

"I think healing this might take a while." Theo smiled, strained. "Your heart is still racing."

Kade nodded. His pupils were huge and unfocused. "Shaky guy. Loud heart."

Theo could see every one of his dark eyelashes. It was so quiet. Not even birds interrupted the silence. Like they were the only ones in the world.

Kade's gaze dropped to Theo's mouth.

It couldn't happen. One kiss would burn Kade to the bone. And yet, Theo wanted it. He wanted it like he never wanted anything.

"Kade," Theo said softly, regretting the words even as he said them. "I...we *can't*."

A loud bark echoed through the clearing.

Kade startled, jerking out of Theo's arms so fast his hand skimmed Theo's bare neck, hissing as it burned him.

"Ow, shit—" Kade stopped and stared as a dog padded through the trees.

Not a dog—a *puppy*, paws too big for its body, ears too big for its head. Its fur was short and endlessly black, the way an abyss was black. It looked like a strange cross between a doberman and a rottweiler and its eyes were smoldering orange, gazing up at Theo expectantly.

"Uh," Theo said. "Hi?"

The dog woofed happily. Its tail wagged. Something stirred in Theo's chest. Familiarity. A bone-deep knowledge: *this is mine.*

"Huh," Kade said thoughtfully.

"What?"

"Nothing." Kade rubbed the burn on his hand. "Told you it'd be a dog."

TWENTY-NINE

TWENTY DAYS after Theo Fairgood died, he met Kade Renfield in the woods.

Kade didn't notice him at first. Theo stood for a while, watching Kade smoke and pick at the dark blue polish on his thumbnail. It made him strangely calm. Like wandering in a foreign land and spotting someone from home through a crowd.

Theo had come home the night of the ruined basketball game with a puppy (dubbed Sparky, due to her fiery eyes) and a horrible flu that meant he was staying in bed for the next few days. His parents had given him disappointed looks and stocked up on his least favorite soup and cheap dog food. Theo had been eating local wildlife and doing the homework Felicity emailed him and googling how to look after a dog. Every night he'd checked the tears in his chest, and every night they were thinner. Yesterday they were still scabbing. Today they were lines of raised skin. Tomorrow, hopefully, they would be nothing. No reminder of Hawthorn's claws ripping him open. Theo was looking forward to it.

Next to him, Sparky barked.

Kade whipped around, cigarette falling out of his hand. He stomped it into the dirt, swearing.

"Shit! Walk louder!"

"Get better ears." Theo grinned. "How are you?"

"Hydrated." Kade slapped his neck, breaking into an endearing smile when Sparky bounded over. He bent down and rubbed frantically at Sparky's ears. "Hi, girl! How's my favorite satan spawn? You look so good, yes you do!"

"We should bring her into school," Theo said. "Your badass rep would be gone in five seconds once they see you cooing at her."

"Yeah, let's not." Kade straightened, looking Theo up and down. "You look better. Back to school soon?"

"Guess so."

Kade nodded. He picked at his wrist cuff. There were a few of them, bracelets stacked on top, covering him halfway up to his elbow. Was he hiding a bruise?

Theo frowned, sniffing the air. "Has Aaron been bothering you?"

"Nope." Kade's lips smacked around the *p*. "Think you really freaked him out. He won't even look at me now."

"Good," Theo said firmly. They hadn't talked about

Kade and Aaron yet. Theo had tried to bring it up the first time they met after that night, only for Kade's face to immediately close down. He'd let Theo feed on him and then walked off the moment Theo healed him. Theo hadn't dared ask a second time.

Kade scuffed a platform boot against the grass. "Parents forgiven you yet?"

"They'll forgive me when the town forgives me," Theo said. "So, no, never. No rescheduling this time, we just lost. Our team's got no chance without me. Not against the Wayside Hawks."

"Assholes," Kade said mildly. Theo didn't know if he was talking about the Wayside Hawks or his parents.

Theo pushed away the looming knowledge of his parents' punishment, yet to come.

"Still no word on the bodies?"

"Nooope." Kade's teeth tug into his chapped lower lip, muffling the word. "They got substitute teachers in. The cops are looking. Don't think they'll find anything. I mean, if *we* can't—and we know where they died. So."

He sat down, beckoning Sparky back over. Theo followed.

Kade's gaze flickered up as Theo sat down, Sparky wriggling on the grass between them.

"Everything okay today?" Theo asked.

"Always." Kade ruffled Sparky's thin fur, a reluctant smile creeping in when Sparky licked his hand. "Aunt Sundance knows something's up. Just doesn't know what. She won't shut up about you coming over for dinner again."

"You and the Fletchers, man. I *love* pretending to eat."

Sparky rolled onto her back. Kade rubbed her stomach, making soft cooing noises he couldn't seem to hold back. His hand roved her furry belly. Theo reached out, careful to keep his hand on her chest.

Kade's petting slowed, growing more careful. The burn he'd gotten during Sparky's introduction was still vivid on his wrist. Theo had offered to heal it and Kade had called him an idiot, waving at Theo's injuries.

I can deal with a little burn, he'd told him.

Kade rubbed his face. He had bags under his eyes again, and he was paler than usual.

"You look tired."

"Bad dreams." Kade smiled crookedly. "So, you burning me is part of some big vampire plan."

"Apparently."

"And we have a year to figure out how to stop it."

"Looks like," Theo said. He tried to think of something cool to say, something fun and witty, but he was tired after days of healing on nothing but deer blood, and he was never good at this. Not like Kade was. He wanted to tell Kade how scared he was. How terrifying it was to lie in his bed at night, not sleeping, not knowing who was out there and when they would come for him. For him *and* Kade. Knowing they were doomed, the clock ticking down, with no idea how to climb off this path strangers had forced them on.

"Milly texted me," he said instead. "She wants us to come to the bookshop tomorrow. She has something to show us."

"A cure-all for our doom, I hope." Kade fondled Sparky's big paw, pressing on his black toe beans. "You know what I figured out?"

"What?"

"Stories are only fun afterward. When you're living them, they scare you shitless." Kade shot him a smile. Only a hint of sharp. The rest of it was all soft. Afternoon light filtered through the trees, washing Kade in pale gold, and Theo wanted to kiss him so much he could taste it. It made him think back to the last time they were in this forest. Standing there, surrounded by blood and death, Theo would have given anything to kiss Kade and not hurt him.

But that wasn't how this went. *Your story was never going to end well,* Hawthorn had snarled, slurring around all those terrible teeth. *You were always going to kill him.*

Kade sighed, stretching out his legs until he was one long line of pale skin and ripped black clothing. Today's shirt was a flowy black blouse that exposed his collarbones, that pale blue vein fluttering under his skin like a siren's song.

"I know *that* look." Kade stood with a flourish. He waited until Theo followed him up, then extended his neck.

Theo sighed, hands on his hips. "Have you eaten enough?"

"Big meal, all the water in the world." Kade jerked his head. "Go for it, blood boy."

"Call me Theo."

Kade paused. A sly look passed over his face.

"I don't know," he said. "You sure we're there yet?"

"You're growing on me," Theo admitted. "Like a fungus."

Kade's teasing smile turned delighted. "Holy shit. *Mushroom* boy."

"No," Theo tried, but Kade was already laughing, face creasing with it. "Alright, calm down."

Kade wiped his eyes, still chuckling. He tilted sideways, neck bared. "Okay. Seriously, go on. We need to get you healed up for school."

Theo leaned in. He paused for a moment, letting himself enjoy the warmth emanating from Kade's skin. Then he bit down, and the world narrowed.

Kade's grip slackened as Theo sucked. His hands shifted to grip the small of Theo's back, a hot, shaky press.

Like we're slow dancing, Theo thought muzzily. He brought his arms up to circle Kade's shoulders. They stayed there as Theo pulled back, the sizzle of skin fading into silence.

Kade groped at his healed neck, the way he did sometimes, like he was checking it was smooth skin. He swayed against Theo.

Theo thought once more of dancing, then stepped back. "Can I try something? I just..."

Kade gave him a bleary look. "Depends what it is."

Theo pulled out a pair of knitted gloves.

Kade laughed. "I hope you know how embarrassing this is," he said as Theo slid them on. "They're *so* bad. Like, *so*..."

He trailed off, smile falling as Theo lifted a hand and touched Kade's cheek. Slowly, gingerly, feeling the bone with his thumb. He made sure not to press too hard, so his skin stayed behind the thin wool barrier.

"I just wanted to see if this would work," Theo admitted.

Kade stared at him, chapped lips parted in a surprise Theo wanted to swallow. Then he jerked back, sucking in a breath. "When you come back to school... do we..."

Theo hesitated.

Kade twisted out of his grip. "Great. Fine. I'll just go."

"Aaron's involved," Theo told him. "But I don't think he knows it. I...I should stick close. Maybe I can make him see there's another choice that isn't following his family into hunting, uh, me."

"Right. One less person aiming silver arrows at you when the time comes. Can't talk him into the light side with Monster hanging around." Kade's thin smile wobbled. There was no sharpness, just bitter resignation.

He gave Sparky one last scratch and turned away. "See you at the bookshop after school?"

Theo wanted to drag him back. Wanted to tell him he'd burn all his bridges to walk hand in gloved hand with him in the halls. Do *something* to prove they weren't doomed.

"See you tomorrow," he said instead.

He watched Kade walk away until his shape vanished through the trees, too far for even a newborn vampire to see. He walked home, Sparky ambling at his side.

Then he lay on his bed with the bundled gloves under his nose, breathing in Kade's soft, metallic scent until it finally faded.

SPECIAL THANKS

Thank you so much for reading BLOOD TETHERED! You can grab the second book in the trilogy, VENOM BOUND, on Amazon, B&N and KU.

If you want to support me, please leave a review on Goodreads, Amazon and any social media of your choice.

You can get updates on my upcoming books by subscribing to my newsletter! Sign up by visiting my website at isbelleauthor.com. (by signing up you also get a free sapphic novella!)

You can find her on Tiktok @i.s.belle_writes or on Instagram @isbelleauthor.

ACKNOWLEDGMENTS

First off, let's give it up for my Kickstarter backers! I was blown away for the support this early-access campaign got. Let's go down the line:

Eden Mason, Milo N, Ashley Binder, Victoria P, Ary, Michelle B., Briar, Valentine, Ashleigh Wolfe, Bee Marie Chase, Lisa Herrick, Ayanna W, Ayla Peyrot, Ember, Maggie Callow, Persephone Embers, Katie Olive, Lucy Holland, Maddie Murray, Xander Beck, Kym Saunders, Hann K, Paige L, Katherine Nichols, JJ, Korvus F. M., Effy, Franchesca Caram, Michael Anthony, You, Steffi Happy, Mal M., Rowan Knight, Craig Esser, Marie C, Caitlyn Manning, Faith Dam, Gabriel De Jesus, Eric McCurry, kishaya wicks, Jor-Jor, Jess Autiero, Sophia, Maya Tohill, Jessica Williamson, DangerDays, Hailey Robinson, Clarissa, Finn, Virginia Queen, Gwyny Rankin, Stuart Turnbull, Jordie, Rafa Apolo, Stephanie Lucas, Raul Alonso, Breaker Chittenden, Millie, Phoenix, Gee Rothvoss, Fergus (the dear kitty cat), Jessi Heimer, C F Chan, Ashliicat, Noal, Urna Mukherjee, Nico, Lily Schnur, Rachiel Rosser, Chris Mobley, Rebekah Roennfeldt, Jack Schiller, Mish

Phillips, Tara W, Tiffany Culver, Tayva Case, Dead Fish Books.

And of course my formatter, Edward Giordano, my cover artist Nani (shinirikaya on Insta), my editor Catriona Turner, and lastly my wonderful betas, Donna Taylor (author of the San Nico Slayers series), Chloe Spencer, Eleanor B and Jamie Sands, among others!

ABOUT THE AUTHOR

I. S. Belle writes Young Adult and New Adult books that are sometimes spooky, often romantic, and always gay.

She works in a bookstore in New Zealand and stops to pat dogs in the street. If you have a dog and your local bookshop allows pets - for the love of booksellers, please bring them in.

She has a Creative Writing Masters from the International Institute of Modern Letters. You can find her on Tiktok @i.s.belle_writes or on Instagram @isbelleauthor.

ALSO BY I. S. BELLE

I. S. Belle

LGBT+ Young Adult Fiction

BABYLOVE SERIES

BABYLOVE

SUGARSNAP

SWEETHEARTS

ZOMBABE

ZOMBABE

HONEYBLOODS SERIES

HONEYBLOODS

HONEYBITES

HONEYCRAVES

BLOOD TETHERED SERIES

BLOOD TETHERED

VENOM BOUND

SOUL BURN

GIRLS NIGHT

GIRLS NIGHT